TALES OF REVERBA: A NEW EMBER

THE STORY OF FIRE

JORDAN SPICER

Edited by Iris Marsh,
https://www.irismarsh.com/editing-services
Cover design by Nirkri, fiverr.com/nirkri
Formatted by Nola Li Barr

ISBN 978-1-7377928-0-2 (ebook)
ISBN 978-1-7377928-1-9 (paperback)

This book is dedicated to my mother who raised me into the man I am today. Without her, I don't know where I'd be in life. Thank you for all your love and support. I will always love and cherish you.

ACKNOWLEDGMENTS

I would first like to thank my writing coach Barbara Hartzler, my editor Iris Marsh. I would also like to thank my family and friends who encouraged me and assisted me with cultivating my ideas and fine tuning my writing. My mother, sister and my dear friends. I would like to thank my launch team for their help and all their hard work. Most importantly I would like to thank you, the reader, for supporting me on this journey. I hope to see you again in the next book. If you wish to see more join my mailing list at:

jspicerwriting.com

PROLOGUE

December 6th, 2015

Weiler sat on his couch, his dark green jersey sat loosely on his chest. Stains of pizza past decorated it. He sported a standard issue jar head haircut and a ruby red heart tattoo with a ribbon on his bicep that read "Mom". The TV blared in the background. A freshly delivered pizza sat opened in front of him. The salty, oily smell of pepperoni and the spice filled red sauce filled the air. The game was in overtime. Giants vs Jets.

Weiler leaned forward, he clutched his hands together.

Come on guys. You can do it.

He tapped his Jet's bobble head for good luck as the team's kicker got into position.

The ball was snapped, the holder caught and positioned the ball.

The kicker smashed it.

Weiler stood up.

"Come on, come on..."

The ball floated to the left inching ever so closer to the post.

"Come on..."

The ball continued on its path, Weiler held his breath.

The loud dial tone of the emergency alert system came crashing through his TV and phone. The footage of the game got snatched away by the logo of a local news station before a distraught reporter appeared, her eyes darting across the sheet of paper in front of her. She looked at the camera, her face tense.

Weiler deflated, "What. The. Fuck!?"

"We have a breaking story. Moments ago, over the Atlantic Ocean a mysterious object punched through the sky and has encircled the world. You heard me correctly. A mysterious object is currently encircling the world. We have footage of the first sighting. We shall play that now."

The footage transitioned to an aerial view somewhere over the ocean. There was a bright light and from that, a large black metallic object emerged.

"Is that a train?"

Three blades creating the appearance of a spearhead surround the head of the object. At the top of the head sat a thick smoking stack. The wide body was divided into sections.

The reporter continued, "What you are seeing is this metallic, almost 'train' like object coming into view. As of right now, there are no reports of destruction or casualties. We will continue to monitor the situation and bring you the latest updates."

Weiler's phone continued to ring. He turned the TV off, grabbed his things and rushed out the door, hopping into an already overcrowded truck filled with other army soldiers who were being called in.

May 10th, 2016

The scent of polished metal, the roar of the engine, and the rumble of the plane filled the air. Weiler stared at Smith in front of him, seat eleven, second to last to jump out of the plane. At the front of the line sat Jackson. Her bright blonde ponytail peeked from under her helmet. She looked down and brought her hand to her mouth. Probably giving her good luck charm a kiss. It was a necklace given to her by a little girl in Syria, in hopes America would leave her country alone. Their orders weren't unique, but the destination was.

A voice came in on the headset.

"Approaching Drop location. T-minus ten minutes."

Weiler inhaled. His heart was pounding. He tapped his foot as they approached the destination.

Ten minutes later, the back of the plane opened, everyone stood and awaited the order.

Shortly a voice came over the headset, "DZ in sight you are clear to jump."

Micheals, the commanding officer, jumped on the mic next. "Move, Move, Move." He waved everyone forward.

One by one they jumped until only Weiler was left. He hesitated. The pit in his stomach got worse, he felt Micheals hand on his back. With a sharp inhale, he threw himself off the back and into the skies.

The group spread themselves out as they fell. Jackson turned around and signaled the group before changing her course. A few seconds later, the landing zone came into view. The Train. Its massive, black, metallic body devoured the surrounding light. Jackson pulled her chute and shortly after, everyone followed suit.

The pit in his stomach grew bigger until it ached. Jackson was the first to touchdown. She made it closer than any missile the U.S government shot. Her feet touched down, she slipped into the body of the train.

"She went through it?"

Fear shot through his body. He reached up toggled his radio, but hesitated. He gave it a second.

The second in line slipped into the body, then the third.

He toggled his radio, "Jackson, Mark, Jen come in."

No response came as the seventh and eighth person slipped inside. When the tenth person came into contact with The Train, he noticed something. Something so small he wouldn't have noticed had his panicked mind not been razor focused. As the tenth person slipped into the train, their parachute wires twisted violently while the top stayed still.

He toggled his radio again, "Smith abort. Abort!" He yanked his steering lines, hoping to get away from The Train. Smith couldn't react in time. His feet touched The Train despite him yanking his steering lines and struggling to not fall in. His body stayed where it was, and eventually he slipped inside.

As Weiler drifted away from The Train, his heart broke. He toggled the radio off. Before he knew it, he landed. His body collapsed under its own weight; his eyes never left The Train not even as he sat there, back against a tree. He reached up to his radio and toggled it.

"Command, this is Ty Weilers. I have something to report."

Jul 3rd, 2016

Weiler sat in a booth, his head low, his eyes stare past the barely sipped stout of beer in front of him. A half-eaten burger with dry, cold fries remained of his overpriced and under flavored dinner. His hair dangled just in front of his eyes as he looked down at his plate.

He barely heard the clack of high heels approach his table, "How was everything?" The curly haired waitress asked. Her eyes glanced at the half-eaten food.

He lifted his head and smiled warmly at her. "It was good. I just wasn't as hungry as I thought." He checked his watch:

20:08 pm.

"He's late."

He turned his attention back to the waitress. "Can I get a box to go, please?" He asked.

She smiled. "Sure, I'll be right back with that box, and I will bring you the check." She walked off.

His attention turned to the murmur of the television that hung in the bar's corner. The barkeep set it to the news. He couldn't hear the TV but could make out the captions.

"Temperatures reach record low in areas obscured by The Trains shadow prolonging nighttime in various parts of the globe. This Train is the same one

4

that appeared back in December last year. As you may know, the American gover-"

The welcome bell on the front door ringed, his eyes snapped to the door. A tall man walked in, salt and peppered beard reached to the center of his neck. The man walked straight and with authority, hands sat in his jacket pockets. He turned and the two men locked eyes; he approached with a friendly smile.

The man stopped at the table, and his smile disappeared. "Corporal Weiler."

Weiler stood from the table and saluted, "Sergeant Marsh."

Marsh smiled, "At ease, Ty, I'm not in the military anymore."

Weiler relaxed, then frowned. "You're late. Last time I was ten minutes late you made me dig a six-foot hole."

Marsh smiled, "And it was the last time you were late."

Weiler tilted his head and raised an eyebrow. "Last time that you know of."

Marsh scoffed. "So, what did you call me out here for? I hope it wasn't just to see if I would be late."

Marsh motioned to the empty booth in front of him. Marsh sat down and picked up a cold fry.

Weiler slid the ketchup to him, "They suck but help yourself."

Marsh took a bite. "You weren't going to waste this, were you?"

Weiler shook his head, "No sir. You taught me better than to waste any food. It was your first rule of survival. 'Secure food and never waste it.'"

"Good, you remembered. Though I wasn't concerned you didn't. So, what do you want to talk about?"

Weiler pointed at the TV, which still had the news on about The Train as the headline.

"Ah... our mysterious visitor from... somewhere. What about it?"

"What do you know about it?"

"The basics, what they told all the civvies and what is common information. It showed up December, encircled the world and has done nothing since then besides floating in the atmosphere. Despite our worthless attempts at aggravating it with missile fire and radio waves. I also know about that little boarding attempt we made two months ago."

At the mention of the boarding attempt, Weiler clenched his fist. "Yeah, that's what I wanted to talk about. What all do you know about it?"

"Eleven people airdropped onto The Train and we are still awaiting the news from the boarding team."

Weiler shook his head, "I don't think we are getting anything from that team."

Marsh lifted his head. "Why do you say that?"

Weiler opened his mouth to speak but noticed the waitress speed walking back with a check and a Styrofoam container.

"Sorry about the wait sir, the machine had a little trouble printing out your ticket." She smiled at the new face. "Oh, did you want me to get you something or...?"

Marsh waved off her offer. "No, I'm just sitting with an old friend. I'll eat his leftovers."

The waitress giggled, "You two take your time. When you are ready to leave, you can pay up front." She turned on her heel and gave the men their privacy.

Once she was out of earshot, Weiler continued, "There were supposed to be twelve people to board The Train. Eleven including me, I... didn't finish the jump."

Weiler hung his head in as the memories came rushing back. He recounted the jump back in May. Making sure to leave nothing out; despite being under a gag order but after all that has happened; it felt pointless to abide by it.

Marsh nodded as Weiler finished his story. "So, you got discharged for abandoning your duties. Should you even be talking about this?"

Weiler scratched his head. "Honestly, I don't care. I stopped caring what the military thinks for a long time now. I was bound to say no and walk away from a mission at one point, I was just surprised when and how it happened."

Marsh raised an eyebrow. "You were unhappy?"

Weiler nodded. "Been unhappy for a long time now. It wasn't so bad at first. I had you to look up to, and the squad kept my spirits high. Especially Jackson. She was the team's courage. Always first in, last out."

Marsh laughed, "Ah, Martha Jackson 'The Golden Sun'. She was always pushing you all to work harder."

Weiler smiled, "I would have followed her anywhere... but not that Train. And I followed her through multiple hells. Iraq, Afgan, Syria. Syria was the worst, by that point everything we did stopped making sense."

Marsh frowned, "We?"

"The government, our government. I wanted kids, I really did, but I don't deserve them, not after what happened there. And once Jackson got that necklace, our 'Golden Sun' didn't shine so brightly. We were lucky to get pulled early and stationed somewhere else. It took a while for our Sun to shine again."

Marsh finished the last bit of Weiler's leftovers. He stared at the empty plate as silence overtook them drowning out the rumblings of the surrounding diner.

Weiler chuckled, "How's Tim?"

Marsh's eyes lit up. "He's good. Finishing up high school, we actually have another camping trip planned in the next few weeks. He's a natural survivor, that one, though I need to work on his cooking skills."

Weiler felt his eyes watering. "That's good. He's a good kid."

"You should join us on that trip. He misses you, told me so a few weeks ago, actually."

"Yeah, that might be nice." Weiler looked up at Marsh, "It's getting late we should get going."

Marsh smiled. "I ate all your leftovers, so I owe you a meal."

Weiler chuckled, "You sure did... guess I'll have to take you up on that."

Weiler grabbed his check and stood up. "I'll meet you outside, just have to pay really quick."

Marsh nodded and left the diner while Weiler got in line.

When he got to the cash register the cashier looked up at him and made the usual small talk.

"Cash or credit?"

"Credit."

"And are you a part of the military? We have a fifteen percent discount for vets and their families."

Weiler thumbed over his military id, then pulled out his credit card. "No."

1

A NEW WORLD

Jul 6, 2016

Jordan sat in his room, the screen of his computer illuminating his face as he typed away. In the bottom corner a small notification box popped up: it was a message from Kyle, one of his friends. A link was the first thing he saw followed by a message that read.

"Lol"

He opened the link which took him to yet another article about The Train, this one talked about The Train being a messenger of God to usher in his return to Earth. It went in detail about the Thrones class of angels. Referred to some scriptures from the bible, mentioned how the world is filled with sins and pointed out various things such as gay marriage, porn use, interracial marriages.

He opened the message and typed a quick reply.

"They are doing that thing again where they act like God couldn't just snap us out of existence if he was really upset."

He closed another tab, referring to The Train as a being from another dimension. Between that or the belief that it is God's messenger, he chose to believe an interdimensional train came to Earth. For what? He didn't know, but he had one hope.

A ping grabbed his attention, a reply from Kyle.

"Whatever it is, it just needs to hurry up and do it. I'm trying to leave… at the rate we're going we destroy the world in like 50 years anyway so what's the point?"

Jordan laughed and replied.

"It needs to grab us and go or just crush the Earth like a watermelon between some thicc ass thighs. Either way, I'm tired of being here. There's nothing here for us bro, our gen becomes 25 and we have quarter life crisis's, what a fucking joke. I'm 25 with enough debt to put a down payment on a house and all I've done is go to college. I'm just trying to leave and throw some fireballs or some shit at people."

"Shit… same… nothing like waking up in your 'prime' feeling like you fell down some stairs. I'm trying to get that wind magic doe… but anything at this point would be good imo."

"Shit true!!!!"

Jordan checked his phone.

5:34 pm.

He sighed and turned to the computer.

"Ight I gotta head off supposed to meet up some people to hang out. I'll catch ya later."

As he stood up, one last notification popped up

"Peace."

––––––––

A WHILE later Jordan was walking around downtown. He glanced up at The Train. It sat in the sky, softly bellowing smoke.

"If you gonna clap Earth please hurry."

Up ahead, a group of his friends stood waiting. He drew his hand out of his pocket and waved to get their attention. The world shook as The Train blared its horn. He placed his hand on the side of a nearby building.

He felt his body get hotter. His stomach boiled with nauseated and agitated acid; his food failed to find a place in his stomach to rest. He could feel it pushing against the roof of his stomach, threatening to break free. He hunched over, his esophagus burned as a brownish pile of bile slapped the ground, chunks of a chewed-up meat and melted cheese swim in the mixture, remnants of tonight's dinner. Its sound being muffled by the roar of The Train that coiled overhead, threatening to squeeze the Earth. The smokestacks on top of the spear-like head of the Train bellowed a deep white smoke that fell to earth clouding the air. His legs felt weaker than a newborn fawn, his eyes filled with pained tears blurring his vision.

"Why does everything hurt?"

He placed his hand on his stomach.

"It's okay... you're fine. Breathe."

He lifted his head and saw his friends rushing towards him, their eyes trained on him. Before reaching him, they jump in unison and look off to the side. His eyes followed. A car had slammed into a parked car. The parked car took the hit for his friends. They reached him and tried to lift him to his feet.

He mouthed.

"I'm fine..." but failed to say it out loud. His mind focused on surviving.

His eyes widened as a new sensation echoed through his body, followed by pain that made his eyes roll back. The sensation of a constant crunching, like a mouth full of nut clusters, vibrated his body as it cried in pain and his heart panicked. A deep chill froze his body.

Lava rushed through his veins. His shirt couldn't absorb all the sweat from his body. He dug his nails into his arms as he held himself close.

"I'm not fine."

Another pile of bile erupted from his mouth and slammed into the ground. Even through his blurry vision, he could see something wiggling in the acidic mixture. Chubby, white worms. The pain continued, and he collapsed. His breathing was shallow, his body paralyzed itself to stop the pain, and his mind filled with haze. He could see people running and panicking while the streets filled with the white powder from The Train. Soon his world went dark.

A SOFT BREEZE cooled his skin, He sighed in relief before his body got hot again. His breathing was slow as he inhaled this scent. It was fresh; it reminded him of spring. Something tickled his nose, causing him to wake up swatting at his face. His eyes stung from how bright the area was. He looked around and saw that he was outside in what looked like a meadow. A deep sea of green grass with splashes of vibrant flowers surrounded him on all sides. He tried remembering where he was before passing out, or at least how he got here. He was wearing tennis shoes, black jeans and a simple shirt, the bottom of which had some dried puke on it. Besides the puke, this was his normal wardrobe for going out with his friends. They had wanted to go to a restaurant downtown. He remembered the sound of The Train followed by intense pain, then nothing. He brushed the dirt and foliage off his dark skin then picked a few blades of grass from his thick wool like hair.

He inhaled deeply.

"Crazy bastard did it."

He laughed and rubbed his head. "Well, shit."

His glasses sat on his nose, covered in a light coating of dust. He took them off and reached into his pocket, pulling out his glass's cleaner. As he wiped down the lens, he noticed how sharp his vision was. He waved his hand in front of his face, then scanned the area. Everything seemed crisp and clear, as if he was wearing his glasses. He held his glasses up and peered through, his vision blurred.

He scratched his head while he thought, his thick curly hair quickly wrapping itself around his fingers. After a moment he shrugged and put them in his pockets, which still had his phone, wallet, keys and handkerchief. His phone showed no signal, 60% battery and the time read 3:05 AM. xWith no way to check where he was and no one around, he picked a random direction to walk in.

Despite not knowing where he was, being surrounded by nature was calming. The warm sun, calm breeze, sounds of insects and birds surrounded him. The area shimmered in the bright sunlight as it reflected off the morning dew. All this brought a soft smile to his face. He grew up in cities, but he spent time out in nature. Earth had its moments when it was beautiful, but the air never smelled this good. It was always as if there was a layer of rot encasing it. The more he thought about his situation, the happier he got. Was he free of that world?

———

AFTER WALKING FOR THIRTY MINUTES, according to his phone. He stumbled upon some figures in the grass; he approached, squinting his eyes to get a better look from a distance. In the grass a group of people stood, one paced back and forth, their arms moved erratically. Another stood with one hand on their hip, one on their head. Two others stood looking downward at something in their hands. He straightened his back, lifted his head, and approached them.

He kept his hand in his pockets as he approached. "Yo."

The group turned, smiled and rushed over towards him.

"Hey. Another person. Thank god, I was so worried we were lost." A blonde girl spoke up. Her skin was tanned and sprinkled with freckles. Her warm brown eyes gazed upon him with hope. A gold necklace shined around her neck.

"Hey, bro, is your phone working?" another one asked. This one was about as tall as him, hovering around the 6ft range give or take. He had black eyes and hair, a firm chin and a warm white skin tone.

Jordan scanned the rest of the group. "Nah, I don't think anyone's phone will work here, or anywhere."

In the back stood a meek teenager who looked to be in his early years of high school. His small, delicate frame hinted he didn't do much athletic activity. Though, he did have a decent tan like he spends his time outdoors a lot. Behind him, stood a chubby girl with a cute, round face and pale skin. She looked around the same age as the meek teenager.

The blonde-haired girl spoke up again, "Oh, I'm Cindy by the way." She extended her hand.

Jordan gently grabbed her hand and shook it. "Jordan."

The rest of the group spoke up.

The black-haired boy stepped forward. "Jason, nice to meet you man."

Next was the chubby high-schooler Stacy, and the meek one was Tim. With their introductions done, Jason asked Jordan what he meant by their cell phones not working here or anywhere.

Jordan looked at Jason, "We aren't anywhere with coverage; I mean, mine says it's past three am, but it looks like high noon." He had other reasons to suspect the phones wouldn't work, but this was the easiest.

The group nodded in agreement. Jason double checked his phone before sighing and stowing it away.

"Can I ask or test something with everyone?" Jordan asked. "I'll say where I was last night before waking up here and everyone does the same. How's that sound?"

The group nodded after a moment.

Jordan smiled. "I was in San Antonio, Texas."

Cindy glanced at the group before chiming in "I was in Austin, Texas."

"I was in New York, New York." Tim said.

"San Fran California…" Stacy said.

"I was in San Fran too, actually." Jason replied, staring at Stacy.

Jordan rubbed his chin. "What was everyone doing last night? I was meeting up with some friends to hang out."

Jason was the first to answer this time. "Oh… I just did a beer run. Me and some friends were having a bonfire on the beach, and we ran low."

Cindy chuckled. "Well, nothing as fun as that. I was turning on the TV to watch… something I hadn't decided what yet."

Stacy rose her hand, "I was having dinner with my parents, we ordered pizza and some wings that night."

Tim also rose his hand, "I was buying some stuff online. My dad and I were planning a camping trip."

Jordan lowered his eyes and thought for a moment.

"This makes sense, we were all in America it was around six pm."

He looked back up. "Everyone heard The Train blow its horn, right? And if so, you had pain immediately afterwards, correct?"

Stacy shuddered. "Ugh, I threw up these fat worms."

Jason gagged. "Oh bro, don't mention those things. I thought someone brought some bad tequila I was like 'when did I drink tequila?' that was awful."

Cindy showed the bottom of her shirt, which was soiled in puke. "I didn't make it to the bathroom."

Tim sighed. "I passed out with my head in the toilet, so I didn't see what I threw up. All I knew was how tired and in pain I was." He glanced at Cindy's shirt, "Maybe we can find a river to clean your shirt off." He looked at Jordan's shirt. "Looks like you had the same experience too."

Jordan chuckled, "Yeah... it was rough." He shivered, remembering the image of them wiggling in his puke before he passed out. "I hope there isn't any more inside of us."

"So, I was right. The Train did something. Which means it might have really been from a different dimension."

Jordan got lost in his thoughts until Jason spoke once more.

"So... did you have any more questions or... are you thinking? What's going on?"

Jordan came back to reality. "Right. Sorry, I was thinking. So, if you all remember when The Train first came to Earth, it kind of punched a hole into space and coiled around the planet. There were some theories about it being an alien machine, a hidden weapon made by another country. But I think the ones about it being from another dimension makes the most sense to me." He frowned for a moment. "I think for the lack of better words, the Train has abducted us, and either put us on a different planet or a different realm all together."

He scanned the group's faces. Tim wore a blank expression, as though he was thinking himself. Stacy scratched her head but seemed over all confused. Cindy stood wide eyed. She softly clutched the pendent on her necklace.

Jason frowned. "How do we know we just aren't in some field somewhere, why does it have to be some new strange planet?"

Jordan nodded, "Fair." He reached into his pocket and took out his cellphone.

The time read 4:12 AM.

"What time does everyone's phone say?"

Everyone took out their phones and glanced.

Cindy looked up, "4:12 AM"

Jason was next. "2:12 AM"

Stacy nodded, "Same."

Last was Tim who replied, "3:12"

Jordan raised an eyebrow at Tim. "AM, right?"

Tim's eyes widened, "Correct, sorry."

Jordan smiled. "It's fine just wanted to make sure." He looked at his phone and turned it off for thirty seconds. "Let's turn off our phones and see if it updates the time."

Everyone followed suit, after a moment they turn their phones back on.

"*I thought so.*"

"Anyone's time changed?"

The group shook their heads.

Jason looked around. "Still doesn't mean we aren't on Earth. We could just be away from a cell tower or something."

Tim frowned. "Well, we don't have phone signal so that may be true, but our phones should have updated when we were moved."

Jason looked at him, "What if the signals were blocked by some government signal blocking thing or they were off while they kidnapped us."

Jordan tilted his head upwards and looked at Jason, "They as in...?"

Jason looked back at Jordan, his face getting redder as time passes. "I don't know China or whoever controlled The Train. They could have knocked us out and abducted us. Then dropped us in the middle of nowhere."

Cindy seemed lost; her hand kept messing with her necklace.

Stacy sighed. "But if we were all in different locations, how did they grab us and move us before we woke up?"

Jason groaned, "Who knows what kind of technology China has."

Jordan frowned.

"But…"

Jordan looked at Jason, "Why?"

Jason turned his attention to him. "Why what?"

"Why would… let's say China. Invent a huge train that can encircle Earth. Why would they knock out a bunch of no named Americans to then drop them… somewhere in a meadow with what-ever was in their pockets, including their phones? It makes little sense to me."

Jason glared, "What do you mean by 'No name'."

Jordan sighed.

"I should have worded that better."

He calmed his nerves and took a deep breath. "Are you someone important? A scientist, an inventor, son of a billionaire heir to multiple tech firms? Some kind of researcher?"

Jason scrunched up his face. "No, I work at some office basically filing papers."

Jordan nodded. "Right, I work in IT but my job is brainless and honestly progresses nothing significant that another country would want. Especially not some tech powerhouse like China." He turned to the others. "Anyone else? Anyone's name have any weight to it?"

Jason shook his head, "The news said The Train wasn't ours. We even tried to attack a section of it. Hell, we sent troops to go board it and we never heard back from them. They were probably captured by the terrorist on The Train or something."

Tim looked up. "My dad was a military vet. He actually knew one of the 'Lost Troopers', he actually met with the survivor three days before The Train blew it's horn."

Jordan's eyes lit up. "Oh… Tim. Tell me everything."

Cindy looked at Tim. "I heard the boarding forces all disappeared during the operation, was that not true?"

Tim nodded. "That's what they said, but my dad's friend was supposed to board The Train but saw something strange and aban-doned the mission. He kept trying to contact the ones who… I think dad said 'slipped' into The Train. But he got no reply from them. He was glad he chickened out at the last second."

Jordan tilted his head, "Slipped? Like they went through it?"

Tim nodded, "Yeah like, you know how things sometimes clips through walls in video games? They just went through the body but not the other side."

"So, are they still on the Train or did they get moved here?"

Stacy chimed in, "I remember watching all those missiles fly at The Train. It felt like the start of a world war."

Cindy seemed to relax a bit. "It was kind of spooky when the missiles didn't even reach The Train, they just kind of... blew up in front of the Train. It was even spookier when you realize the Train actually didn't do shit for six months until it blew it's horn and suddenly, we are here."

Jordan held up a finger. "So... besides Tim. Does anyone else remember anything important?"

After a moment of silence, Jordan continued. "I noticed my vision is better, so I don't need my glasses anymore. Anyone else have any issues fixed?"

Tim patted his shirt pocket where his glasses sat snug. "Yeah, I can see so much better than when I had my glasses. Even better than before this whole ordeal."

Everyone else shook their heads.

Tim looked up. He noticed the sun had moved in the sky, "We should find somewhere safe to sleep before it gets dark. We should also find some food or at least water."

Jason looked around, "Isn't it better to stay put when you're lost?"

Tim nodded, "Typically yes. But sense we don't have any supplies on us I think we should at least find a river or something."

Jordan rubbed his chin.

"We could wait for help but, I doubt any is coming. But what if we leave and we miss help."

Stacy tugged on her shirt letting small puffs of heated air escape, "Maybe we should at least find some shade before it gets too hot?" She glanced up at the clear blue sky.

Jordan looked back up. "I think Tim is right. Whether or not we are on Earth doesn't matter if we don't last long enough to get rescued. So, we do need to move or at least explore. Maybe there is a town nearby?"

Jordan surveyed the area around him, the tall blades of grass, constant noise of insects flying around, and lack of buildings didn't give him much hope in finding a town. Though he hoped there is a small village for them somewhere in this wilderness.

Jordan looked at the rest of the group, "Shall we get going?"

Cindy frowned, "Where though?"

Jordan motioned in front of him, "Forward, I guess? Hopefully we find something?"

The group agreed and began their march for food and safety. Everyone besides Tim was chatting. He seemed lost in thought, as if chewing on a problem he hasn't brought up yet. Even when asked questions, he would jump in surprise and mutter out an answer.

AFTER WALKING FOR ABOUT AN HOUR, hunger set in just as a forest came into sight.

Tim perked up. "This is good. A forest should have lots of food to forage and a river running through it somewhere. Which also means the land is fertile, so maybe we can grow some crops?"

Jason punched him in the arm. "Look at that, the nerd finally speaks up."

Tim shrank a bit as Cindy hit Jason's arm.

Jordan frowned. "Tim is right, this is good for us. Do you know a lot about nature, Tim?"

"Y-Yeah, my dad and I used to go camping a lot, so I learned a lot about edible plants and survival."

"Cool. Good shit man, I wanted to forage during college, but I never had the time. You can be our expert, okay?

Tim nodded, "Sure."

They entered the forest. Jason and Jordan walked in the front, with Cindy and Stacy in the middle and Tim bringing up the rear.

As they walked Jordan's mind drifted into the clouds, thoughts of exploring this place flooded in. His skin tingled with anticipation. He wore a soft smile as he continued to scan the area.

Jason's voice brought him back down to earth. "So, what do you do for fun?"

Jordan glanced at him, "Played games, fenced, a little bit of rock climbing, stuff like that."

Jason raised his eyebrows, "Fencing like the..." He wiggled his hand in the air as if swinging a sword.

Jordan chuckled, "Yeah sword fighting."

Jason smirked, "I bet I can beat you in a match."

Jordan beamed with joy, "Sure, when we get back to civilization, we can have some matches."

Jason's smirk faded and after a few seconds of silence he spoke again, "I-I was joking when I said that."

Jordan's smile faded, "Oh." He smiled again, "That's okay. It's a fun sport you should try it out, I'll even teach you somethings if you want."

Jason chuckled, "Nah, it sounds like it'd hurt being stabbed."

Jordan shrugged and chuckled back, "Sometimes but that's part of the thrill I guess."

From the corner of his eye, he spotted a paw print in the dirt. Before he could call it out, Tim spoke up.

"Stop."

Everyone turned around and saw Tim holding a small berry in his hand. Upon closer inspection, it turned out to be an elderberry. Tim explained how black elderberries are edible but to avoid any green ones as they will make you sick. The group cheered as they started grabbing some berries.

"Woah, woah... Only take a few, we might need to come here again." Tim grabbed two small bushels.

Everyone nodded, grabbing a few of them. Jordan turned to look at the footprint he saw earlier but couldn't locate it.

"Shit, where did it go?"

They had covered the ground in fresh shoe prints. The area where he thought he saw the print had been disturbed and the evidence destroyed. Jordan kept an eye out for more tracks as they walked.

While they were walking and making sure not to eat any green berries, Tim had migrated closer to the front as he scanned the area, looking for any other edibles or any signs of water nearby. Everyone helped by also scanning the area.

Stacy called from the back, "Hey Tim, what's that?" She asked, pointing up at a tree.

In the tree, snow-white leaves grew, red orbs complemented them. Tim looked and studied the tree; it was nothing he had seen before. The bark looked as if someone carved lines into the sides of it but was smooth to the touch, like that same person stained and polished it.

"I am not sure what this tree is, and I can't see the leaves or those red things. They seem like fruit, but if I want to know for sure, I will need some samples." Tim looked at Jordan and Jason.

Cindy patted Jason on the back. "Jason can do it, he's in good shape."

Jordan shrugged and stepped back. Jason, spurred on by Cindy, approached the tree. After sizing it up, he tried to wrap his arms around it and climb but fell back. He then tried to jump and reach for a branch, but his hands slipped, and he fell.

Jason placed his foot against the trunk of the tree, he shifted his weight and started to bounce in place.

Jordan's eyes widened as he watched, he opened his mouth to say something then shut it and just watched.

"Don't slip Jason."

Jason hopped and put his weight onto the foot that's on the trunk as he reached for the nearest branch. His foot slipped from underneath him a split second later.

Jordan inhaled sharply as he watched Jason crash headfirst into the trunk of the tree.

"God damn it."

The group rushed over to check on him.

Jordan knelt, "You alright?"

Jason rubbed his head, a bright red spot blossoms on his forehead, the damaged skin and small trickles of blood confirm that's where he hit his head. He gently tapped the wound then checked his fingers for blood.

"Yeah, I think so."

Cindy leaned in and moved his hair out of the way so she could get a better look. "Well, it's not bleeding that much. Hopefully you didn't hit it too hard."

Jason sighed, "Sorry, I tried."

Tim frowned softly, "It's alright. It's probably not worth the effort to climb this since we don't know what this is."

Jordan glanced up at the tree.

"Lots of berries up there. Maybe it's a fruit tree?"

Cindy and Stacy helped Jason to his feet.

Cindy slowly let go of Jason's arm. "Can you walk?"

Jason nodded slowly, "Yeah. I'm fine."

Tim sighed in relief, "Alright, let's keep moving. Sorry about that Jason."

Jordan stood up, "Let me try."

Tim looked at Jordan, "You sure? I don't think it's worth it. I don't know what kind of tree that is."

Jordan glanced at the nearby trees, "I think that's why we should figure this tree out. I don't see any other trees like it nearby. Maybe it's a fruit tree or something. But I think it's something we should know."

Tim opened his mouth, but Jordan continued. "Plus, I'd feel bad if Jason got hurt and we had nothing to show for it."

Tim sighed, "Alright just be careful."

Jordan smiled, "Where's the fun in that Tim?" He winked and turned towards the tree.

He rubbed his hands over the tree's surface, examining every part he could. After studying the tree, he bent down and covered his hands in dirt then wiped them off on his pants.

"Okay, my hands should be dry enough."

He dug fingers into the small grooves and hoisted himself up, climbing at a decent pace. He grabbed a small branch of berries and leaves and jumped out of the tree.

Everyone clapped but Jason who winced from the sudden noise.

Cindy's eyes beamed in amazement, "That was great. How did you do that?"

"Oh, I used to rock climb in college, once I understood how deep the grooves in the tree were. I figured I could climb it. If only for a few moments." Jordan said, handing Tim the sample. His fingers trembled from fatigue, cracking every time he bent them.

Jason frowned. "Why didn't you go first then?"

"Cindy said you had it and I thought you did to, if I knew you were going to get hurt, I would have tried first. My bad."

Cindy rubbed Jason's back. "Sorry Jason, I put you on the spot there."

Jason rolled his eyes, "Yeah, well… just handle the tree climbing from now on."

Jordan smiled softly, "Sure, sure." He glanced over at Tim, who was studying the plant.

Tim's face scrunched up. He pinched the skin of the berry and gave it a light squeeze. The liquid was milky but smelled sweet. Disappointed, Tim dropped the berry on the ground. "Usually when the juice is milky, it's poisonous, at least to humans. Also, the berry is red, so it was a fifty-fifty chance of it being safe to begin with. As for the leaves? They are pretty, but most likely useless. We can take them though and use them to start a fire once we find a place to settle. Sorry you wasted your energy guys. And sorry Jason got hurt."

Jordan shrugged. "It's fine, we need all the info we can get."

Jason smoothed back his hair. "Yeah… don't worry about it."

Tim's eyes widened as his face dropped. "Shit. Let me know if you start to feel any tingling by the way. I don't think this is poisonous, but the branch you grabbed shows some characteristics."

Jordan swallowed his worry. "Like what?"

Tim pointed to a few stems. "Poison ivy and poison oak like to grow in pairs of three. This branch is following a similar pattern. I should have thought about that before you grabbed some. Sorry."

Jordan put on a brave smile. "No problem, it was better we find out now than later."

Stacy stepped forward. "So, what happens if it is like poison ivy?"

Tim bit his lip and looked off to the side.

Jordan smiled. "It's fine, we'll cross that bridge when we get to it."

Though not the best response to that question, the group marched on. As the sun got lower in the sky, the shadows of the trees grew larger, encircling the group with darkness.

Jordan looked at the orange sky, he could see flocks of birds flying down into the forest. Probably heading to their nests for the night. He went to wipe the sweat from his brow but only found dried dirt and leftover salt from his sweat.

He looked back at the group; fatigue was eating away at them. Lips dried and cracking, with tired legs and of course Jason's head wound. The progress has gotten slow.

"We have to rest, but this isn't a good spot."

He glanced at Tim who seemed to be on the same page.

Tim inhaled deeply, "Okay it's getting dark. But we still have some time left. Hopefully we find a spot to rest and maybe some water or food."

The group groaned in unison.

Cindy dryly looked at Tim, "We've been walking for hours, can't we rest?"

Stacy leaned against a tree, "Those berries weren't filling, we should have grabbed more. I don't have the energy to walk all day."

Tim glanced around, he seemed to deflate in place.

Jordan mustered up his energy, "I'll go scout ahead. You guys rest, if I can find something close by we can move there for the night. If not, then we can just stay here. How's that sound?"

No one tried to argue they just motioned for him to do what he wanted.

"Alright I'll be back."

Jordan turned and walked at a brisk pace.

Thankfully, he found an open spot in the forest, he had lost track of time, but the sun hadn't set yet and he felt he was still reasonably close to the group.

"Good, we can sleep here tonight."

The grass covered ground died out as soil took its place, in the center of the clearing a tree stump rested just big enough for someone to sit on. The trees surrounded the area on all sides, the darkness of the forest lurked just a few steps beyond those trees.

Jordan stretched his legs and mustered up the last bit of his strength.

"Alright, let's go get the others."

A FEW MOMENTS later the forest had succumbed to darkness, forcing Jordan to walk slower, his hand out in front to guide him forward, while making sure his feet doesn't catch an exposed tree root. The ambient noise of the forest made him tense. Every snapping twig, rustling bush or animal noise pulled his attention and halted his steps.

A twig snapped ahead of him; his eyes widened as he dropped down.

"What's that?"

He held his breath and watched; from the shadows the group came into sight. He exhaled in relief then stood up.

The group jumped as he stood up.

Stacy clutched her necklace, "Jesus Jordan."

Jordan chuckled, "Sorry I didn't mean to scare you. I was coming back to get you all. I found a spot for us to rest."

Jordan glanced at Jason, "How are you feeling?"

Jason shrugged, "Alright, not too bad I guess."

Jordan smiled, "Good. Let's get going."

ONCE THEY WERE at the camp Tim stepped forward and surveyed the area. "This is good. We can make a camp here, maybe even turn it into a small base until we get our bearings or Jason is healed up."

He started collecting rocks, "I know it might be a lot to ask but any chance you guys can go get some firewood while I prepare camp?"

Jason sighed, "Yeah. I guess."

Cindy wiggled her legs, "I'll go too."

Jordan nodded, "I can help too."

Cindy looked at Jordan, "You sure? You've been doing a lot and you haven't rested."

Jordan smiled, "If I sit down, I won't want to get up later so I might as well help as much as I can."

Cindy looked him up and down, "Alright just don't pass out on us. I'm not dragging you back."

Jordan simply gave a thumbs up. With that Jordan, Jason and Cindy got firewood while Tim and Stacy stayed to prepare camp.

AFTER WALKING FOR A WHILE, picking up any twigs that they found, the wood gatherers find another clearing in the forest. The area was ripe with fallen trees, dead plants, and other materials useful for starting a fire. They spread out and the air was filled with the soft murmur of wood clunking against itself, feet crunching leaves and the occasional sneeze as they picked up sticks.

Eventually, Jason looked up at Jordan, then at Cindy. "Hey Jordan, we're gonna check over here for some more wood."

Jordan hummed a response. He chose not to look up from the pieces of wood he was picking up. He could hear leaves crunching underneath their feet as Jason and Cindy moved to another location. After a moment he stopped and stretched his back, the constant bending over was wearing on his lower back. Eventually he made a game of kicking twigs and branches into a messy pile, only bending over to pick up the occasional log.

He eventually sat down on a tree stomp, wiping his brow clean of dirt and sweat. Once he got his breathing back under control, he realized how silent the area was. He only heard faint rustling of plants caused by a gentle wind and the soft murmur of insects.

The silence reminded him of the woods near his grandparents' house, he reached down and pulled off a loose piece of bark from a log he found. He could hear his grandfather's voice in the back of his mind.

"You see how easily the bark came off? That means this wood is dry and should burn clean, it's also not too big either making it easier to carry."

He sighed like he always did after receiving an impromptu lecture from his grandfather. For he knew another one was right around the corner; he just didn't know what would trigger it. But he always listened, he knew his grandfather meant well with his flood of lectures.

He smiled and whispered one of his grandfather's many phrases.

"Never stop learning."

A few moments passed as he tried to dig up any other survival lectures he received. His exhausted mind drew blanks. While no lecture or tip came to mind, something did. A realization followed by a chilling question.

"I can't hear anyone. Why can't I hear anyone?"

He lifted his hand and snapped his fingers by his ear. The sharp sound flowed into his ear, then silence returned.

"So, it's not me, the area is just silent."

He could hear no sounds of wood being gathered, no sneezing from dust, crushing of leaves or twigs snapping under a heavy foot. Only the light chorus of insects in the night.

He stood up and surveyed the area. "Where are they?"

He started walking around the area in search of his missing companions; he left the wood on the ground for the time being.

"Cindy, Jason." He called out and scanned the area. "Where the fuck did they go?" His face grew tighter. He stomped deeper into the forest, "These motha fuc-" His skin grew cold, and his heart skipped a beat.

"Not this way..."

He turned around. In the pit of his stomach, fear burned, warning him of unseen danger. He couldn't figure out why, but he believed he was being watched and if he walked that direction he would die. Forgoing any more wood, he scooped up what he had in both his arms, and he raced back to camp, checking his surroundings on the way.

———

A WHILE later Jordan made it back to camp. The sense of being watched long gone but fear still lingered.

Stacy looked up at Jordan as he walked into camp. "Welcome back."

Tim also turned to him to see the wood he collected. They were sitting together, both smiling as a fire burned behind them. He approached Tim and dropped his medium-sized bundle of wood. "This good?"

Tim examined the wood with a satisfied smile on his face. "Perfect." He looked around. "Are Cindy and Jason behind you?"

"Nah, they ditched me in the woods." He rolled his eyes, "Or they might be lost."

Stacy crossed her arms. "Assholes."

Tim frowned, "Yeah, that wasn't smart. Did they just walk away?"

Jordan shook his head. "They said they were going to look for wood eventually I realized how quiet it was and when I turned around, they were gone. I called for them, but I guess they moved out of vocal range. It's fine though, as long as they bring back some decent firewood it doesn't matter."

Tim picked up some wood, tossing it into the fire. "You picked some good pieces; Dry but not rotten. Have you ever been camping before?"

Jordan chuckled, "Nah, my grandfather used to lecture me about things like this."

Tim chuckled, then his eyes grew sad as he became fixated on the ground. "So, are you really okay with just losing all your friends and family like this? Not even being able to say goodbye?" His eyes were watering up.

"A goodbye wouldn't have hurt... but it might have been too hard, maybe a little too selfish."

Jordan put on a brave smile, "Well, I believe a good friend of mine is definitely here." Jordan's words are confident, but his voice is hopeful. "As for my family..." His expression grew less open. "They'll probably freak the fuck out, actually." He laughed; a smile spread across his face. "My poor mother."

"She is probably still trying to call my phone or send me texts."

"When... if we get cell signal again, I wouldn't be surprised if my phone just vibrates for ten minutes cause of all the messages from her. I just hope she's safe somewhere."

Tim smiled, "Did you guys have a good relationship?"

Jordan wiggled his head as he thought, "It could have been better. But we did worry a lot about each other, so I guess it wasn't bad. What about you and your dad?"

Tim nodded, "We did, after he left the military that is. I think he worked hard to keep up appearances while he was serving but when he retired, he just wanted to spend time with me. We went camping a lot, we were supposed to go on a camping trip on the 9th but... you know."

Jordan nodded, "Yeah."

They sat in silence while Tim fed the fire.

Jordan watched quietly then after a moment turned to Tim. "Hey, do you mind teaching me how to start a fire?"

Tim smiled, "Of course." He grabbed some wood and bark, placing the supplies near the fire he had started earlier.

He gave Jordan some basic instructions before letting him try. Stacy, eager to help, also attempted to make a fire. Soon there were three fires burning in camp.

"There you go. With more practice you will be faster at it." Tim assured them both.

Jordan smiled, "Thanks man."

Stacy threw the twigs she used into the fire. "Yeah. Thanks Tim."

"I never asked, but are you okay with this? Chances are you will never see your father as well."

Tim smiled, "Well, he'd be jealous that I somehow ended up in a strange forest without him. And disappointed that I did so without so much as having my pocketknife." Tim sighed, staring into a fire as his face betrayed him with a powerful display of depression.

Jordan smiled softly and patted him on the back, before turning to Stacy. "What about you Stacy?"

"My mom is probably bawling her eyes out, dad..." A smile crossed her face as her eyes grew soft, "He's probably being dad." She gently twisted her pendent in between her fingers.

As they sunk into their thoughts, a soft realization washed over them. It told them they had no choice but to be okay with it, at least for now.

The twinkling of Stacy's pendent caught Jordan's attention. He squinted his eyes to get a better look at the pendent, it was a simple black stringed necklace with a copper crescent pendant. The tip of the crescent hung a pentagram. "What does that symbol mean?"

Stacy looked down, "This? It is the symbol of Wiccans" She held it up, so he could see it better.

Tim beamed with curiosity, "Wiccans? As in witches? So, can you do magic and cast spells?"

Stacy smiled and told Jordan and Tim all about Wiccans.

STACY SAT DRAWING in the dirt with a stick. From the woods, two familiar voices came crashing in. Jason and Cindy had returned with a disappointing amount of firewood, considering how long they been gone. Tim had expected them to bring back more wood, or at least bigger pieces. Instead, they brought small twigs and a few branches. Some of them were still fresh and looked as if they had just gotten ripped off a tree.

"Welcome back." Stacy said, not looking up from her dirt drawing.

Jason tossed the wood onto Jordan's pile. "Hey Tim. We got you some wood."

Cindy added to the pile. "Yeah, here you are."

Tim looked at the wood. It was mostly green wood, terrible for burning. He swallowed his disappointment. "Thanks."

Jordan looked them up and down, then glanced at the amount of wood they brought. "So what the fuck?"

Cindy and Jason looked at him.

Cindy glanced around, "What?"

Jordan frowned, "Why did y'all leave me in the woods alone? Where did y'all go?"

Jason shifted in place, "I just wanted to search a different location for some wood and I just... ya know lost track of time."

Jordan glanced at Jason who was avoiding looking at him. Then he glanced at Cindy searching her face for answers.

Cindy stepped forward and placed her arm in front of Jason as if shielding him from something. "I went with Jason to go look for some wood, we took a break and just kind of lost track of time. Then we rushed to try and get back to you but saw the fire and just came back here. Sorry."

Jordan opened his mouth to say something else but his eye focused on the wound on Jason's head.

"Let it go."

He sighed, "Just don't do it again please. We already had one injury today we should try to avoid any others."

Cindy and Jason nodded.

Jason looked around. "So, um, what's to eat?"

Tim stared at Jason, confused by the question. "Nothing. The only edible thing we found was that berry bush. If you ate all of your berries, then you are going to have to wait until tomorrow to eat again."

Jason sunk into the ground, the situation they were in still not fully hitting home. "Aw... man, I'm hungry, I should have saved some berries." He looked around for a moment. "What are we gonna sleep on, by the way?"

Again, Tim looked at Jason before patting the ground. Jason groaned and flopped onto the ground. Tim and Jordan just shook their heads as Cindy sat with Stacy in the back.

Tim threw some white leaves into the fire as he laid down on the ground. Everyone found a small spot and curled up into a tight ball on the ground. They tucked their arms into their shirts for extra warmth. Jordan sat against a tree, his breathing slowed, he blinked.

2

NEW DISCOVERIES

Jason's voice rang out, "Ugh... my head."

Jordan sat up. His eyes shot open. The sun blinded him and forced them shut once more. "Fuck...." He groaned, rolling over.

"When did I fall asleep?"

He sat back up.

Everyone else stirred awake, stretching painfully, the signs of poor sleep obvious in everyone's eyes.

Jordan's muscles ached as he forced himself to his feet, he tried to lick his lips, but his mouth was uncomfortably dry.

Tim sat up and looked at the group. "We can backtrack to the berry bush for breakfast, and we should explore for more food, water and supplies." He stood up and dusted himself off.

He glanced at the cooling embers where their fires once raged. Everyone grouped up and walked towards the bush when a loud crunch like glass breaking echoes into the forest.

Stacy looked under her foot. "What the fuck?"

Cindy walked over. "What's wrong?"

Stacy moved off the ashes. "Someone threw glass into the fire, and I stepped on it."

Confused, Jordan, Tim, and Jason walked over and examined the scene. Sure enough, covered in ash were pieces of glass broken by Stacy's foot. Tim picked one up and looked at it closer. It had the same texture and shape as a leaf, but it was hard and brittle. Tim could break the glass with his fingers.

Jordan leaned in, "Is it possible those white leaves you threw in harden, if exposed to heat?"

Tim frowned. "Yeah, but... that sounds impossible. Why would a plant evolve in such a way?"

Cindy rubbed her chin, "Don't know, but you also said you have never seen that plant, and Jordan said we might be in a different dimension or planet or something. So, a lot of things could be different for all we know."

Jason rolled his eyes at the mention of Jordan's theory.

Tim looked at Jordan. "No rashes or anything, right?"

Jordan smiled and shook his head.

"Do you think you can get more of these?"

Jordan nodded, "Sure, I can grab a bunch on the way back from the berry bush."

With that, the group hurried to the berry tree. Sadly, the tree was running low on berries and the group could only afford one handful per person. The juice from the berries flooded their mouths with much needed moisture. On the way back, Jordan climbed the white leaf tree, grabbing multiple twigs of these strange leaves and berries. When they got back to camp, Tim, Jordan and Stacy started three fires to experiment with.

Cindy walked over, bending down to get a better look. "So, what is the plan?"

Tim glanced at her. "We are going to light three fires. In one fire we will just put the white leaves in it, in another we put just berries and another we put berries and leaves in it."

Cindy tilted her head, "Why the berries? I thought the leaves were the things that hardened?"

Tim nodded, "Yeah but plants don't waste resources on useless things. So, maybe the berries have a purpose too."

Once all the fires were lit, they placed the samples on rocks and placed them inside their respective fires.

Tim stood up, dusting his hands off. "Okay, while these are burning, we need to gather more firewood and start scouting the area. We also need someone to stay here and keep watch on the fires."

Jason's face scrunched up; Jordan noticed the change of expression. "I can go forage for some food." Jordan blurted, "I have a slight idea of what is edible and what is not. But I will still need you to help me test for sure. Jason, can you go get more firewood?"

Jason looked over and raised an eyebrow. "... Sure, I can go get firewood."

Tim nodded. "I will go look for food as well."

Stacy bounced to Tim's side. "I can come too."

Cindy smiled, "I guess, I will stay here and make sure the fires don't go out."

Jordan smiled, "We shouldn't go solo... yet, so why not use the buddy system? Jason and I will get firewood and bring back whatever looks edible." He then pointed at Tim and Stacy. "You and Stacy go find some food and hopefully water."

Everyone agreed and the two groups went their separate ways, leaving Cindy alone in camp.

JORDAN AND JASON walked in silence for what seemed like hours, their ability to tell time gone with their phones last bit of battery life. They picked up any dried wood they could find, Jordan found some more elderberries and wild onions; they were small, but beggars can't be choosers. Jason broke the silence with a harsh question.

"So, Tim is kind of a bossy little know it all, huh?" He snatched up another bundle of firewood.

Jordan sighed faintly. "What do you mean?" He knew the answer to that question.

"I mean he has been like ordering us around, he didn't use mine or Cindy's firewood that we worked hard to gather—"

"The wood was fresh and healthy wood. It wouldn't have burned well, and the fire might have gone out faster. So, it's better to let it dry out before using it."

Jason rolled his eyes, his hand open, and twisted in disbelief. "And that shit last night, what is up with that?"

Jordan smiled weakly. "What happened last night?"

"The whole 'you gotta wait until morning to eat again', like he should have told me not to eat all the berries and that rude ass way he patted the ground when I asked what we were sleeping on. I mean, he should listen to us. He's the youngest here." Jason huffed while he snatched up more wood from the ground. "And another thing!—"

Jordan rolled his eyes.

"Okay… guess we are doing this."

Jordan stood up and looked at Jason. "To be fair… To be fair, we thought we would find more food, and we didn't. So, telling you to hold off on eating the berries could have been bad since you'd be depriving yourself of energy for no reason."

Jason scoffed, "I wouldn't have wasted energy if he didn't tell me to try climbing that tree."

Jordan recoiled back and scrunched his eyebrows together, "He… he didn't ask you to climb that tree."

Jason looked back, "Yes he did. He said… something like 'we need to climb this tree' then patted me on the back and said I can do it."

Jordan's face softened.

"Oh shit."

"Then I hit my head trying."

Jordan took a step forward, "Jason how's your head feeling?"

Jason rubbed his forehead and squeezed his eyes shut, "My head hurts really bad bro."

Jordan moved closer and grabbed his arm, "Why don't you sit down for a second?"

Jordan helped Jason down on a nearby log, Jason placed his hands in his head to shield his eyes from the sun.

Jordan took off his shirt, "Here my shirt is kind of dark so it should help block some of the sun." He draped it over his head.

Jason took some deep breaths, "Thanks."

Jordan patted him on the back, "You rest, I'll keep foraging then we can head back okay?"

Jordan tossed a small bundle of wild onions in a pile next to a few bundles of elderberries. Next to the food he placed a small bundle of firewood, enough to refill the fire pit while still being easy to carry with one arm. Jason had been sitting still for a while now. Jordan approached him and placed a hand on his shoulder.

"You feeling better?"

Jason sat up slowly, he inhaled deeply as he slowly opened his eyes. "Yeah, a little."

Jordan passed him some berries, "Eat some of these before we head off. Just so you have something in your stomach."

Jason took the berries and ate them slowly, while he ate Jordan kept watch. After a moment he glanced at Jason.

"Listen about Tim."

Jason looked up, "Hmm?"

"He probably was just tired and maybe frustrated. He is used to camping but I don't think he's used to having four other people rely on him like this. We have no camping supplies, and we might be in a different world. Cut him some slack, he probably didn't mean it."

Jason chuckled, "Yeah, I guess you're right. Man... my bad, I didn't mean to suddenly rant. My head was just killing me and... I don't know I wasn't thinking straight."

"It's fine, I prefer you to rant in private than to flip out randomly."

"Yeah." Jason chuckled, "That wouldn't be so good." He handed Jordan back his shirt. "Thanks for that. It helped a lot."

Jordan put his shirt back on, "No problem. Let's head back to camp." He bent down and picked up the wood. "You got the food?"

Jason nodded, he glanced down, his lip tightened.

Jordan raised an eyebrow, "Something wrong?"

Jason frowned gently, "Hey, can we keep my little... rant between ourselves? I don't want the others to be worried or feel bad about me hitting my head."

Jordan thought for a moment, "Fine, but if it gets worst let me or someone else know. We are a team so we should help each other out."

Jason nodded, "I will. Thanks man,"

Jordan nodded, "You ready to head back?"

Jason grabbed the food, "Let's go."

The two of them turned back and backtracked their way to camp.

On the way there they heard, some grunting and the sound of small roots being ripped up.

Jordan held out his hand stopping Jason. "You hear that?"

Jason pointed off to the side, "I think it's coming from this way."

They crouched down and sneak forward, just beyond some bushes a small animal rooted around the ground. It was a little larger than a fat house cat, it had reddish fur and a large hump in the center of its back. Sharp claws helped it dig in the dirt. It used its snout to move dirt around as it hunted for food.

Jordan's eyes widened and his mouth opened in awe.

"Holy shit it's cute."

Jason looked over, "Should we try to hunt it?"

Jordan glanced around the area.

"There's only one. It's small so it's probably fast. But those claws look very dangerous…"

He glanced at Jason.

"Neither of us are in good shape, Jason is already struggling due to his head injury."

Jordan shook his head, "No, let's not push our luck. Once we make some tools we can come back and try hunting it. At least we know it exists, we could also try hunting some of the birds we've seen around the forest too. But first, we need tools."

Jason nodded and they backed off slowly before they continued walking back to camp.

JORDAN AND JASON arrived at camp first. They see Cindy staring at the fire, bored. When she heard them approach, she perked up, "Hey, you're back." She stood up and rushed over to them.

Jason puffed out his chest. "Yeah, we got some good shit too. Lots of wood and some food. We also saw a pig... Thing in the woods that we can hunt."

Cindy smiled, "You guys are great. What did the animal look like?"

Jason glanced at Jordan, "Like a red furry pig, right? Kinda small?"

Jordan nodded, "Yeah kinda cute too."

Jason turned back to Cindy, "We are going to hunt it once we get some tools."

Cindy smiled wearily, "I guess that would be good. Just try not to hurt yourselves."

She looked at the fires, "The fires are still going strong; How long should we burn those leaves for?"

Jordan walked over and placed the food down somewhere safe. "Well... we had them burning overnight, but I have no idea how long they actually need to burn for. Maybe we could use a stick or something to pull some samples out?"

"Sure." She grabbed a stick from Jason before making her way to the fire. She used the stick to take out the berries and leaves from inside the fire.

They gathered around and examined the results of the experiments.

First, she fished out the samples from the berries only fire. The once vibrant red berries have charred, its fleshy insides are now black ash. The remains exploded in a black puff if they were squeezed.

Cindy hummed, "It looks like the skin popped open in the fire but other than that nothing really happened. They just burned." She pressed down on another one which puffed leaving behind a small circle of ash.

She moved to the white leaf sample. After struggling to fish out one of the leaves she flicked one out of the fire. It flew a few feet before landing into the dirt. Once it cooled, she picked it up.

"Yeah, it's hard kind of like an eggshell."

She broke it effortlessly between her fingers.

The last fire with the berries and the leaves yielded much of the same results. The berries busted open before charring, the leaves turned hard and brittle.

Cindy held up a leaf from that experiment. On the very edge she noticed that some of the leaf is dyed red, which made it transparent instead of opaque. She tried breaking the leaf by snapping it half. The leaf snapped but the break went around the red part.

She hummed as she thought.

Jordan looked over, "What's up?"

She grabbed the red part carefully and bent it, she felt it resist her longer before it snapped in half. The snap was noticeably louder than before.

She looked at Jordan, "Why don't we try another experiment?"

Jordan tilted his head up and smirked, "Whatcha got in mind?"

She smirked back, "Let's put the juice of the berries on the leaves? Maybe that will do something? After all Tim said plants don't waste resources on useless things, maybe he's right?"

Jordan nodded, "Good idea. I think we have some berries and leaves left over."

Jordan grabbed some loose bark to use as a bowl, he then squeezed the berries gently hoping to get most of their juice inside the back. He placed a few leaves inside to soak up all the juice. Once the leaves turned blood red Cindy picked them out of the bowl and laid them on a rock to be put into the fire.

After covering the rock in red leaves, they carefully placed the rock back into the fire, throwing a few more pieces of wood to keep it strong.

They watched the fire burn and listened to the sound of liquid popping and sizzling in the flames.

"What's going on?" A soft voice came from behind them. They turned to see Tim and Stacy with shirts filled with mushrooms.

The three walked over and explained the situation.

Tim rubbed his chin, "That's pretty awesome, it's a little weird that the leaves react to fire like that but... it's worth a test."

Jordan lifted one of the yellow mushrooms in their shirts. "I see you guys had some good luck with finding food."

Stacy smirked, "And water."

Tim pointed down south. "Yeah, we found a moving river. The

water tasted fresh. We saw some fish and turtles. It's not too far from here, we can make a trip every morning unless we want to get closer to it."

"I can show them." Stacy volunteered as she began walking towards the river. The rest of the group quickly followed, leaving Tim behind to watch the fires and checked the foraged food for edibility.

AT THE RIVER, Jordan knelt and scooped a handful into his mouth. He lowered his head, gulped as much as his mouth could hold. He didn't realize how thirsty he had gotten until this very moment. Remembering to breathe, he leaned up and filled his lungs with air as his stomach felt heavy with water.

"I needed that."

Jason belched next to him, "God that tasted good."

Jordan smiled and looked at Stacy, who was rummaging in some nearby bushes. "What are you looking for?"

Stacy popped up, holding more mushrooms. "I found some more Chant... Chann...? Chearn...?"

"*Ah.*"

He recognized the mushroom, "Chanterelle mushrooms."

Stacy smiled and pointed at him. "Yes. I found more, so I was going to bring them back." She smacked the tops releasing some spores into the air. "Tim said that you should do this while harvesting mushrooms so more can grow later."

Cindy wiped her mouth. "I'm glad we found a river. Don't forget to wash your shirt Jordan." She had the bottom of hers in the water as she rubbed the sides together before giving it a hardy squeeze.

Jordan followed suit, getting it as clean as possible. He glanced over at Jason who was still gulping down the water.

He chuckled and patted Jason on the back, "Don't drown Jason, I still need you for the sacrifice."

Jason lifted his head and wiped his mouth with his sleeve, "The what?"

Jordan smiled and shook his head, "Nothing it was a joke."

Once everyone drunk their fill and gathered more supplies, they made their way back to camp. Before they left, Jordan spotted a large flat rock on the ground away from the river. He had an idea; he retrieved the rock.

Jason looked at him. "What's that for?"

Jordan smiled. "Cooking, we can use it as a cutting board or like a stove top you know?"

Jason hummed a response with a nod. "Smart."

Once they made it back to camp, they could see Tim had organized the supplies into neat piles. Cindy smiled as she got closer. "So, is everything safe to eat?"

"Yep, everything is perfectly safe. Most of the food is safe to eat raw, but some stuff is safer if we just cook it. Sadly, I can't cook."

Hearing the words "Cook", Jordan's ears perked up. "I can cook. Leave it to me." He grabbed some mushrooms and onions.

Stacy walked up. "You know how to cook?"

To which Jordan nodded. He walked over to a nearby tree. Snapping off sturdy looking twigs. "Yep, I learned mostly on my own. Though my mother, grandmother and aunt taught me a fair bit as well."

She maneuvered in front of Jordan. "I always wanted to learn how to cook but my parents weren't really the home cooked meal types."

Jordan took the hint with a chuckle. "I can teach you."

Stacy's eyes lit up again as she nodded. "Yes. Teach me everything." She clenched her hands and bounced in place. Waiting for her lesson to start.

A smirk crossed Jordan's face. "Great, your first lesson." He bent down grabbing mushrooms and onions, "Go wash these and we can go from there."

Stacy placed them in her shirt and ran off. Cindy followed, to make sure she didn't get lost.

Jordan sat down and started shaping the branches into crude skewers. He used a rock to sharpen the ends into a point. He hummed to himself while he worked.

Tim sat next to Jordan. "I'm surprised you know how to cook."

Jordan gently pressed the tip of a finished skewer against his finger. The sharpened point threatened to break skin. Satisfied, he placed the finished product to the side and starts working on another one. "I'm surprised you don't. Figured your dad would have taught you." he slid his hand up, removing thin twigs from the outer edge.

Tim shrugged, "My dad did all the cooking, I was happy to just help by gathering plants, he also did all the hunting so I'm not great there either, but I loved fishing with him so I'm good at that."

Jordan nodded. "Mmm, that's fair. I have been fishing too, probably not as much as you. But we can use that as our main source of food. As for hunting, we will see how those leaves in the fire turn out later. If we can get some tools maybe we can hunt that cute pig thing Jason and I found earlier."

A flock of birds took flight somewhere in the forest, the two looked up and watched them fly into the sky.

Tim rubbed his chin as he watched the last one disappear from sight, "We could also raid some bird nests."

MOMENTS LATER STACY and Cindy returned with the washed mushrooms and onions; Jordan explained how to cut food and what to look for in ingredients that show they aren't fit for consumption. Stacy studied as Jordan made mushroom and onion kabobs, placing them near the fire to cook. He rotated them until they were golden brown on all sides. After a final check, he handed a skewer to everyone.

Jordan watched as everyone took a bite. The expression on their faces was all Jordan needed to tell that he did a good job. The group devoured their kabobs once they finished. They joyfully tossed their skewers into the fire. When Jordan finished eating, he leaned up against a nearby tree, his mind begun to work through the edible things they have found so far.

"Birds and their eggs are probably safe to eat. That pig most likely is as

well... Fish is tricky but also a possibility. Tim can figure out which plants are safe to eat so we can rely on that for some time."

His thinking quickly progressed from what is safe to eat to how he will cook it.

"Pieces of pork with an egg on top? That'd be fun... I could use some of those mushrooms and onions too. Oh... if it has a good amount of fat that would be really good. I just need a knife."

He smiled and hummed to himself as he continued to think of dishes to try.

THE SUN SETS, the forest is cloaked in darkness. A crackling campfire the only defense from the shadows that surrounded the young survivors as they slumber. Jordan once again placed his back against a tree and slipped off to sleep.

Tonight, he experienced something different; It started as a quiver but grew into a full body tremor. His ears had a constant ringing, his eyes ached, he choked on the air in his throat. His eyes shot open, and a world of darkness greeted him.

"Where am I? What happened?"

His head was stiff and immobile, so he used his eyes to look around, there was no sign of the group nor the camp anywhere. Just an ever-expanding world of darkness. The only light source is a misshapen circle floating in front of him.

He tried to move his body, it resisted him.

"Sleep paralysis?"

He continued to try and move his body, his body ached from the strain of it. Eventually he took a break and caught his breath.

He scanned the area again, though nothing has changed. He could feel something watching him. The light in front of him continued to bob slowly in the air. His eyes were drawn to the ugly edges, something deep inside of him wanted to fix it.

He went to call out, his voice slammed into his lips unable to escape his closed mouth.

He groaned and rolled his eyes.

"Of course you can't talk Jordan. You can't even move your head."

His eyes continued to dart to the light, even when he tried not to stare at it. It called to him.

"God I want to touch that thing."

His fingers twitched as the urge grew stronger.

"Come here, let me touch you."

The light moved closer.

His eyes widened and he focused more.

"Come here."

The light moved closer; his fingers begun to move more.

Jordan continued to will the light closer until it was in his hand, he could feel the paralysis melt away as he touched the light. Soon he was able to sit up, his body was still stiff but at least he could move freely.

He brought the circle closer to his face as he examined it.

It was slightly transparent, flat with jagged edges. Jordan rubbed the edges. He felt a small nick on his hand.

He yanked his hand back and sharply inhaled, he checked his hand and noticed a small break in his skin. Though, there was no blood. He then turned his attention to the spot where he rubbed. The edge was smoother, and the pure white color was tainted with a faint smudge of purple.

He glanced at the wound on his hand and took a deep breath. Then placed his hand back on the circle.

He moved his hand over the edge once more, he could feel the pain in his hand increasing. He steeled himself and continued smoothing out the edges.

"It's okay, you can take this. If not, you'll wake up so there's no risk."

He spent an unknown amount of time shaping the circle, the rounder it became, the more the purple bled into the white. The smaller the circle got. Once it got to around the size of a large dinner plate it became perfectly round and a deep royal purple.

Jordan looked down at his hands, a deep laceration sat in the middle of his palms. He inhaled sharply as he cradled his arms.

"Might have fucked up there."

From the darkness a bass filled feminine voice echoed all around.

"You finished faster than I expected."

He jumped in place and looked around, "Who's there?"

A blazing orange glow bathed the dark world in its light. Jordan looked up squinting his eyes as he did.

He couldn't see the person the voice belonged to; the light was too bright.

From the sky, tendrils of fire reached down and wrapped around his hands. He felt the warmth of their embrace. His hands tingled as the wounds started to heal, the more they healed the more his body quivered from the sensation. As the lacerations on his hands closed, he let out a deep and relaxed sigh.

He inhaled deeply shaking off the mind scrambling sensation, "Good god, that felt good."

The voice chuckled, "I'm glad. Now stand up, you have much to learn tonight."

Jordan stood up and glanced at the light in the sky, "So, who are you?"

"Don't worry about that."

Jordan frowned, "Not a fair thing to say to someone in this situation."

"I disagree, you don't need to know who I am yet, you just need to learn a single word."

Jordan rolled his eyes, "And that word is?"

"Gao."

"G-Gao? What's that mean?"

"Speak it into the circle and find out."

Jordan glanced at the circle then approached it.

He touched the circle and it shined brightly, when he moved his hand, it followed it. He touched it with his other hand, and it followed that one. He continued swapping hands, even testing to see how fast it can swap.

The voice spoke once more, "It doesn't matter which hand its in. You can summon it in any hand."

Jordan softly glared at the light, "I was having fun."

He stuck his hand out, the circle hovered in front of it as if awaiting a new order.

"Gao."

The circle exploded and Jordan was launched back into the air. He flew for a few feet before landing roughly on the ground.

The voice giggled, "It's always a treat watching someone's first time."

Jordan sat up with a huff, he glanced at his right hand.

"She said I can summon it…"

He snapped his fingers and the circle reappeared in his hand.

The voice cooed, "A fast learner. I like that, but you don't need to snap to summon it. You just need to will it."

Jordan stood back up and held the circle out in front of him. "Gao."

———

JORDAN PUSHED himself up onto his knees panting as sweat dripped down his body.

"Never sweated in a dream before."

He had lost count of how many times that circle has exploded. At first, he wasn't pronouncing the word right. Then he wasn't confident enough and now his voice is lacking a certain authority.

He groaned has he pushed himself up.

"Okay, once more."

He summoned the circle. After taking a deep breath, he went to speak the word again. But first, he glanced up to the sky, the raging fire was calm, and he hadn't heard the voice in a while.

He glanced at the circle then back towards the sky, "You still there?"

"I am always here."

Jordan nodded, "I'm going to do it this time."

The voice grunted in amusement, "I wait with bated breath."

He focused his mind, steeled his will, puffed out his chest and lifted his head. "Gao!"

The circle shimmered; a loud ringing flooded the world. Jordan kept his resolve. The ringing stopped and a symbol appeared at the top of the circle.

Jordan laughed and grinned up to the sky, "I did it."

The voice chuckled, "I saw."

Jordan looked around, "So what does it do?"

"Figure it out."

Jordan shot the voice a confused look.

From deep in the void an explosion rung out, a different light flooded the world. A shock wave lifted Jordan into the air. The last thing he heard before the brilliant light overtook him was.

"Congratulations."

3

TOOLS AND MAGIC

JORDAN'S EYES SHOT OPEN, he let out a loud gasp.

The others jolted awake and sat up.

Tim was the first to speak, "What happened?"

The adrenaline from waking up faded and fatigue took its place. Jordan rolled over and tried to push himself up. His body trembled under its own weight.

He glanced up and saw the worried look on everyone's faces. He gave an embarrassed smile, "Sorry, had a weird dream that's all."

Cindy placed a hand on her chest, "Geez Jordan, you gave me a heart attack."

Jordan wanted to reply, but he found it hard to even keep his eyes open. Every blink came with a sleepy nod. His nose ran and his eyes watered as he fought to stay awake.

"Why am I so tired. Was it from that dream?"

He checked his hands for any scars or wounds, despite the dirt his hands were normal.

He felt a hand on his shoulder he jumped and looked up to see Cindy looking down at him. "Hey... You alright? Your eyes are so bloodshot."

He wasn't sure if he was okay, the events from last night still clear in his mind. "Yeah… Just tired is all. Guess I didn't get good sleep."

Cindy rubbed his back, "Rest up while you can."

Jordan glanced over and saw Stacy digging into the fire.

"Hey guys. Come look at these leaves."

They gathered around and examined the results of the experiments. The leaves soaked in berry juice have turned a crimson red, they were transparent compared to the opaque white leaves. Despite the covering of ash, they shined brilliantly in the sunlight.

Jordan raised his eyebrows as he examined the changed leaf. *"It looks like a ruby, you could make some pretty stuff with that leaf."*

Jason picked up one of the leaves, he rubbed his fingers on the top and bottom cleaning off the ash. "It's pretty hard." He gripped the leaf with both hands and tried to bend it.

Slowly he applied more pressure until the red leaf broke with a hard satisfying,

SNAP!

Jordan's eyes lit up and he grabbed one for himself, he ran a finger on the edge.

"Sharp."

He grabbed one of the wild onions and using the leaf as a knife to cut it. Just as he thought, the leaf cut into the onion easily he could even cut the onion thinly. While it wasn't a chef knife it would definitely get the job done.

Jason grabbed the slice on onion and held it up to the sun while he peered through. "Dude… that's amazing."

Jordan smirked, "This is fucking amazing. We can use these for so much, we might not die out here after all." He laughed at his own morbid joke, he stopped laughing as he ran out of breath and fatigue took over once more. He choose to lean against a nearby tree for support.

As the others chatted about the possibilities of these new "Blood Leaves" Jordan closed his eyes for just a moment. He felt his shoulder sliding backwards on the tree.

"I think I'm falling."

His shoulder continued to slide backwards.

"I should..."

His knees buckled and his body fired off warning signals to wake him up. His eyes shot open, and he tried to grab something to stop himself from falling.

Luckily, Cindy caught him and slowly lowered him to the ground. "Woah... Okay, just take it easy today. We can't have you getting hurt. We still got some mushrooms left, maybe you will feel better once you eat." Cindy leaned Jordan against the tree and sat in front of him.

Jordan's eyes were half closed as he fought to stay awake.

"Gao. What does that even mean, and who was that voice? Why did she congratulate me?"

He realized it was futile to try and figure out the answers when he could barely keep himself awake. Tim's voice drew his attention.

Tim touched his chin as he thought, "You might be suffering from poor sleep and being exposed to the elements so much, plus you have been working hard."

Jason kicked a rock and stuck his hands in his pockets. "So, what are we going to do?"

"Well, we need to make camp more habitable, but we also need tools for that. Without Jordan we can't get any more blood leaves so-"

Jordan cut in before they get carried away. "Once I eat something, I should have enough energy to climb the tree."

Jason raised an eyebrow. "Are you sure, bro? You look like you can barely stay awake."

"Yeah, plus if it is because of poor sleep then it won't get fixed until we make some crude beds or tents."

Cindy shook her head. "Isn't it better to just rest when you aren't feeling well?"

Jordan chuckled, "I don't have a fever or anything, I'm just a little tired. Plus the faster we get these leaves cooking the better for all of us.

Tim frowned. "If we let you climb the tree, will you just rest until you feel better?"

"I will rest until I feel better, I promise. Now lets stop wasting time, lets eat and go get those damn leaves." He forced his stiff body to its feet.

After eating mushroom and onion kebabs again, Jordan felt a tad bit better. After stopping at the river to drink before they set off to the blood leaf tree.

When they arrived, Jordan lazily walked up. He placed his hand on the tree and hid a deep, silent yawn.

"Fuck..."

He looked up at the tree, sniffling and panting.

"Okay, we can do this."

He dug his fingers in the grooves and hoisted himself up. He moved quick before his body gave out. Once he stabilized himself on a branch, he started tearing as many twigs and branches off as he could reach, before gently tossing them down. The others gathered them up.

As he worked, he noticed claw marks on the branch; he was currently sitting on.

"What caused these?"

He ran a finger along the marks. The start of the marks were deep and as the scratch continued, the depth decreased. He looked at a nearby tree to see if he could spot any more marks. Unsuccessful he searched around the area and sure enough found marks going up the trunk and around the branches.

"Shit."

Stacy called from below. "You alright up there?"

"Y-Yeah, just thinking sorry." He ripped off some more branches and tossed them down.

As everyone gathered the branches he tore off, Jordan spotted more claw marks heading up the tree.

"There's even more?"

He followed the marks with his hand, he looked up and something fell from the tree. He leaned back as it came into sight. A ball of reddish fur, covered in deep orange spikes fell towards Jordan.

"Oh shit."

His mind flooded his body with adrenaline flushing the sleep from his mind and allowing him to react to the situation. He twisted his body to dodge, he felt himself lose his balance on the branch. His mind raced as the spikes continued their descent towards his chest.

"I can't dodge this."

The spikes were a mere couple of inches away, he felt the tips press against the skin.

His mind scrambled to find a solution to survive, it searched and searched. Finally it reached something hidden, something new and arcane.

A royal purple circle flashed into existence; it was snug against the creature's body. Jordan knew what he needed to do, he needed one word to survive.

"Gao."

The circled flashed and the creature was pushed away as the tips of the spikes scraped across his chest tearing his shirt in the process.

He clutched the branch and regained his balance, he looked down and shouted. "Watch out."

Stacy had been grabbing a bundle of branches unaware of the surprise attack, Tim lunged and grabbed her shirt. He grunted and with all his might, he yanked Stacy out of harm's way, the creature's spikes cut her forearm as she is pulled to safety.

The creature slammed into the ground, it springs back up and jumps at the group backing them up while it bared its teeth. It snatched up a mouthful of twigs from the blood leaf tree and took off running into the bushes.

Jordan chuckled and caught his breath as he scanned the area above him before looking down. "Everyone alright?"

Tim tore the end of his shirt and wrapped it around the wound on Stacy's arm.

Cindy looked up, "Stacy got cut on her arm but other than that we are fine. What was that?"

Jordan gave her a weary smile, "That was the cute pig thing Jason and I found."

After everyone's blood pressure returned to normal and everyone had a bundle in their arms. They called him back down. Jordan sloppily jumped out of the tree, landing with a slight tumble. He dusted himself off and gave two thumbs up and a lighthearted chuckle before scooping up the rest of the harvest. Satisfied with their haul, they made their way back to camp. Jordan surveyed the trees as they walked, looking for more of those "Drop Pigs".

ONCE THEY RETURNED TO CAMP, Tim started a huge fire while Cindy and Stacy squeezed the berries over the leaves, turning them blood red. Jason used the Blood Leaves from earlier to cut dried grass while Jordan bandaged his chest wound with some of his shirt. Afterwards, he braided dried grass into rope, nodding off every so often.

THEY SPENT the entire day making supplies that ranged from rope to fishing spears to a skeleton of a tent. Stacy found out that you can shape the white leaves before turning them into blood leaves to make unique shapes like hooks or crescent blades. Everything was shaping up nicely. Thanks to the blood leaves, they jumped to the stone age and were making their camp more habitable. By the time they got done with all the crafting, it was dark. Jordan used the last bit of mushrooms and onions to make kabobs again. He slept on his side close to the fire making sure to keep pressure off the side of his chest where his wound was, thankfully he quickly fell asleep.

THE NEXT MORNING CAME QUICK, and with-it Jordan's energy. He woke up before Tim and the others. While he waited, he braided rope he took his mind off the pain in his chest by thinking of fencing.

He smiled at the memories, his fingers worked steadily making sure each braid was tight and secured before moving onto the next section.

"Reminds me of braiding body cords, that was the fun part about making them, the ends were always the troublesome parts."

His mind drifted back to the Drop Pig attack; his body tingled with a familiar sensation. He smiled while basking in it, his mind kept replaying the attack repeatedly. Each time he reached the climax of the fight he replayed it in his head. This feeling... **The Thrill of Combat.**

He sighed, "I could really use a good fencing match right now."

"Maybe I can convince Cindy to make me a sword once we get the basic tools made."

A twig snapped behind him, his hair stood on end and he spun around with a mischievous smile plastered on his face.

"Oh? Round two?"

He sighed and dropped his face when he saw Tim walking towards him.

"Oh."

Tim rubbed the sleep out of his eyes while he approached, "I'm glad to see you're feeling better."

Jordan gave him a warm smile, "Yeah, I feel much better. My chest kind of hurts but I suppose it could have been worst."

Tim sat next to Jordan and picked up some grass to turn into rope. "Did your grandfather teach you how to braid?"

"Nah, I learned for fun in high school. I experimented on some of my female friends. I also learned how to do it when I used to fence. I made my body cords, so it was easier to just braid them than glue them."

A gleam appeared in Tim's eyes. "You know how to fence? Is it fun?"

Jordan smiled, "It's intoxicating at times."

Jordan dived into his fencing stories, his wins, his losses, the people he's met. Tim listened with glee asking any question that came to mind.

After regaling Tim with another heroic comeback victory, he noticed the others had woken up.

He smiled at Tim, "Ah, well we can talk more about fencing later. For now it looks like we better get to work."

Tim bounced in place. "That was so much fun, Jordan. Tell me more later."

Jordan smiled, "Sure anytime you want."

The sound of rumbling stomachs signaled the need to go gather food. They grabbed the makeshift fishing rods and spears and headed towards the river. Jordan and Tim took the rods while everyone else took spears. They spread out along the river, hoping to cover more area.

BY THE TIME Tim and Jordan had gotten set up, the sun was already peeking over the trees, warming the earth as it continued to climb high in the sky. With non-baited hooks and little time, they tried their best to catch food. They focused solely on the task, only taking part in small talk.

THE SUN CLIMBED OVER HEAD, the heat cooked Jordan and Tim sapping them of energy, driving their thirst forward. From upstream they could hear a ruckus from the other three, a lot of screaming, some laughing, some cussing, and a lot of splashing.

Tim sighed. "I guess they won't be bringing back any fish."

Jordan yawned. "Nonsense. They probably have a dozen fish by now. Either that or they are dying up there." He sarcastically covered his mouth in shock.

Tim tilted his head "Why would they be laughing?"

Jordan rubbed his chin, "Hmm, maybe their minds are broken by the trauma?"

Tim stifled a laugh. "Makes sense."

Jordan watched the water wiggle his line. He gave it a few test pulls just to make sure something wasn't messing with it. No luck. With a sigh, he threw the line back in. He glanced at Tim and saw a pensive look on his face.

Jordan checked his line once more before recasting it out into the lake, "What's wrong."

Tim looked over, "How come you're so... okay with this? We might really be in a new world, and you seem perfectly fine with it?"

Jordan chuckled, "Well the thought of not paying student loans is quite a nice one."

Tim's face scrunched up with confusion and a hint of anger, "That's it? You're happy about not paying off loans? Aren't you scared?"

Jordan's smile faded away, "No, not exactly. The... better answer and probably the one you are actually looking for is, I couldn't see a future on Earth. You're... how old are you?"

Tim relaxed, "I'm seventeen."

Jordan nodded, "Seventeen... alright then you're still in the 'Don't talk to girls, get good grades, go to college.' stage, right?"

Tim nodded.

Jordan smiled, "I'm twenty-five. I'm in the 'Where the fuck are my grand-kids and how come you aren't making six figures?' stage."

Tim grunted in amusement, "You don't want kids?"

Jordan thought for a moment, "I did when I was younger, probably around your age." His eyes lowered, "But you felt it too, right? Your age group is inexperienced but not stupid. You all felt it, the way the world was spinning, the way the older generation kept fucking things up, the way they sneered at anything that made our lives a little bit happier, while at the same time blaming us for the consequences of their actions in a world, we didn't ask to be born in."

Tim lifted his head; his lip trembled a bit. He stopped it with a deep breath, "Aren't you scared?"

Jordan leaned in and looked him in the eye, "Of course I'm scared. Anyone in their right mind would be at least worried, I almost died yesterday. But deep down a part of me feels like my future here will be better than my future on Earth."

Jordan leaned back, "I didn't have a bad life. If you broke it down to its fundamental pieces you could argue it was a good life or at least average. I had no father but a loving mother who worked her ass off to provide. A loving family that I saw frequently, I had a job and my own place which is better than most people my age due to no fault of their own. I just got lucky. But every time I looked at my future all I saw was unhappiness not just for me but for everyone in our." He motioned between him and Tim, "Generation. Understand?"

Tim nodded, his lip kept trembling.

Jordan placed his hand on his shoulder, "Listen, we are going to be fine here. Of all the possible places we could have landed, we landed in a pretty decent spot. It's okay to be scared but we will make it work alright?"

Tim took a deep breath, his lip stopped trembling. He gave Jordan a stern nod. "Alright."

At that moment, Tim's rod suddenly bent as he was tugged forward. Jordan grabbed the rod and helped Tim get his balance back. Together they pulled until they yanked the fish from the water. It landed on the ground with a thud before flopping towards the water.

Tim yanked it back as Jordan ran up and secured it.

He held up the small pike and looked at Tim. "See? We'll make this work. We will survive. "Tim's face tightened as Jordan spoke. Jordan smirked, "I promise, we will get through this. Alright?"

Tim smiled, "Thanks."

Jordan smiled back, "Anytime. Don't forget we are in this together, if you need my help just ask and I'll do what I can."

———

ONCE IT GOT DARK, Tim stared at the pitiful pike he had caught earlier. "You ready?"

Jordan sighed and pulled in his line. "Yeah..." He stared at the empty hook. "Let's hope the others got something. They have been quiet for some time now."

"Hopefully, they aren't dead."

When the spear fishing group came into sight, Tim and Jordan let out a depressed sigh. Seeing no fish being carried.

Jason waved, "Hey. How did you guys do?"

Jordan put on a brave smile. "Hopefully worse than you three?"

Jason's face revealed what they were afraid of. "Nah, we didn't catch shit."

Tim held up his single fish. "We need to go fishing earlier."

The group marched back to camp in silence. They attempted to find more food, but as night had already started to cloak the forest, they cursed their luck and increased their walking pace. Once they got back to camp it was evening, Jordan got to work on preparing the fish to cook, descaling and degutting. Stacy watched until the degutting part. Jordan chuckled as she looked away in horror.

Cindy knelt in front of Jordan as he prepared the fish, "So, how are we gonna split the fish?"

Jordan glanced up then glanced around, he saw the hungry looks on everyone faces. Even his own stomach growled at the thought of eating some fish.

He idly tapped the blood leaf he was using as a knife on the stone tablet he found earlier. He lined up his hand with the fish it was just slightly longer than the palm of his hand.

"Five of us, two thin strips if I cut it right."

Jordan shook his head, "I can't split this tiny fish five ways. It's a small fish probably a baby one. I'd be lucky to get one decent chunk out of this.

Cindy shrunk in place, "Oh, not even if you cut it in half?"

Jordan motioned to the size of the fish, "There's no half to cut. It'd be different if I had proper tools and maybe some other things to cook but, I don't. It's a small nibble for everyone versus a meal for one person."

Jason tapped a couple of sticks on the ground. "So, Tim is the only one who gets to eat tonight?"

Tim flinched at the sharp question and held up his hands, "I was going to share."

Jordan glared at Tim. "No." He looked at Jason. "We need Tim to identify edible plants for us, we need him in the best of health possible." He said, placing the fish on a stick.

Jason's fist tightened up, "So, we go hungry tonight?"

Jordan gave him a stern look, "We should have caught more fish or found more food. Going hungry for tonight won't matter too much if we get food for tomorrow."

Stacy raised a finger as an idea popped into her head, "Maybe we can make a soup? That way everyone can get something in their stomach."

Jordan sighed a little louder than he meant to.

"Come on guys, I don't like this either."

Jordan shook his head, "I would need some kind of pot or bowl for that. Neither of which we have. We can just drink water to help ease the stomach pains, but I don't see a way to split this in a way that makes it worth it. And if there was, I'm not good enough to do it correctly."

The air got tense and suffocating.

"I'm sorry, I really am but I think this is the best play. Tim is our best bet at surviving this."

Stacy hung her head and quietly rubbed her arm.

Jordan gave her a weak smile, "The soup idea is great, we just need the tools for it. I promise y'all I worked this fish in my head over and over again. I don't know a good way to split it to make it worth it for everyone."

The camp quieted down, only the crackling of wood filled the air. Jordan held his breath waiting for any more objections. His hair stood on edge, he felt like he was one word away from being beaten down by a very hungry mob.

Jordan leaned forward, "We good?"

Jason backed off with a roll of his eyes, he sat on the ground, pouted and stared off into the forest. Jordan scanned the group, Cindy stood up and walked away. Stacy kept her head down, Tim stood in the center of camp unsure what to do.

Jordan shook his head in disappointment.

"Damn it. God damn it."

His stomach growled loudly in a final protest.

"Don't you start."

Once the fish finished cooking, Jordan handed it to Tim. "Eat."

Tim opened his mouth to say something, but Jordan reinforced his command with a stern look. Tim reached up and took the fish from him. After eating, Tim tried to lighten the mood, but Jason was still brooding.

With the mood soured, everyone surrendered to sleep. Everyone but Jordan who looked at his hand. He focused on it before whispering.

"Gao?" He waited a moment, but nothing happened. Again, he tried. This time with a little more authority in his voice. "Gao."

Repeatedly he spoke that word, but no purple circle appeared. He took a deep breath and envisioned the circle in his mind. A purple circle shimmered into existence slightly above the palm of his hand. It spun slowly, as if waiting for a command.

"This is it… it wasn't just a dream."

At the top of the circle there was a symbol, it resembled the top left half of a round arch with a line going up from the center. Though it had no letters underneath it he could still read it.

"Gao."

The circled flashed, and he felt a slight breeze, but nothing else happened. He looked around for something to test this ability with. Looking around, he found one of the blood berries that hadn't been used yet. He placed the berry in his hand and focused his mind once more. The circle appeared. The berry sat in the middle of his palm with the circle spinning around it.

"Oh?"

Jordan poked the circle and watched as his finger passed through it and met his palm. He smiled and uttered the word again.

"Gao."

Again the circle flashed, and it launched the berry about a foot into the air before it smashed into the ground. Jordan picked up a pebble. Once again, he caused the circle to appear before launching it into the air. Curious about how far away he could use this spell from he placed the pebble on a rock and sat two feet back. He held his hand out in front of him and once again muttered.

"Gao." but this time instead of pushing the berry into the air, it pushed the berry off the rock.

"*Oh… it's a pushing ability. No, it's magic. Amazing…*"

Jordan's mind buzzed with excitement he wanted to keep practicing. He grabbed another pebble and focused his mind again.

"*Gao.*"

Darkness overtook him.

TIM'S VOICE came crashing into the darkness, "Alright guys. Let's go get food."

Jordan sat up with a sharp gasp, drawing attention to himself.

Stacy rubbed her eyes. "You alright Jordan?"

Jordan turned and smiled. "Y-Yeah. Just got surprised by Tim is all."

Tim chuckled, "Sorry."

"No worries."

Jordan looked away and felt unease flow through his body.

"*When did I fall asleep? The last thing I remember… was practicing that spell. Then nothing. What happened?*"

He placed his hand in his lap and summoned his spell circle. It appeared in his hand and spun slowly, he could see the symbol for Gao at the very top.

From the corner of his eye, he saw Jason bend down and pick up a fishing spear. Jordan beamed with joy. "Oi, Jason, let me spearfish today. I wanna try it out. You can fish with Tim."

Jason shot an ugly look. "Don't think I can do it?"

Still riding his high, Jordan pressed on. "I know you can do it, but I want to try something. So, humor me on this, will ya?"

Jason sucked air through his teeth and snatched the fishing rod from Jordan and shoving the spear into Jordan's chest. Jordan didn't mind, though. If he was correct, he could catch a fish.

THEY MARCHED TO THE RIVER, Jason and Tim went to a deeper area to fish away from the spear fishers. Jordan began removing his shirt, socks, and shoes.

Cindy averted her eyes. "Why are you taking off your clothes?"

"I'm going to be at least waist deep in water, so I figured it'd be better to take what I can off. I will be here, you guys go to a shallower area."

Stacy grabbed Cindy's hand, and the girls took off down the river-bank in an embarrassed rush. Once Jordan was down to his boxers, he stepped in river feeling the cold water embrace his skin sending chills and goosebumps all over his body. Once he was waist deep, he stood still and watched the fish swim around him, getting used to his presence in the water. Once they started to idle around him, he scouted potential targets.

He spotted a decent sized fish.

"Oh, you're a good size."

He carefully adjusted his body to make sure his shoulders lined up with his target, once it stopped moving, he stabbed at it. The fish around him scatter at the sudden movement including the one he was aiming for. He groaned before setting himself up to try again.

HE TRIED A FEW MORE TIMES, each time with varying degrees of failure. Sometimes he would move too much, and the fish would run before the tip was even in the water. Other times he missed, sometimes he would strike the fish but not hard enough to actually secure it. He tried in shallower water and on shore both gave him the extra strength for his thrusts and hid his movements better but at the cost of accuracy. He took a break and contemplated his next attempt.

"So, I can aim better in the water, but I don't have the strength to really nail the fish without a lot of movement. So..."

He summoned his spell circle.

"What if I launch it with the circle?"

He clutched his spear and crouched down into the water. He let the fish surround him once more, slowly he loosened his grip on his spear. It was just enough to have it slide out of his hand but not enough for the river to carry it down on its own. His body relaxed as he watched the surface. He waited there for a while until he found his next target.

He focused on the head of spear; his circle appeared around it. Its shimmering light drew the fish's attention.

"Gao."

The circle flashed and the spear shot forward, the blade smacked the fish leaving a gash on the side of its face. It's blood exploded in the water obscuring Jordan's vision. He stood up and saw a trail of blood leading downstream. He grabbed his spear and sighed.

"Close."

He moved locations and tried again. This time he planned to throw the spear through the circle while casting Gao.

He gripped his spear tightly and lowered himself into the water while using his hand to hold on to the bottom of the river and guide him towards his prey. Once close enough, he began focusing in front of the fish. Just like last time, the purple circle shimmered into existence. The fish took notice of the circle and became mesmerized by it.

After a moment, Jordan tossed his spear with a sharp flick of the wrist shoving his spear forward.

"Gao."

The circle flashed; the spear gained a burst of speed as if pushed by an invisible hand. This time the spear traveled through the fish tearing it in half as it did.

"Holy shit."

He rushed to grab his spear and what was left of the fish. He stood up and inspected his catch, what was left of it anyway. His plan of attack not fully thought out.

"Damn that's really powerful. What if I actually threw it?"

He walked out of the river and wrapped his fish nugget in a leaf for safe keeping. His muscles ached from hunting. He looked up and saw the sky is turning orange. He let his skin dry off then redressed himself. A few moments later Stacy and Cindy came up from downstream. Each carrying a fish with a strand of braided grass through the gills.

Cindy held up her fish, "Hey Jordan how'd ya do?"

Jordan gave her an embarrassed grin and lifted his fish nugget. "I caught one."

Cindy laughed, "Did you take a bite out of it? What happened?"

He glanced at the fish, "I uh..."

"What should I say?"

He looked back at Cindy, "Got a little overzealous with hunting." He chuckled.

He glanced at Stacy, "I see you got one too."

Stacy held up hers, "Yeah, I actually got lucky on this one. I think it was already injured or something attacked it." She pointed to a large gash on its face. "It wasn't moving all that great."

Jordan smiled, "Welp, too bad for it. Cause it's dinner now."

Stacy smiled.

Jordan looked upriver, "So shall we go get Tim and Jason?"

Stacy and Cindy nodded, and they began their march upstream.

WHEN THEY MET with Jason and Tim the sky is a fiery orange. In Tim's hands two small fish, in Jason's a broken fishing rod.

Tim smiled as they approached, "Hey how did you all do?"

Everyone showed their catches, Tim eyed Jordan's fish suspiciously. "Please don't tell me you ate raw fish."

Jordan chuckled, "No I just went a little overboard stabbing it."

Jordan motioned to Tim's fish, "I see y'all had some luck."

Tim frowned, "Yeah, we would have had more but Jason hooked a big fish and it broke his rod."

Jason cut a look at Tim before looking away, "It was a flimsy stick, not my fault."

Jordan shrugged, "It's fine we can just make another rod. Let's head back and don't worry I'll be eating the small fish nugget." His stomach growled in protest.

After eating and building another sturdier rod. They spruce up camp a bit more before going to bed.

THE NEXT MORNING Jordan stood in the river, the current felt stronger today. His stomach ached from the lack of food. His grip on his spear was weak and with every passing second the current threatened to knock him down.

"I gotta do good today. We can't afford to struggle for food everyday."

He sunk down into the water, leaned back, aimed his spear towards the surface and summoned his circle.

"They like the light."

He placed the circle in front of the spear and waited.

It didn't take long for a curious fish to wander over, it darted around the tip of the spear before taking hesitant bites at the circle.

"Wait for it."

It moved in front of the circle, Jordan slowly pulled the spear back. He felt his chest get heavy from lack of air.

"Almost there."

The fish stopped moving, with a flick of the wrist the spear flew through the circle and into the stomach of the fish. Jordan grabbed the end of the spear and shot up out the water. He held the spear high towards the sky, water rained down around. At the end of the spear, was the fish. Its blood trickled down the shaft of the spear towards Jordan's hand.

Jordan roared in victory.

"I did it! I can use magic. I can use magic to hunt. We'll survive. I'll make sure of it."

He lowered the spear and secured his kill. Once the fish was tied to a nearby tree, he took a deep breath and continued the hunt.

HIS BODY SHIVERED WITH EXCITEMENT. He marched out of the water, in his hand his spear and at the end of the spear was his third catch of the day. After drying off he threw his pants back on. He gutted and cleaned the fish. As he finished the process, he threw the guts into some nearby bushes, then dipped the corpses into the water to rinse them off. After attaching the fish to the front of his pants, he sat on the ground and rested before meeting up with the girls again. His body was exhausted. He let out a large yawn. He smiled and blinked.

FROM THE DARKNESS, a voice spooked him awake. "Oh, goddamn it."

Bushes rustled nearby.

He felt a soft, slightly damp hand touch his arm, and his body shook as it nudged him.

"Hey. You alright?" Another voice asked.

Jordan's eyes shot open. He had fallen asleep; his sore back ached from being hunched over for so long. He looked up and saw Cindy and Stacy looking down at him. He grinned, "Yeah, I am." He sat back and showed them the fishes he caught.

Cindy blinked in surprise. "Holy shit. You got three of them?"

He chuckled. "Yeah, I will tell you all about how I did it back at camp. I'm exhausted." He followed up with a big yawn and a twist of his body. He popped his back, sending a wave of deep relaxation through his body.

Cindy helped Jordan up.

Stacy picked up his spear and handed it to him.

Jordan took it and looked around, "Have you seen my shir--" He spotted it on the ground the end of which just barely in some bushes. "Ah nevermind." He bent down and picked it up, when he went to shake it off, he noticed two small dots above two larger almost oval like dots on the very end of his shirt.

"Is this... a partial paw print?"

His heart raced and his eyes widened.

"How close was this beast to me? When was it close to me?"

He glanced at the spot where he was sleeping at.

"While I slept?"

A wave of dread washed over him.

Stacy touched his shoulder and he jumped.

Stacy flinched, "You alright?"

Jordan turned with a warm smile, "Yeah just got lost in thought sorry." He shook off his shirt and threw it on. "Let's go get Tim and Jason, see if they had good luck too."

AS THEY WALKED UPRIVER Jordan threw a glance over his shoulder, just in case. Though he saw nothing, the sense of dread lingered over him.

They marched towards the fishing group. Jordan with his three-fish hanging by his belt loop and Stacy carried the only one they caught in her hands, gutted and ready for consumption. After a moment the fishing group came into sight. Even from range it was plain to see Jason's annoyance. The scowl on his face, his clenched fist, his refusal to look straight but down and to the left. Even though Tim held up a final fish in one hand and a few stalks of river leeks in the other. Jason's rage damped the achievement. Jason's eyes noticed the three fish hanging from Jordan's waist.

His face reddened, "Bro. How did you--?"

Jordan raised his hand to stop him. He smiled, "It's easier to show than tell. But, before it gets dark Stacy, and I will clean the fish and some leeks for dinner tonight."

Jason sucked air through his teeth and started walking back to camp. Tim looked at Jordan as if to say, *"He tried..."*

Jordan replied with a shrug.

He looked at Stacy, who smiled with an eagerness to learn. Stacy was fine with the descaling, but the gutting still made her squeamish. Jordan just chuckled at her reactions. After cleaning and inspecting the fish, they gathered all their prepared ingredients. But something caught Jordan's eye. Across the river, something was watching them. It had dark green fur, yellow eyes, and a stern-looking face. It laid low to the ground, as if studying Jordan and Stacy. Jordan and the beast locked eyes. A murderous chill ran through his body.

"Shit, how long has that been there?"

Jordan tried to hide his sudden fear from Stacy, unsure of how she'd react to the beast.

Stacy didn't seem to notice; she was still feeling the high of learning how to gut and descale fish.

The beast started to stand up and lean forward as if it's about to pounce. Jordan slowly reached for his spear, his eyes widening as he kept his eyes locked onto the beast. Slowly he put his weight on his front foot readying his body to move at a moment's notice.

The beast lifted its head then looked off to the side for a moment before retreating back into the forest.

Jordan relaxed; it was only now that he realized Stacy had been rambling about something. He put on a brave smile, "Hey, let's... let's head back to camp."

Stacy nodded and returned his smile. "Sure, let's go."

She tilted her head, "Are you alright you look... pale?"

Jordan nodded, "Yeah just hungry. Let's hurry up and cook these."

Stacy nodded and bounced off towards camp.

As they headed off, Jordan looked over his shoulder and saw the creature had disappeared.

Back at camp, Cindy had made some "Umbrellas" out of branches and rope. She also did another experiment with the Blood Leaves stacking them on top of each other to create a thicker and hopefully stronger blade. Tim had started a fire and Jason sat off by himself. Jordan looked at Cindy, then glanced at Jason before furrowing his brows back at Cindy. Cindy replied with a shrug of her shoulders and a soft shake of her head. When Jason noticed Jordan was back at camp, he stood up and marched over to him. Cindy's eyes grew wide, and Stacy took a step back, Jordan stood his ground.

"So, are you going to tell everyone how you got three fish?"

"Jesus, I just got back to camp." He chuckled. "Once I get the fish cooking, we can talk all about it Jason." He walked off with a coy smile.

Jason glared but dropped the issue for now.

Jordan softly sighed in relief.

"Sorry Jason but I want to produce results before getting your hopes up."

He felt he couldn't perform magic now. His body is exhausted, and his mind felt burnt out. It almost felt like his mind was strained, he needed to understand the limits of his magic better.

AFTER STUFFING the fish with leeks and running a stake through them, he placed them near the fire to cook. Jordan gathered everyone around, Jason's eyes burned with impatience. Jordan tried to stall for more time to gather his energy; he still felt tapped out.

Jordan turned with a grin. "Okay, good news and bad news guys, which one you wanna hear first?" He tried to lighten the mood but was met with a stick snapping.

"Tell us about the fish." Jason's face was red. He dropped the stick, his glare trained on Jordan.

"I saw that coming… but why is he so mad?"

He sighed, "Fair enough. How I caught the fish is complicated, but it could prove very effective for us if we all can do it. Let me..." Jordan grabbed a leek and walked over to the fire to roast it.

Everyone watched in silence after the leek was roasted Jordan ate as much as he could.

This brought confused looks from everyone. To stop questions, Jordan held up a finger as he swallowed and took deep breaths. The food helped, but he still wasn't sure if he could do magic.

He focused like he did earlier. Soon his Spell Circle appeared in his hand, its color is faded compared to the circles he summoned earlier. It spun slowly, as if waiting for a command.

"I can barely focus on this right now."

He took a deep breath. "Two nights ago something happened while I was sleeping. I heard a voice, and it told me a word."

He told them how the following day was the day he felt extremely exhausted and later that day is when he learned that he could use magic now. Everyone sat with wide eyes as Jordan showed them the circle in his hands. They tried to touch it, but their fingers simply passed through.

Tim looked up. "Why didn't you tell us?"

Jordan shrugged. "I was afraid of getting your hopes up. Even though I practiced one night, I still wanted to make sure it wasn't some fever dream."

Jason scoffed. "And you think that's a good reason to keep that a secret? How do I know you aren't lying? Show us something." His voice caused everyone near him to flinch.

"Okay, Imma be real with you Jason. I fucking can't deal with you right now. I caught three fish today, if I practice more, I can keep providing food. That's a good thing. Chill out."

Jason opened his mouth to say something else, but Jordan held up his hands, "Stop. We're too hungry to be forcing arguments, just shut the fuck up and let me cook the damn fish."

"Jesus, why did that turn so sour? That should have been good news."

Before Jordan could make it back to the fire to check on the fish, Jason threw out one last comment. "Next time you better tell us right away instead of hiding shit from us."

Jordan smirked in annoyance.

"I tried."

He turned around and looked at Jason. He crossed his arms and leaned back a bit. "Jason, why are you mad? Let's talk about this."

Cindy frowned, "Yeah, you've been constantly angry since like yesterday, what's up?"

Jason shot a hurt look at Cindy as he angrily fixed his hair, trying not to make eye contact with anyone.

Jordan nodded to himself, as he studied Jason. "Is it because you feel useless?"

"Jordan!" Cindy and Stacy both snapped at him.

He looks at them with an upturned hand. "It's a serious question. He only seems to get mad when someone performs better than him in any area. Well, he gets mad at the men of the group, anyway."

Jason glared. "I do not."

Tim frowned. "No, he is right. You do get mad whenever we do something you can't."

Jason's knuckles were white as he turned to Tim. "Like when?"

Tim, unphased by Jason's aggression, continued. "Like now? You were furious he came back with three fish and you couldn't catch any. This entire argument started because you were so hung up on how Jordan caught three fish in one day."

Jason got up and moved towards Tim, who leaned back, trying to put distance between them.

Jordan stepped forward. "Jason..." He summoned his Circle. "You touch Tim and I will put your head through a tree."

Jordan glared at Jason.

"Please back off... this doesn't need to get violent..."

He felt guilt flow into his stomach.

"I really shouldn't be doing this."

Jason stared for a moment before succumbing to the threat and sat away from the group. Stacy jumped up and rushed to the fish, the smell of burnt flesh hanging loosely in the air. She reached them in time and hurried them away from the fire.

With tension still high in the air, everyone but Jason grabbed a fish skewer and ate quietly. Cindy took Jason a skewer, but he refused to eat. Finally with a full stomach but with heavy hearts, the group went to sleep filled with mixed emotions, hoping tomorrow will be better.

4

TREE BOUNCING

THE NEXT MORNING CAME, and though the sun shined its gentle rays provided no heat, each soft breeze caused more goosebumps to form. Jordan sat up slowly and looked at the group. Jason had eaten his fish from last night. His eyes were bitter. Cindy laid on the ground, eyes open but filled with sadness. Tim sat with Stacy. Their eyes had a small flicker of hope that today would be better. Without words, they gathered fishing supplies and made their way to the river. Jason and Tim with the fishing rods, Jordan, Stacy and Cindy with spears. They said no farewells, just glances as the two groups went their different directions.

The river looked different today; the waters rushed faster, fish leaped constantly before belly flopping back in.

Stacy dipped a toe in, "Maybe it rained somewhere?"

Cindy scratched her head, "Or a dam broke. Look at how strong the river is and all the fish, if we had a net, we could catch hundreds of them in a single day."

Jordan kicked off his shoes. "Well, it looks like I won't have to use magic today, so that's good at least."

As they worked on catching their dinner, they did so in silence until Cindy spoke up. "So, I think when we get back to camp, we all should gather around and air some things out."

Jordan stabbed the water, missing a large fish that darted off down the river. "Yeah, my bad about last night. I should have handled that better. I was just... I don't know I brought good news and he basically shitted on it. When we get back, I will try to apologize to Jason."

Cindy stopped hunting for a moment. "I think his head wound might be to blame. Remember when we left you alone in the woods?"

Jordan looked over, "Yeah?"

She shuffled in place, "Well, Jason wanted me to follow him, so I did but... It was like he forgot what he was doing. He was just super confused, and we ended up kind of lost because of it."

Jordan thought for a moment, "He was unnecessarily mad at Tim like the day after that. Maybe we're just pushing him too hard, we're stressed and not eating as much as we should be."

Cindy frowned softly, "So what do we do?"

Jordan sighed, "... First things first we need to--"

Stacy held up a fish on a spear. "Got one." She glanced over at the two before blushing. "Sorry. Keep going." She turned around to stab the water some more.

Jordan chuckled, "We need to get food."

Jordan summoned his spell circle, "Follow my lead."

⸻

THE SUN WAS high in the sky, the trio marched upstream, making small talk and carrying four decent sized fishes. Their smiles faded as they came upon a still angry Jason and a timid Tim.

Jason scoffed. "Only four fish this time? I expected more."

Jordan smirked. "Well, **we** got four and figured Tim could catch one. Looks like he caught three so there is no need for us to catch anymore."

Cindy popped him in the arm. "Stop."

He looked at her and rubbed the spot, "Ow..." He gave her a

playful look. To which she rolled her eyes and shook her head. Jordan shrugged in response.

Jason glared. "Tim didn't catch all three fish. I caught one."

Jordan gasped and opened his eyes wider. "Progress... I'm proud of you."

Cindy rolled her eyes. "Guys, can we not fight? We got food, let's go back to camp, we still have a lot to do."

Jordan shrugged and walked back to camp, followed by Tim and Stacy with Cindy and Jason in the back.

AS THEY WALKED TO CAMP, Jordan kept scanning the foliage for the animal he saw, but he was also worried about Jason starting another fight. Every snapped twig causes him to jump in his skin. He could feel himself grinding his teeth, the look in his eyes grew fiercer by the second.

"Damn, why am I so agitated right now? This isn't good or helpful, I'm popping off at the mouth too much. I need to relax."

He saw something black blocking their path; he stopped abruptly taking the rest of the group by surprise.

Jason snickered as he walked to the front. "Did you get lost or something?"

Jordan continued to look at the mass in front of him. "Not the time Jason."

In the middle of the path sat an animal, dark green fur with yellow eyes. Its front paws were enormous, and each sported a thick nub that could be a thumb. The front legs were long and skinny. Its hind legs looked full of muscle. Its head was small and aerodynamic. Two thick fangs peeked from under its upper lip. It sat there with a stern look on its face, as if expecting something.

Stacy moved behind Jordan. "What do you think it wants?"

Tim unhooked one fish and tossed it to the feline. Who bent down and picked it up with its mouth before walking away. Jordan noticed the hind legs appear shorter than its front legs. The group walked faster to camp, hoping they satisfied the beast.

ONCE AGAIN, the beast appeared before them, with the same expecting look on its face.

Jason growled, "We just gave you some fish, fuck off."

The beast seemed to ignore Jason until he bent down and picked up a rock. He brought his arm back.

"Jason no."

Jordan lunged to grab Jason's arm but was too slow. The rock flew from Jason's hand and hit the beast square in the face, just above the right eye, causing it to stagger. Blood dripped from the wound. The air was suffocating as the beast glared at the group. Jordan felt the murderous aura of the beast once again. The beast jumped into the bushes, seeming to run off.

Without saying a word, the entire group ran to their camp, their minds filled with fear as their legs carried them home as fast as they could. Once they saw the remains of their fire, they stopped and caught their breath while scattered throughout the camp. But all eyes were on Jason.

Once Jordan gathered enough breath, his eyes grew sharp as he glared towards Jason. "Have you lost your fucking mind?"

Jason glared back. "What? You just wanted to give that thing another fish?"

"We had seven fish, seven fucking fish. We could have given it one more and everyone would still have food. Instead, we now have a pissed off animal."

Jason looked around confused. "I didn't know you were such a pussy. You wanted to just give that cat food? We didn't spend all day, hunting just to give it away."

"You are really stupid if you think pissing it off was a better idea."

Stacy moved towards them, edging ever so slightly. "Guys. Chill out."

Jason's grip tightened around the fishing pole as he got into Jordan's face. "Fuck you."

Jordan deflated with a snigger. "Great point Jason. I'm seeing your side of the argument."

Tim jumped in between them. "Jordan, let it go."

Jason shoved past Tim. "Yeah, listen to the fucking nerd."

Jordan's voice cracked with frustration. "At least—", He cleared his throat and tried to calm down, "This is fucking stupid Jason." He took a step forward, "Either you calm the fu--" His attention was stolen. His head slowly turned to Cindy as his face dropped.

Cindy was red in the face. "Guys chill the fu--"

She goes to yell, only to realize they were no longer fighting among themselves but staring at her, their eyes wide and mouths agape. From behind Cindy, the enormous cat from earlier embraced her. Its massive paws wrap around her body. A mouth filled with ivory daggers opened wide before crunching down on her neck as it tackled her to the ground.

Her scream shook the group to their core and froze them in fear. She clawed at the ground then at her neck, trying to escape the clutches of the beast. It shook its head in defiance, pulling her back whenever she tried to crawl away.

As the beast tore into her neck, holding her down as it had its way with her. Stacy and Tim slowly backed away, reeling from the sight before them. Jason and Jordan stood in fear, forgetting to breathe. Cindy reached out for the group with a desperate plea as she cried.

She gagged, her eyes were filled with terror, blood leaked from the sides of her mouth. She forced two words from her mouth. "Help me!"

Her plea snapped Jordan back to life; he brought the spear over his head, summoning his spell circle in front of the head.

"Save her."

He threw it with all his might into the circle, the spear flew at a great speed. Cindy, in her struggle to get away, leaned up right as the spear was in front of her. Silence fell upon the camp as the spear ran through her chest.

"Ah.. a... h.." Cindy tried to speak, but all she could muster was a bubbling groan. She went limp as the light faded from her eyes.

The beast, no longer interested in her, let go and sat on top of Cindy's lifeless body and gave the surviving members a disdainful look.

"I-it's making a statement?"

Jordan's mind raced.

"Do we run or fight? What's the best move here?"

Jordan desperately tried to reach a solution.

"Run or fight, run or fight, run or fight, run or fight, run or fight."

Jordan was in a full-blown panic as the beast readied itself to pounce again.

Jordan chose, "Run."

His shout was the bell for round two. Everyone bolted into action. Tim and Stacy turned and ran, Jason turned to follow them, Jordan ran to the right to grab another one of the Blood Leaf spears. Jordan reached the spear. His fingers clawed the ground as he snatched it up. He turned to face the beast, but it was no longer in front of him. He spun around and he flinched with shock to see the beast dividing the group.

"What?"

Tim stopped and realized the situation. "Guys?"

Stacy grabbed his arm. "We have to run." She yanked on him and got him moving again.

Jordan and Jason stared at their hunter before turning around and running in the other direction. Jordan glanced back and saw the beast staring at them as if giving them a head start before it jumped into the bushes.

As Jordan ran alongside Jason, his mind worked overtime.

"Why go after me and Jason? Tim and Stacy would be the easier prey. I understand Cindy, she was isolated."

At the thought of Cindy, the image of the spear killing her appeared in Jordan's mind. He shook his head defiantly as he kept thinking. He glanced at Jason, whose face gave him the answer he was looking for. Jason is traumatized, his face distorted with panic. When he glanced at Jordan, the panic became focused and delusional. A betraying smile crept onto his face.

"I get it... We aren't a team, so you're guaranteed to kill at least one of us. If it came to it, Jason would leave me to die to save himself."

He scoffed.

"Tim would try to help Stacy, Stacy would try to help Tim. That makes them more of a threat than me and Jason. This beast is cunning. How long had it been watching us?"

A sad chuckle leaked from his mouth as he ran.

"This is bad..."

The sound of a rushing beast behind interrupted Jordan's thoughts. He turned to his hunter, who was running full speed at him. If this continued, it would catch up to them. Once again Jordan glanced at Jason, who seemed to have arrived at the same conclusion.

"I just have to..."

Jordan summoned his spell circle and started to turn towards the beast.

"Trip the beast."

The light of the spell circle shined brightly in the dark forest, illuminating the area. As Jordan turned his eyes caught Jason's face. The light cast traitorous shadows over Jason's face, Jason's eyes opened wider he gripped his rod and went to trip Jordan. Jordan caught the attempt from the corner of his eye. He instinctively went to block, the sudden refocusing of his mind caused him to accidentally cast Gao while he tried jumping out of the way. The rod is pushed downwards into Jason's legs tangling them up and causing him to fall. Jordan landed and lost his balance, he tumbled backwards but managed to recover. He looked up and saw the beast was already pouncing. His heart sunk as the beast chomped down on Jason's shoulder.

Jason screamed out. In his desperate rage, he threw his rod. "You fucking bastard. How could you? Help me!"

Jordan stepped forward; he gripped his spear tightly readying himself for a fight. The beast looked up and released Jason. It leaned forward readying a pounce, its ivory teeth now coated with blood.

Jason's shoulder squirted blood onto his face and the ground. This image stopped Jordan, his mind reminded him of a word.

"Run."

Jordan swallowed his remorse and ran. His mind only focused on survival even more so when the rod Jason threw entangled itself in his legs, causing him to stagger but he recovered and kept running as fast as he could. His arm bled from his earlier tumble.

He ran to the sound of Jason screaming while he was being mauled. He ran aimlessly, taking random turns to lose the beast. Up ahead, there was a clearing. Jordan ran as fast as he could. Hoping to get away from all the trees. When he stepped into the clearing, he instead found a steep hill. Losing his footing, he tumbled all the way down, clutching his spear in his right hand as he slammed into the rushing river below, getting carried downstream.

IT WAS dark when Jordan came too, his right hand still clutching his spear, although enough of it had broken in the fall to make it more of a dagger now. He stood up, wincing as sharp pains shot through his entire body. He looked at his left arm, which hung low. Sighing, he popped it back into place. His vision flickered. With his arm popped back in, he wrapped his arm in his shirt to stop the bleeding as he limped away from the shore. Finding a small spot to set up camp, he quickly started a fire with nearby wood and leaves. Glancing at his dagger, he noticed the blade was thicker.

"Must be one Cindy made by stacking the leaves on top of each other."

He sighed and sat alone in the dark for the first time since he got here.

"Seven days… it took Seven days for this to all go to shit."

Jordan clutched the dagger as he stared at the ground. He slipped deep into his thoughts.

"What do I do now?"

The Burning voice spoke to him, *"To the left."*

Jordan's eyes opened wide as he looked over, hoping to see the person the voice belonged to. Instead, he is met with giant paws reaching out to him. Instinctively he leaned back and cast Gao, causing the beast to fly over him, missing its pounce. The beast tumbled to the ground before regaining its stance, unphased by the spell. Jordan got up and got into a deep fencing stance. His eyes opened wide as he focused only on the enemy in front of him.

The voice spoke once more. *"Only one use of Gao left. What are you going to do?"*

Jordan readjusted his position, keeping his eyes trained on the beast, "If you aren't going to help, shut the fuck up."

The beast readied itself to pounce.

The voice chuckled. *"If it hits that pounce you will die."*

Jordan gripped his dagger tighter. "Shut... up."

Sounding amused, the voice spoke again, *"The final round... will you survive? Don't disappoint me."*

Jordan ignored the voice this time. He focused all his energy on this next casting of Gao. The Spell Circle swelled under his feet as his muscles tensed, readying his coup. His vision grew dark, obscuring everything besides the beast in front of him.

The world grew silent as it watched the conclusion to the duel. The beast jumped forward, claws outstretched; fangs bared. Jordan lunged forward, his spell pushed him with extreme force.

It happened in the blink of an eye, but to Jordan and the beast. The events took an eternity to unfold.

Jordan's eyes homed in on a sweet spot in the beast's attack, a small area offering the best place to sink a dagger into.

"There."

He braced for impact. His lunge had placed him past the beast's claws. Propelled by his spell his dagger crashed into the beasts' chest, caving it in and knocking the predator back. Razor-sharp claws scratched Jordan's arm on the way out. The collision threw both combatants away from each other. Jordan's lightweight body gets shoved back near the campfire. While the bulky cat fell backwards and cracked its head on a nearby tree before falling onto its side.

The voice cheered. *"Wonderful."*

Jordan struggled to sit up on the ground, his body exhausted and shaking with fatigue. His breath heavy, his face flushed and his eyes bloodshot. They struggled to stay open.

He felt his conscience drifting away, but heard the groaning of a dying beast. He forced himself to stand up. His world spun as he lumbered towards the beast laying on the ground. Blood pouring out profusely from its chest. A gaping wound revealing where Jordan had hit. The adrenaline faded from Jordan's body, the sense of danger flowing away like the beast's blood. He knelt over the beast who stared up at him; it looked almost like the beast was proud of Jordan.

Jordan bowed his head softly. "Thank you." He raised his dagger and delivered the coup de grâce, ending the battle. Jordan fell onto his side. Finally, he could rest.

5

FERAL MINDED

IN THE DARKNESS, Jordan stood. His mind was still. He felt warmth coil around his body; it lifted his right arm into the air while being guided by these warm strings.

In a loving, almost motherly way, the voice spoke to him. "Focus now, you don't have much time."

Instinctively, Jordan summoned his circle. Its purple hue illuminated his regretful face. He sighed and the spell circle flickered as he lowered both his gaze and his arm. A fiery hand stroked his hair and lifted his chin.

"No, focus."

Jordan tried to look for the body attached to these hands but could never quite get a good look. It was always just beyond his vision. He gave up and allowed his head to be lifted. "Why didn't you tell me?"

The hands moved to his arm lifting it slowly, he could see there was no body attached. Instead they were simply floating hands.

The voice spoke again, "Tell you what?"

"What would happen."

"I'm not all knowing nor am I all powerful. A gambler would have bet on you guys giving the beast a fish and that gambler would have lost their money."

Jordan clenched his fist, "Why didn't you give them all magic?"

The voice chuckled, "Various reasons but I suppose the biggest one is… interest."

Jordan's face scrunched up, "Interest?"

"Correct. I wasn't interested in teaching them anything, if one of the others were, I suspect they would have reached out. Plus not all can learn, whether or not they could I don't know. Like I said, I wasn't interested so I didn't check. Now focus."

A bright orange light flooded the room. Jordan turned to look. A colossal orange spell circle hovered in the air. Compared to his, it was like a dinner plate next to a deep space radio dish. Next to him stood a titan silhouette cloaked in a raging fire. She stood straight up, her shoulders back and head tilted up. Her arm outstretched as tendrils of flames danced around her. Fire waved in the air behind her head, giving the appearance of a full, thick head of hair. Her feet and hands were clawed. But that was all Jordan could make out. Her fire burned too brightly for him to stare at for too long. In this dark void she was the only light. Jordan wished he could stand closer to her, he felt inspired by her.

"Focus and repeat. Ver."

Jordan looked in front of him and repeated the word. "Ver."

A new symbol appeared in the middle of his circle. It glowed, and its shimmering grew louder and louder before it shattered. The dream collapsed; and Jordan fell to his knees in exhaustion. He looked at the Burning Queen as his vision faded. In the darkness he saw two figures staring at him, one small and curious, the other… proud?

Jordan awoke the next day, exhausted, stiff as a board and his head pounding. But he was alive, and that's all that mattered to him. He looked at the corpse of the beast he had slain, his dagger embedded triumphantly in the head. Grabbing the handle, he skinned the beast. Being careful to get it all in one piece. He was oddly good at this, even though it was his first time. After he finished cutting the head off as he laid the pelt on the ground fur side down. He got to work cutting chunks of meat off, laying them on the pelt. Afterwards he started harvesting bones he could sharpen into tools and weapons. Last, he harvested the stomach, hoping he could use it for a makeshift water bottle. After starting a new fire, he skewered the meat and left them to cook while he dragged the carcass away from his camp and went to clean his pelt, stomach and his dagger.

AT THE RIVER, he washed off as much blood and dirt as he could, making sure he cleansed his wounds. He drank his fill of water and cleaned the pelt. The pelt is simple to clean. Jordan used the blade to scrape any bugs and burs he saw while trying to keep the skin intact. The stomach proved tougher. After washing the outside, he turned it inside out and saw the lining.

He tugged on the lining, feeling it pull slightly away. "Shit, I wasn't really expecting this."

He grabbed the lining and gripped his dagger. Carefully, he cut it away. While he focused on the tasks, he remembered to keep checking on the meat, which was slowly turning a deep brownish red. He let some pieces cook longer than others to dry them out, hoping to extend how long they last. After he finished cleaning the stomach, he stripped and cleaned his clothes.

As he stood naked by his campfire, chewing on freshly cooked meat, he thought about his next move.

"I shouldn't stay in this forest for long. That... Tree Bouncer is dangerous and even that Drop Pig almost killed someone. Should I try to find Tim and Stacy?"

His mind flashed back to Tim and Stacy running away, he shook his head.

"They most likely made it out of the forest and probably won't enter again."

He looked around and thought back to everything he's seen in this forest, nothing seemed familiar, his mind reminded him of his tumble into the river.

He nodded.

"My best plan is to get out of the forest as fast as possible. The river carried me downstream so hopefully I'm close to the edge. Alright let's prepare."

Once his clothes dried, he tested his stomach water bottle. To his satisfaction, the bottle didn't leak. He tied one end of the stomach tight and filled it with water. Next, he wrapped the over cooked meat in his pelt, piercing it with small, sharpened bones to pin the pelt together. Using his belt, he hung the package in a tree for safekeeping. By the time he finished preparing everything, the sun was setting. Before he went to sleep, he summoned his spell circle. Next to the symbol for Gao sat another symbol.

He grabbed a stick and placed it in the dirt away from him, he focused.

"I believe it was... Ver."

The symbol flashed in the middle of the circle. The stick in the ground came flying at Jordan, hitting him in the face as if someone threw it at him.

He inhaled sharply while holding his face. "Son of a bitch."

He placed the stick back into the dirt and focused again.

"Ver." The stick again came flying to him. This time he caught it.

"A pulling spell?"

Jordan threw the stick into the air, and he opened his palm as if taking aim.

"Ver."

The stick suddenly changed direction and came towards him, landing on the ground.

"Yep, pulling spell."

He felt a wave of excitement flow through his tired body. While he was exhausted from the fight he didn't feel as tired as he normally did after casting four spells.

After dumping more wood into his fire, he sat down against a tree. He wanted to go to bed early, hoping he could make it out of the forest in one day.

HE WOKE up the next morning, tears stained his cheeks. His eyes held more tears that were waiting to roll down his cheeks, his stuffed nose gurgled when he tried to breathe through it. He reached up and wiped his tears away. He felt the remains of a sad dream flowing away.

"Why am I crying?"

Try as he might, he couldn't remember what he dreamt of last night. Wanting to waste no more time he quickly gathered his things. He stuffed his pockets full of dried meat, filled his stomachs with water. He wrapped the pelt around his body like a cape and marched. With no way to tell his direction or his position, he decided on a very simple plan. He was going to walk in a straight line until he escaped.

SADLY, this forest was thicker than he imagined. After five days of travel, he was running out of food and had to substitute it with more water. He was having troubles sleeping and every morning he'd wake up with tears on his face. His heart and mind conspired to suppress his emotions and to keep him moving through the forest. The only objective was surviving.

Every day and every night, he tried to contact the voice. Whenever he focused his mind, an image wafted into his mind. He could see a silhouette of a great being surrounded by smaller beings of various sizes. Focusing on the being, he could hear muttering, but couldn't make out any words. As much as he wanted to, he didn't practice his magic. The thought of wearing himself out and suffering for it overrode his eagerness.

On the sixth day he felt strange, his body ached and burned. It exhausted him. He looked at the wounds on his arms. They were swollen and red. Any pressure would cause pus to leak out.

"Infected."

The only word Jordan could think of as he drained the wounds.

Slowly, he marched on. His mind deteriorating from his wounds.

The voice came in hazy and broken. *"Yo...ing..."*

By the seventh day, he forgot to drain his wound, he only focused on walking. By the eighth day he had forgotten why he was walking. His body ached with every step, it begged him to stop moving but the last bit of survival instincts he had forced him to keep moving. He would only stop to gulp down more water.

In his daze He didn't notice that the trees looked bigger; the wind danced differently; the creatures sung louder, and bushes are stocked with fruits and flowers. At night, the sounds of the forest lulled him to sleep while the cool earth provided a soft bed for him to lie on.

When morning came, it was gentle, like a mother's kiss on the forehead. The sunlight energized instead of burned. But Jordan couldn't appreciate the beauty in his current state. He had become oblivious to all non-threatening stimuli. His vision was a black tunnel, only seeing the dimming light in front of him.

ONE GENTLE AFTERNOON, while walking through a clearing, he heard a buzzing sound and what sounded like high pitched screaming. He turned and followed the noise.

He came upon a spider's web, in the web a small person struggled. Their tiny butterfly wings flapped desperately. In the web's corner, a spider the size of a beach ball crawled closer towards the trapped being.

Jordan glanced at the spider as he approached. He slowly raised his hand, weakly clutching his dagger. He stabbed quickly, destroying a section of web but not freeing the trapped creature. The spider's legs curled inwards, trembling as it embraced death. Jordan sniffed it and gagged.

"Can't eat it."

He let it slide off the blade and fall to the ground.

He walked over to the trapped creature and plucked it off the web. It was a small humanoid with white hair and small butterfly wings.

The small humanoid squeaked in his grip, "Isal veri atil me."

Jordan couldn't understand the language. He just flipped it around in his hands, inspecting and removing small traces of web. His mind only focusing on whether he could eat this thing. He gently squeezed it and felt bones underneath the flesh.

"Can I eat this?"

"Mekah tei u li?"

A twig snapping refocused Jordan's attention. He turned to see another "Tree Bouncer" sitting in the grass, staring at him to start a challenge. He could see a partly healed wound just above the right eye.

Jordan loosened his grip on the squeaking creature and turned to square up with his new foe.

The small humanoid struggled in his hand before breaking away and pulling on Jordan's shirt. *"Rau muy waiq ti."*

The Tree bouncer got into its usual pounce stance; Jordan mimicked. Instead of jumping forward, it jumped towards the nearest tree and started ricocheting in various directions around Jordan.

A moment of clarity flooded into Jordan's mind.

"Shit, what am I doing? I can't fight this."

He saw the beast turn and pounce towards him; he lifted his hand to cast Gao, but the circle wouldn't fully form. In a ditch effort, he dodged out the way. The beast jumped back into the forest and begun circling again.

"Why didn't it work?"

He dodged another pounce from the tree bouncer, but his arm gets clipped by its claws, reopening the infected wound from earlier. In a panic, Jordan rushed into the thicket and placed his back against a tree.

His jellylike mind informed him of his error as he realized the situation.

"Am I fucking stupid? Why did I do this?"

He heard the bushes around rustling and the sounds of claws digging into wood. He focused on his hand again, failing to summon the circle. The sound of footsteps snatched his attention. He looked towards the sound and is greeted by a large swipe from the beast.

Razor-sharp claws rake across his chest. The pain makes him buckle at the knees and fall on his back. With a sharp growl the beast leaned forward but hesitates, it looked around and jumped back into the bushes. The world became unstable, every movement made it spin and distort. His mind focused on every little movement and sound. He forced himself to his feet. The sounds were coming from all around. His heart drummed loudly in his chest. He lost track of the beast; the area was oddly silent besides the beating of his heart.

From a nearby bush, the beast shot out, its claws outstretched, fangs bared. Eyes deadly focused.

It slammed headfirst into the tree next to Jordan and collapsed to the ground.

Jordan stood next to it, wide-eyed. He looked around in confusion. *"Wait what? It missed? How? Why?"*

The beast struggled back to its feet and started wildly swiping at the air away from Jordan.

Jordan backed away. "What are you doing?"

The beast turned around, its face bloodied, eyes unfocused. It hissed and swiped at the air once more. Its head snapped around and it continued hissing and swiping at ghosts.

Jordan gripped the dagger tighter and slowly approached from behind. He took aim and stabbed it in the neck. It reared up and roared loudly. Jordan fell back and pushed himself away. The standing beast suddenly went limp and fell to the ground. Jordan waited and approached it slowly.

It laid there unmoving, mouth agape.

"Wha—",

The air cracked, and a sharp pain followed. It spread from his back to over his collarbone; he screamed and felt the area. A deep bleeding lash like from a whip, the world melted and warped itself around him. A few feet away he could see something wiggling. It was large and green. Deep green strands danced around it. After a moment, it faded from sight. Unsure of what that was, Jordan forced himself to his feet and out of the thicket. Something snagged his ankle, and he tripped.

He was tired, his blood soaked into the earth. His body was shutting down. His heart struggled to move the scarce blood to all his organs. Something tugged on his ankle and his body is dragged for a moment. He couldn't turn his head around; he could barely keep his eyes open. Something fleshy exploded behind him.

He laid his head down. His breathing grew shallower by the second.

"*I can't move...*"

As his eyes closed, he heard rustling from the bushes.

"*Fuck.*"

Darkness overtook him as he lost consciousness.

6

NEW FRIENDS

JORDAN OPENED HIS EYES, it's dark and the world is silent. He looked around and realized he is in the middle of camp. His head ached as he tried to remember. All around him the camp was in disarray, he felt like he was forgetting something, or he was searching for something. He rummaged around, lifting rocks and leaves in search of this object.

A voice echoed behind him, "Hey Jordan."

Jordan turned around to see Cindy standing upright with a warm smile on her face. He relaxed and smiled back. "Hey, what's up Cindy?" He glanced around for this phantom object.

She continued to smile. "What are you looking for?" She stood oddly still, her hands behind her back, and she tilted her head to the right. Her eyes are wide and quizzical.

"Oh, I am looking for…" It dawned on Jordan that he did not know what he was searching for.

"Is it your fishing spear?"

A sudden realization barged into Jordan's mind. "Yeah. I think that's what I'm looking for. Have you seen it?". His eyes focused on Cindy, who was still in the same position with the same warm smile.

Her voice echoed with a slight distortion. "Yes, I have."

Jordan noticed something strange on Cindy's chest; it looked like a brown dot. Cindy smiled as her hand reached up and pulled on the dot. The sound of flesh being slowly ripped apart flooded the world. Jordan hadn't noticed that the light had faded.

Cindy's voice cracked. "You left it here, don't you remember?" Blood flowed from the wound and down her chest.

Jordan took a step backwards and suddenly felt his body tighten up.

Bite and claw marks appeared on her neck and shoulders. "Don't you remember throwing it at me while I was getting mauled to death?"

More blood flowed from her body as a giant Tree Bouncer appeared behind her. It embraced her like a lover before sinking its teeth in her neck. Cindy cried as her warm smile trembled. The spear appeared in Jordan's hand as he watched her being ripped apart once again.

"Here, try again. I'm sure you can do it this time. After all, you have magic, don't you?"

Her voice was hollow, her eyes cold and piercing, her smile was no longer warm but manipulative. Jordan's hands trembled as they clutched the spear. He raised his hand like a puppet obeying its puppeteers' commands. His eyes watered as he took aim, summoned his spell circle, and threw the spear. The spear flew straight for the tree bouncer before changing direction and impaling Cindy in the chest, who lets out a world-shaking screech. The sheer loudness of it vibrated every bone in Jordan's body. Once the screeching stopped, Cindy looked at Jordan and smiled again.

She smiled as the spear appeared in Jordan's hand. "It's okay, try again."

Jordan shook his head, "I don't want to Cindy."

Cindy wrinkled her nose and smiled, "Why Jordan, you don't have a choice."

Controlled by an unknown power, Jordan once again lifted the spear, his spell circle shined bright. He threw it. Once again, the spear found its way inside Cindy. She rewarded Jordan with another blood-chilling screech. This force compelled Jordan to throw the spear, he tried to fight, but he couldn't. Every fiber of his being screamed to save Cindy, and those same fibers trembled whenever he failed. His mind was breaking as he choked back tears.

The cycle continued until a soft hand appeared on Jordan's chest, followed by a soothing voice.

A soft light came from the hand as it spread over his body. "Avu nalo quti."

A Bloody Cindy looked around, her voice oozed hatred. "Don't fucking interfere."

Jordan stared at Cindy in shock as she turned to look at him. Her face twisted back to her manipulative smile, but it seemed almost desperate. "Try again Jordan. You can do it this time; I know you can."

Before Jordan could react, the light engulfed him.

He heard a loud gasp as he opened his eyes. His vision was blurry, cheeks wet from tears only added to his confusion. He looked around and saw a person in the fog of his vision. His heart was in his throat as his mind raced. He clutched a soft blanket. A jolt of pain interrupted his attempt to sit up. He yelped, collapsing back into what felt like a bed. He finally noticed a hand trying to sooth and calm him down once his vision unblurred, he saw the person attached to the hand.

Her tight skin had an earthy cream color to it, her face was almost perfectly round, long green hair flowed down her back and hugged her waist. The areas around her eyes and mouth revealed how often she smiled. Jordan calmed down as this figure entranced him. As he scanned her body, he noted she was tiny, with small breasts, short arms, and legs. She was also thin. Her body reminded Jordan of a very short girl. Even stranger were her ears. They were large, and the bottom curved up to a point. The uppermost part of the ears were jagged, like someone broke a chunk off. He estimated her to be about three feet, maybe less.

The girl smiled, "Sil oua meli?"

"*Bitch what?*"

Jordan's blank stare must have given away his confusion.

The short girl smiled, turned away and brought up two flowers.

"Acnm telioo siao." The girl continued to talk as she leaned in with the flowers.

Jordan tensed up as he waited to see what her plan was. When the flower got close to his ear, it wiggled, Jordan reached up to swat at it. But once again his body reminded him he's at the mercy of this little girl. As the flower sunk into his ear, he felt a stabbing pain, followed by a numbing warmth. He could feel the flower digging into his eardrum and taking root. The pain made his jaw tremble as he sharply inhaled, it only lasted for a moment.

"Anc- u understand me now?"

The girl's voice suddenly came in perfect English.

Jordan was dumbstruck, mouth agape and eyes wide he slowly nodded.

"Good. My name is Singka. I am a healer; can you tell me your name?" She gestured to herself and then to Jordan.

Jordan's ears twitched as he looked around, drinking in his surroundings. He appeared to be in a wooden house. Light shined in the doorway, only impeded by a grass curtain. Singka sat there patiently, letting Jordan observe his surroundings. She saw a childlike curiosity on his face, something that she had seen plenty of times.

Jordan had glanced in her direction and remembered she had asked him a question. "Oh, shit." Jordan chuckled. "Sorry, my name is Jordan nice to meet you Singka."

He extended an open hand. Singka sat with a confused look on her face. She then turned around, picking up two more flowers before sticking them in her ears. Her body shivered as they took root. "Okay, now I should be able to understand you."

Jordan smiled and reintroduced himself.

"Jordan... that's a pleasant name, but what language were you speaking? I thought I knew the most common ones." She asked, while inspecting Jordan's eyes and face.

Jordan let her push his eye open. "It's English."

Singka sat back and stared at Jordan blankly. "English... I never heard of that. Where are you from?" She crossed her legs, swaying back and forth.

"Opps."

Jordan thought for a moment before speaking again. "It's complicated... I am not from here exactly."

He scratched his head as he tried to think of a good way to explain his situation to her. He felt like it was easier explaining it to Tim and the others because they also experienced it. But trying to explain it to a native might be harder and possibly dangerous. Singka smiled and patted Jordan's head, her tiny hands running through his thick curly hair.

"It's fine. You can tell me when you are ready. You just woke up so take your time."

This statement brought a flood of questions to his mind. Where was he, how long has he been sleeping, what happened to him? He rapidly fired all these questions at Singka who just responded with a giggle, which gets followed up by a loud rumbling from Jordan's stomach.

"You have a lot of questions, but first let's get you something to eat."

Jordan smiled and nodded in agreement. A pair of bee-like wings stretched out from behind Singka and fluttered. She hovered into the air before turning and flying off.

This sight caused Jordan to lean forward in his bed, ignoring his injuries. "You can fly?"

Singka looked back and wiggled her tush. "You never seen a fairy before?" She winked before flying off.

She returned a few minutes later with a bowl of tear drop shaped food. Jordan picked one up and studied it. At the very top it was thin and curled, it widened as it grew, ending in a smooth round bottom. The color of the food was varying shades of purple and about the size of an egg. Jordan wondered if this was a fruit or a vegetable that she handed him. He glanced at Singka, who was making hand motions to show you can just eat them as is.

Jordan opened his mouth and took a small bite. His mouth filled with a juice that was sweet but also had a spicy kick to it. He smiled as he chewed the food. Glancing down, he noticed that the fruit had layers. Each layer was a shade of blue or red with the most outside layer being purple.

Singka leaned in closer and gently grabbed Jordan's arm. "Let me see, let me see." She stared into the fruit and smiled. "Oh... you got a Kind Queen on your first try, good job." She released his arm.

Jordan popped the rest of the fruit into his mouth. "Kind Queen?"

Singka reached into the bowl and pulled out a random piece, taking a bite into it. Her face scrunched up before she held it to Jordan's mouth. "Try this one." She chewed the rest of her bite.

Jordan leaned forward and took a bite. His mouth burned red hot before a gentle sweetness rolled over his tongue. He fanned the nonexistent flames in his mouth, inhaling and exhaling as fast as he could. Singka laughed and showed Jordan the inside of the fruit.

She showed the difference, "This is a Spiteful Queen."

This fruit had more red layers than blue layers, with the outside layer ending in purple as well.

Jordan smiled as he studied the fruit. "So, what do you call these normally?" He took another fruit from the bowl.

"We call them Queens Drip. A bunch grow around here so when we founded the village, we called it Queens Land. They are our primary source of food," Singka finished the rest of her Spiteful Queen. Jordan took a bite of his, Sweet.

Jordan looked up from his food. "Queens land is the name of this village?"

"Mhm. It's a newish village, but we get by here. I am surprised you found it honestly." Singka crossed her legs as she reached for another fruit.

"I'm sorry, but I don't know how I got here."

"What's the last thing you remember?"

Jordan thought for a moment, his expression growing dark. His head hurt. "What do I remember?"

He remembered Tim and the others, he could remember killing the tree bouncer, he could remember walking for four days, then suddenly nothing.

Singka grew worried at the prolonged silence. "Well, how about this I can tell you everything I know and maybe that will trigger some memories for you."

Jordan nodded and leaned in close, giving her his full attention.

"So, our dear little Juka, was out and about and she got caught in a Tree Spider's web. She was about to get eaten." She grew silent. "But then you appeared." She smiled, "She said you killed the spider." Singka clawed her hands and put a fierce look on her face. "Then a Juk-Juk appeared." She growled playfully.

"Juk-Juk?"

"It's a beast that likes to use the trees to ambush and take down its prey. It has dark green fur with bright yellow eyes."

Jordan folded his arms in contemplation. "Oh. I called it a tree bouncer. Sorry I interrupted you, keep going."

Singka shook her head with a smile. "No worries, so a Juk-Juk appeared, and you fought it in the forest and won, but Juka said she lost track of you, so she ran to get help. We found you collapsed with a vine wrapped around your leg, probably from running through the bushes. You had passed out, the ground was soaked with your blood. Thankfully, I stabilized you and we carried you to the village. You were heavily malnourished and infected, you poor thing. You were asleep for about three weeks."

Jordan's eyes widened as he stared at Singka. "I was asleep for three weeks?"

"Yeah, we cured you of all your infections, but your body was a bloody mess. Honestly, I am surprised you survived."

When Singka finished her explanation, Jordan shared some stuff about him. His survival attempt in the forest. He was about to talk about Tim and the others when a wave of guilt flowed through him, he shook it off and skipped that part. From there, he talked the fight with the first Juk-Juk leaving out his magic for now. He hesitated about the deaths of Cindy and Jason, he could feel the sadness welling up inside of him. He pushed passed it and explained as much of his walk as possible. This information perked Singka's ears. She told him she would be right back as she flew off outside.

Jordan sat and continued looking around. He saw more flowers, like the ones that were currently in his ear. Painfully, he reached out and grabbed onto one with the tips of his fingers. He pulled it close and studied it. It's a pink flower with four long thin petals. It had a fat stigma on top of a wavy style, its stamen is crescent-shaped, it had an odd smell, not necessarily pleasant but also not awful. A neutral scent, the kind you wouldn't notice unless you really put your nose in it and smelled.

A stern male voice comes from the doorway, "We call those Transbuds."

He looked to see a small man; the man was smaller, about half the size of Singka. He had a long grey beard, stern eyes, his back was bent over as he clutched a wooden cane revealing butterfly wings, one of which has a tear in it providing for poor flying ability. He embedded Transbuds in his ears.

Jordan introduced himself before smiling and tossing another fruit in his mouth. Sweet.

"Nice to meet you, young Kree. I am Tong the elder here."

Jordan tilted his head slightly.

"*Kree?*"

Tong gently leapt into the air. His old wings fluttered only enough to slow his descent, turning the movement into a series of aerial leaps instead of outright flying. He landed in front of Jordan, who had chewed on what turned out to be a Spiteful Queen.

"Before we start, I would like to thank you for saving Juka. I fear what would have happened if you had not showed up." Tong bowed his head.

Jordan nodded and smiled. "No problem. How is she doing?"

"She is fine, she was shaken up for a while after the attack, but she came by every day to check up on you. She should be out gathering fruit. With a group, this time."

Singka fluttered over with more fruit, joining everyone on the bed. Tong grabbed a Queens drip, holding it with two hands before taking a small bite, spicy. Tong seemed irked by this. Singka smiled and traded her Kind for his Spiteful. Causing them both to smile.

Tong finished his Queens drip, "So, what brings you to our forest? We don't get many Sli' Krees out this way."

"*So... it's a race?*"

Jordan smiled, "A little adventure."

"What kind of adventure?"

"One filled with mystery I suppose."

Tong lowered his eyes, "What have you seen so far? Anything... weird?"

Jordan raised an eyebrow, "Define... weird. I'm not from around here so weird for me might be normal for you."

"Have you seen anyone else wandering in the woods?"

Jordan shook his head, "Besides the people I was camping with no."

Tong lifted his head, "You were with others?" He glanced at Singka who shrugged before turning back to Jordan. "Where are they?"

Jordan's eyes widened and he started to tear up, "I-uh..." His nose ran and he kept blinking away tears. His heart raced, "No, I meant, I didn't- I..." His breathing grew heavier by the second, "I was alone I didn't... there was no one."

Tong tilted his head, "You said you were camping with people didn't you? So where are they?"

The memories broke in and wrecked his heart, his vision blurred as he drowned in the guilt.

"I didn't, I could have... I fucked up." Tears flowed from his face, "I fucked up bad, so bad. I promised..."

"*I broke my promise... and they died.*"

He couldn't breathe. Tears and snot choked his airways, his heart tore itself apart. His mind forgot to remind him to breathe. He tried to get out of bed, his weak muscles trembled from his weight and some wounds reopened. He could feel Singka and Tong try to push him back down but he fought them off pushing them roughly to the floor. He stumbled and knocked some things off a shelf as he regained his balanced. His weak legs carried him slowly towards the door. Underneath his feet a purple light flickered ominously, and a faint shimmering sound filled the air around him.

A black streak appeared for just a moment and while he didn't see what hit him. He felt a wave of force flow through his body and the world went dark again.

A DISTANT SCREAM AWOKE JORDAN. He sat up; the world was a black dome. He knew where he was, there was no more putting it off. Another scream rung out, this time louder, it caused him to jump in place. His ears perked up and he tried to find the source of the screaming, it comes again this time from a clearer direction. Jordan stood up and ran towards it.

There he found the source and his heart sunk, on the ground mauled into tiny pieces was Jason. Lifeless and floating in a pool of his own blood. From the distance he heard the stomping of running feet. He ran towards it hoping to arrive in time.

Jordan ran aimlessly through the darkness trying to catch up to the footsteps, finally he did. A terrified Jason ran towards him. "Jordan, help!" Jason grabbed Jordan's shoulder.

Jordan looked around, "What's going on?"

Jason teeth chattered, "It's coming."

Fear seeped into Jordan from Jason's hands. "Wha-" Jordan looked behind Jason.

In the distance a large Juk-Juk came barreling towards them, its head cartoonishly big and it's teeth nightmarish in both shape and size. The fear grew stronger.

Jason shook Jordan. "Do something."

Jordan looked around for something to use to help but Jason shook him again.

Jason's eyes grew wider, "Your magic, use your magic."

The beast drew closer.

Jordan nodded and summoned his circle, "I'll trip it, you--" His spell fired and launched Jason towards the beast.

"Shit."

Jason screamed as he desperately reached for Jordan's hand.

The beast pounced and crunched down on Jason's shoulder. Sounds of his bones snapping and cracking from the pressure of the beast's jaw echoed out, it dazed Jordan. Jason wailed; his screams burrowed deep into Jordan's skull.

Jordan ran forward, he summoned his spell circle once more.

"I can make it."

His legs froze in place and his circle disappeared, he was mere inches from Jason. He could just reach out and almost touch Jason, a few more centimeters were all he needed.

Jason looked up at him with tears in his eyes, "Why are you sacrificing me? We can work together Jordan please."

Jordan kept reaching, "Jason give me your hand."

Jason reached for Jordan's hand, the beast looked up and glared at Jordan. Jordan flinched backwards right as Jason's hands reached his narrowly missing it. Jason wailed and Jordan's world shook. He stepped back covering his ears, with each step away from Jason the wailing grew louder.

"I can move?"

Jordan ran forward, the wailing grew softer but once again his body froze just out of reach of Jason. The wailing was softer, less bone shaking than before. But the sight of watching Jason get torn apart was gut wrenching.

When it became too much he tried to run away, but the screaming grew louder draining his energy until he collapsed from the exhaustion of it all. Then the screaming stopped, when he turned around there Jason was. On the ground, ravaged into small chunks. And the cycle would repeat again with a fresh Jason running and grabbing Jordan begging for help. He tried running from Jason but he would always appear right in front of him, latching on with inhuman strength.

Jordan sat in front of Jason as the Juk-Juk continued to rip him apart, his screams became normal in this dark world. Jordan realized if he watched and never turned around Jason wouldn't die, and the cycle wouldn't repeat. So, Jordan watched and watched until finally the dream collapsed.

7

THE CONFESSION

JORDAN OPENED HIS EYES SLOWLY; his cheek was wet from tears. He sat up and looked around. The dimly lit hut provided a soft comfort. Outside the windows he could see the twilight peeking in. After some self-motivation, a lot of groaning and a slew of curse words, he crawled out of bed and braced himself on a nearby wall. He looked down and saw a cane resting near the bed. He took it and left the hut.

The cool air hit his skin, he had no objective he just wanted to walk and clear his head. Maybe shake off the nightmares that plagued his dreams. The village was still sleeping as he moved through it. While he walked, he spotted a dim blue glow coming from deeper into the village just past the main grouping of huts.

His curiosity carried him towards it. After a moment he came upon a large tree surrounded by dancing blue orbs that faded in and out of sight.

"Wow..."

Jordan soaked in the image, whenever one of the orbs got close enough, he tried to touch it only to have it disappear right before his very eyes.

The ground crunched behind him, he turned around, and saw a figure standing in the darkness.

Jordan turned and clutched the top of the cane; he scanned the figure for any defining features.

The figure was around four feet tall, large wings with a rounded tip stretched out from behind them. Their ears were similar to Singka's and Tong's. Their fists appeared to be clutched.

Jordan opened his mouth to speak but stopped himself as he remembered the language barrier.

The figure spoke, "Wiuat la vetiy?"

Jordan sighed, "I can't understan--"

He stopped as one of the orbs illuminated the figures face. She had short white hair spiked upwards to the sky, she glared at him. On her back stood one black wing. Jordan's mind remembered the last thing he saw yesterday and readied himself.

The woman did the same, "Aj lie aiel ca"

Jordan frowned, "I can't understand you... and you can't understand me either I suppose." He sighed and relaxed.

The woman wings buzzed and she took flight. Jordan readied himself once more and summoned his spell circle.

The woman moved. Jordan blasted her back with Gao.

He looked at his circle shining brightly and huffed, "Now you want to work."

The woman recovered and rushed Jordan again. She reached him in a blink of an eye and cocked her fist back. Jordan shoved her down with Gao and backed up. Undeterred she pushed her body up and kept pressing Jordan.

She threw a punch and Jordan dodged; his body screamed in pain. The air exploded right next to his head.

"The hell was that?"

Jordan grabbed her leg and growled, "Would you relax?" He yanked her down to the ground.

She braced her fall and looked up right as Jordan followed up with a Gao empowered punch aiming right for her face.

The girl watched it come in close then at the last moment dodged forward. She cocked her arm back; Jordan moved his free arm in between them to block his stomach as he finished his punch.

Once she got close, she threw a solid jab into Jordan's stomach. He blocked it with his arm but his body crumbled around her fist as an explosion erupted deep inside. His legs gave up and he fell to the ground. The cool welcoming ground.

A WHILE LATER, he awoke.

"I know this ceiling…"

He sat up slowly, his arm and head felt destroyed, his stomach felt as if he had food poisoning. Luckily, he could remember everything, the walk around the village, the tomboy, the pain, the blackness. He wanted answers; he needed answers. Looking around, he saw some fresh Transbuds on the table. Upon placing them in, he called out for Singka.

Her tiny head popped in with a surprised look. "You're awake?" She raced over, holding two cups. "How are you feeling?" She placed a hand on Jordan's head while giving him one cup.

Jordan took the cup and looked at her. "My body is killing me. Who was that fairy who attacked me?"

Singka's face grew dark as sadness and disappointment filled her expression. "Right, before I explain. I have to ask. What were you doing by our Noble Tree?"

Jordan replied instantly, "I don't know what that is."

Singka frowned, "It was a large tree, with glowing orbs around it."

Jordan nodded, "Right, I don't know what it is. I was just walking around and happened upon it."

Singka thought for a moment, "Why did you attack Dingba?"

Jordan sighed, "She attacked me."

"Look Jordan you have to see it from my side. You show up injured and while a good chunk of those injures came from saving one of our own, the fact you were caught near the Noble Tree and with people disapp--" She stopped and took a deep breath before exhaling slowly, "And you're not even a Sli' Kree, are you?"

Jordan relaxed, "I never said I was."

Singka frowned softly, "You certainly didn't correct us, even though Tong and I knew you weren't right away."

Jordan smiled softly, "Oh? What gave it away?"

Singka pointed to her eyes, "All Sli' Krees have flamboyant eyes, your eyes are too plain looking."

Jordan scrunched up his face, "Ow."

Singka chuckled, "Sorry I didn't mean it in a hurtful way. You'll understand when you see one."

Jordan nodded and for a moment silence over took the hut. Eventually he looked up and Singka.

He gave her a hopeful smile. "Can we start over?"

Singka smiled, "I would like that."

Jordan revealed where he came from, how he arrived here, what race he is and after a moment of steeling his nerves he told her what happened to the others.

Singka smiled and hugged Jordan, "Thank you for sharing and I'm sorry we pushed you hard after you woke up."

Jordan sniffled and hugged her back and slowly squeezed tighter, he felt at peace for the first time in a long time. She responded by squeezing him tighter. They stayed like that for a few moments before they broke the hug.

Singka smiled, "Feel better?"

Jordan chuckled and wiped some tears away, "Yeah, sorry."

Singka shook her head, "No need to apologize. We all need a hug sometimes and you should never be afraid to ask for one. After all a hug a day keeps the bad thoughts away."

Jordan chuckled, "That's a good saying."

Singka smiled, placed her hands on her hips and posed, "Thanks, I made it myself."

"So, what's a Noble Tree?"

Singka smiled, "How about I show you?"

8

NOBLE TREE

THE NEXT MORNING. Jordan accompanied Singka back to the Noble Tree. He put most of his weight on the cane, leaving a trail of cane marks on the ground.

A few moments later, they were standing in front of a large tree. It was just barely taller than the surrounding trees, its leaves shimmered with a soft blue glow. In the center of the trunk lies a massive cavity. Small orbs of light danced inside.

Singka turned and motioned to the tree. "This, is the Noble Tree."

Jordan drunk in the sights he missed the first time. He could see fairies floating around it, trimming and pruning. The bushes and trees around the tree were heavy with fruits, nuts and flowers. "Wow."

Singka giggled. "Wow, indeed."

"The Noble Tree has a lot of uses for us fairies. First it fertilizes the nearby soil, it can even turn barren soil into fertile soil. As it grows its roots spread and so do the effects on the soil."

She landed on the ground and scooped up a handful of dirt. "You probably didn't notice, but the soil here is much darker than other parts of the forest. You can actually see how far the roots have reached."

Jordan leaned in to get a better look at the soil. It had a wet smell to it. The color was a charcoal black; it looked like charcoal dust.

Singka dropped the soil. "It's still a baby tree, but once it finishes growing, you can see it no matter where you are in the forest. At least that's what Tong says."

Jordan nodded. "That's really cool. What else does it do?"

"Well, fairies don't get lost in the forest because we always know where our Noble Tree is. It's hard to describe, but it's like a gentle pull on our minds. Like it's always showing us which way is home."

Jordan rubbed his chin. "So, a fairy can always find their way home?"

Singka nodded. "Yep, I also heard from my mother that fairies can also sense other Noble Trees if they get close enough to the tree."

She waved him forward. "Come, I got more to show you."

She led him into the cavity of the tree.

Inside were little pods about the size of beach balls. Jordan can see the small silhouette of baby fairies in the pods. They varied in color and the number of babies. Each pod had a small wooden sign with what Jordan assumed was the name of the parents.

Singka floated to the middle of the room. There, a wooden pedestal stood. In the center is a bowl-shaped cavity. Jordan followed and stood on the opposite side of her.

"We use this pedestal to collect the Noble Trees sap and infuse it with our life. Together both parents shape the ball and keep pouring their lives into it. It typically goes fifty-fifty, but some couples change the ratio depending on the type of children they want or other circumstances. For instance, if the couple wants a bunch of fighters, the strongest one or the one with the most magic will give more. If one parent is sickly, the healthy one may give more to ease the burden. Afterwards they carry it to an open spot and let the tree nurture it. When its time the pod busts open and the babies are free."

Jordan looked around at all the pods. There were about ten each filled with at least three babies. "So who tends to them all?"

Singka posed and smiled.

Jordan smiled back, "Ah, I see."

Singka nodded, "I have help but I'm here almost every day checking on everything."

Jordan looked around at all the pods, "That's impressive..."

Singka smiled, "Why thank you."

"So, I noticed your wings all differ in some way."

Singka nodded, "Correct."

"That includes color too, right? Cause that tomboy who attacked me had black wings."

Singka deflated, "Oh... right I never told you about her. She's... complicated but let me explain how fairies work. Take a seat." She motioned to a stool next to her.

Jordan nodded and sat down.

Singka thought for a moment then nodded. "So, to start her name is Dingba, not 'Tomboy'. She is known here as an outcast, a thug. Remember how the children are born?"

Jordan nodded.

She continued, "Well, they are normally born in groups of two or more. My birth had six of us." Singka chuckled as she remembered her brothers and sisters. "The reason this is important to understand is so you can get a better picture of Dingba. Her birth was interesting. She was a solo birth, not only that, but she also had one black wing."

"Yeah, I took note of it before she knocked me the fuck out."

Her face scrunched up a bit. "I'm not sure what 'fuck' means but yes she knocked you out."

Jordan sighed, "Sorry that came out wrong."

Singka gave him a soft smile, "It's okay. Well, there are four types of fairies. Two types and two classes." Singka held up her hands with two fingers displayed on each.

Jordan nodded and tried to follow along.

"First, we separate on height. Nix Fairies are the taller ones, Pix are the shorter ones. Simple, yes?"

Jordan nodded, allowing Singka to continue.

"The second separation is the color of our wings, Bright Wings fairies and Black Wings. Our magic is tied to the color of our wings. The brighter and clearer your wings, the less harmful your magic is and the more beneficial it is. But the darker your wings, the more harmful your magic becomes. For instance, my healing palm might decay flesh if my wings were black."

Jordan raised his eyebrows. "Oh? Why is that?"

"No idea, my sister wanted to find it out, but…" For a moment she glared off to the side, "She never did." She smiled as she returned to her normal cheery self.

Jordan stared at Singka's wings, they are a beautiful stained-glass arrangement that is tainted with a soft grey hue. "So, you can harm with your magic then?"

"Correct, but I focus my magic mainly on the healing and protecting." She smiled. "Since I am normally the first person who sees a newborn, I have to be prepared for anything that may harm them. A fairy's wing changes color depending mostly on their experiences in life. A fairy with a good life, lots of friends and happiness will normally have bright wings… But a fairy who has been isolated, mistreated or just had a bad life. Their wings will turn black as their hate for the world grows and festers."

"So, a fairy's wing doesn't turn black like that unless they have had some kind of trauma?"

"Correct."

"Is it possible for a fairy's wing to switch back and forth?"

"Yes, which brings us to the problem with Dingba. Her wing was already black, which means she had experienced serious trauma. We think it was just the fact she was lonely while being born. The actual issue is, even though we have worked endlessly to make her happy, her wing remains pitch black. Also, only one of her wings is black. Normally when a fairy is transitioning, all their wings grow darker. Not just one. A more serious issue is that she lacks the ability to use traditional fairy magic. Which is extremely rare. Especially since both her parents know magic." Singka scratched her head. "I am disappointed in myself for not being able to help her."

All this was a lot for Jordan to take in. He sat, tossing and turning the information in his head. None of this explained why she attacked him. "So why did she attack me?"

A voice called out, "Because I found you sniffing around the tree."

Singka and Jordan turn to see Dingba walking towards them.

Singka clasped her hands together, "Dingba. We were just talking about you."

Dingba scoffed, "I heard."

Singka glanced at Jordan, "Jordan this is the local troublemaker and my niece Dingba." She turns to Dingba, "And Dingba this is Jordan he's a human, his race went extinct a long time ago but now they're back it seems."

Jordan waved, "Sup." He quickly looked at Singka, "Wait extinct?"

Singka nodded, "That's right all gone. Tong knows more about it than I do."

Dingba gave Singka a confused look.

Singka smiled, "He doesn't speak common or fairy, so you have to use transbuds to understand him." She perked up, "Oh, I have an idea. Why don't you teach him fairy? It'll be fun, you guys might even become friends."

Dingba's gaze softened for a moment, but she quickly hardened it, "Not interested." She took flight and flew off.

Singka sighed, "Close." She glanced at Jordan and smiled, "Let's get you back to the hut. You need your rest."

Jordan watched Dingba fly off, "Is she okay?"

Singka raised her eyebrows, "Dingba?" She looked over, "Yeah, she's just a little shy that's all. Don't worry Jordan, we'll win her over."

Jordan leaned on his cane, "Here's hoping."

Singka chuckled, "That's the spirit."

AFTER SINGKA ESCORTED Jordan back to the hut, she helped him take the Transbuds out and provided him with a large bowl of fruit. "If you get hungry, there's some more Queens drip in the other room help yourself. There's also some more water in the other room as well.

Take care okay? I'll be back to check on you later." She patted him on the head.

He smiled back as she petted him, "Thanks for everything and yeah, I'll be here."

With that, Singka left Jordan alone to his own devices. Still exhausted and very sore, he decided to just get some rest, but as he slept, he felt a familiar sensation of the tendrils wiggling into his ear.

His eyes shot open as his Gao-empowered hand came crashing down on the invader. He heard a sharp yelp as he crushed a feminine hand. Following the arm up, he saw a startled Dingba. Furious, he re-summoned his spell circle, but calmed down as Dingba raised her hands as a show of peace. Slowly, she offered Jordan a pair of Trans-buds while putting hers in.

Jordan took the offering, observing her. It wasn't like he could fight her off, even if he wanted to, but he was still cautious. Once they were in, Jordan shot off a question. "The fuck are you doing?"

"Shh..." She looked around. "I am sorry about earlier. I... I didn't know you couldn't speak fairy. But, why were you walking around without Transbuds? And what were you doing by the Noble Tree?"

Jordan explained the situation.

She groaned, "Look, I'm sorry. I shouldn't have attacked you like that. Things have just been... tense lately." Dingba hung her head low, not wanting to look Jordan in the eye.

Jordan sighed, "It's fine, I suppose I can't really blame you. But what do you mean by tense?"

Dingba thought for a moment, "Just... nevermind."

Jordan frowned, "Alright, is there anything else you needed?"

Dingba nodded, "You came from someplace else right? I think that's what I overheard."

Jordan nodded.

Dingba thought for a moment, "Do you happen to know someone named Jul'Cur'Drl. I called him Jul' or Master Jul' for short, he was a Ram Zegigas."

Jordan shook his head, "I don't know what a Zegigas is."

Dingba raised her eyebrows, "Oh, they are an animal race, think Draco, but fluffy."

"I... don't know what Draco's look like to be honest with you."

Dingba stared at him. "You don't get out much, do you?"

Jordan cut a look at her, "I'm not from this world remember?"

Dingba sighed, "Right well did you happen to see a fairy with large moth wings?"

Jordan shook his head, "Singka was the first fairy I've ever seen."

Dingba deflated, "Cuss."

Jordan tilted his head,

"Cuss?"

She looked up at him, "Well, thanks I'll leave you alone now." Dingba got up to leave but Jordan placed a hand on her shoulder.

"Wait, hold on."

She turned around, "What?"

"I know you said no earlier but... can you teach me fairy?"

Dingba messed with her hair as she looked off to the side, "I suppose... I did attack you, so I'll make it up to you."

Jordan beamed, "Oh and spar with me when I get better."

A flicker of light danced in Dingbas eyes, "You mean like... train with you?"

"Yeah, that Zegiga boxing thing was really cool."

Dingba blushed and fought off a smug smile, "Well, you know..."

Jordan leaned in, "So will you?"

Dingba sighed, "Fine, anything else?"

Jordan smiled, "Let me go back to sleep."

Dingba glared softly. She flicked her wings out and hovered out of the hut with a loud "Hmph."

9

NEW WORDS

THE NEXT DAY when Singka and Tong came to check up on Jordan, it surprised them to see Dingba in the tent conversing with him. After clearing up any confusion, Jordan informed them of the resolution the two came to last night.

Singka looked at Dingba, then back to Jordan. "So, you aren't mad she attacked you?"

"Meh, I would have preferred if she didn't attack me, but I suppose I can't be too mad."

Singka looked at Dingba. "And to apologize, you are going to help him learn the language of fairies?"

Dingba nodded. "Yes, and I was going to help him train a bit once he heals up more."

Tong scoffed, "Well, I guess that settles that."

Jordan and Dingba nod with a grin as Tong got up to take his leave.

Singka's wings snapped up, "Great." She flew off into the backroom and started rummaging around. A few seconds later, she popped her head out. "Dingba, catch." She chucked a book at a startled Dingba.

Dingba fumbled with the catch but kept it off the ground. "Why'd you throw it?"

Singka was already grabbing more books. She flew over and dumped them in Dingba's lap, "These are great for beginners, and you can use these to practice writing." She dropped two wooden slabs and two long sticks that had a white puff ball attached to the end. "And you can read to him. Oh. You should read 'The Wussilefluff' to him." She squealed while shaking her legs and hands in the air.

Dingba's face burned red. "Why would I read that to him?"

Singka beamed with joy, "It's your favorite book."

Dingba leaned back. "Isn't this a little much for today?"

"What's the point in waiting? His body is the only thing injured; his mind seems okay."

"W-Well, it's just."

"No time like the present. Come Tong, let's leave them to it." She grabbed Tong and dragged him towards the door. "I'll bring some snacks later. Have fun you two."

When Singka exited the hut, Dingba let out an exaggerated sigh before looking at Jordan. She smiled softly, "Thank you."

Jordan stroked his beard. "No worries, I have a question though."

"Shoot."

"Singka said you couldn't use fairy magic. But during the fight I know for sure I blocked your first attack, and it still felt like I not only got hit. But like a force was flowing through my stomach. If that wasn't magic, what is it?"

Dingba's face scrunched up. "Singka and her big mouth." She sighed and lowered her head, causing her shallow bangs to obscure her eyes. "Yes." She looked back at Jordan. "I cannot use any fairy magic." She grew quiet for a moment. "When I was younger, a man came to our village. His name was Jul'Cur'Drl."

"The... Zegigas right?"

Dingba smiled, "Yep, It was after I had gotten into trouble again. I had gotten into a fight with some bullies. I lost... and I was sulking. Jul found me in my hiding spot."

Her eyes lowered, and her smile weakened. "I was cursing my life. I wanted to tear my wings off, but he stopped me. What he said to me I will never forget, 'If you can't be a normal fairy, become an extraordinary fairy.' It was the first time someone has ever even hinted I could become someone extraordinary. Even without magic."

She smirked; her gaze grew stronger. "After that, he trained me in Zegiga boxing. Eventually I learned…" She turned and threw a punch, causing a visible explosion of air centered on her fists. "To do that. While it's not magic, it's more of an ability or a trait as a result of my training. Master Jul told me it is called 'Temperance' and that even if someone has magic tolerance, I can bypass it because my fists do more internal damage than external. Plus, it's not magic."

"How do you build tolerance to begin with?"

Dingba shrugged, "Use magic, I guess? You'd have to ask whoever taught you magic if you don't have any tolerance, you're in bad shape."

"That's why it hurt so much; I probably don't have any tolerance. So, you most likely got true damage off on me." Jordan rubbed his stomach, this slightly deflated Dingba's pose.

Dingba sighed and ruffled her hair before looking away. "Yeah, sorry again."

"So, how do you resist temperance, if tolerance doesn't help?"

"That I don't know. I remember Master Jul saying something about… Colors or presence or something? I don't remember it too well." She sighed; her eyes glanced at the book in her lap. Her fingers traced the lettering of the title 'The Wussilefluff.' She smiled, "I suppose we can start your lesson." She opened the book.

"There was once a small creature called the Wussilefluff.…"

AFTER A FEW WEEKS of learning the language of fairies Jordan felt he was starting to get the basics but being cooped up in the hut all the time was starting to drive him crazy. After much begging in both English and Fairy Singka finally relented and allowed him to walk around the village. A few minutes later, Jordan walked behind Dingba as he clutched a cane to assist him in walking and to help him rehabilitate his muscles. Under Singka's orders after all. Dingba used these walks to give him pop quizzes, though after a while it felt like a game. She would lead Jordan through the village and randomly point out various things and Jordan would hopefully call out the right word. If he got enough right, he would get a treat when they got back to the hut.

Dingba stopped and pointed to a wicker basket.

Jordan's eyes widened as he searched his mind for the information. *"Basket... so, it'd be..."*

"T... Tòuli?"

Dingba gave him a thumbs up and continued walking.

A while later Dingba stopped once more and pointed at a fruit.

Jordan stood behind her, panting. His body trembled from overuse. He looked up at the fruit. It was round and orange; the flesh is mostly smooth with pinprick blemishes all over. "Um, orange."

Dingba turned back with a raised eyebrow. "What?"

"It's an orange, you know the fruit an orange."

Dingba noticed his breathing and the amount of sweat that was dripping down his body.

Jordan sighed. "Wait, I... I can't remember what this is. It looks like a fruit called an orange from my world and that's all my mind is telling me." His fatigue got the better of him today.

Dingba deflated, "Oh, sorry, I guess I got carried away. I'll give you a freebie it's called 'Criti'." She floated up and positioned herself under his arm. "Come on, let's take a break we can learn something else while you rest, then we'll get you back." After helping him sit she flew off to get some food and drink.

A while later she came back with some bread and some water.

Jordan tore off a piece of bread and popped it in his mouth. It was a little firm on the outside, chewy on the inside. It reminded him of sourdough, both in shape and flavor. Dingba took a huge bite out of her bread.

Jordan chuckled, and she looked at him while she chewed, "Hm?"

Jordan shook his head. "Nothing, thanks for teaching me."

Dingba raised an eyebrow and swallowed her mouthful. "Why are you thanking me? We had a deal."

Jordan smiled, "Still, thank you."

Dingba smiled, "You're welcome." She then turned to her bread and bit off another piece.

After talking and filling their bellies, Dingba grabbed a tablet and dropped a small bag on top of it.

The sound of metal objects is heard as she moves the tablet. "Alright, last thing for today."

She dumped out the contents of the bag. A trickle of coins spilled out onto the tablet. They vary in color from brown to a bright silver. Dingba gave the bag a final shake, and a few rolled up pieces of paper fell out as well.

She grabbed a bronze coin and lifts it. "We call these pints."

The front had an image of a beetle stamped into it, with a very intricate pattern surrounding it. She flipped it around and showed the back. Which contained an image of a tankard stamped on it.

"This is the currency we use here. Well, not here in the village but in other places we can use it for trading. They increase by tenfold. The bronze ones with one tankard on the back is worth one pint and the super shiny ones with four are worth one-thousand bronze pints."

Jordan inspected each coin, from what he could tell the metals were bronze, silver with two tankards, gold with three and finally platinum with four. "So, one, ten, one hundred and one thousand?"

Dingba smiled. "You aren't so helpless after all. That's right. Now let's see if you can get the next one."

She unfurled the rolled-up paper, "These are called slips, they work much the same way but go by fives."

She laid out four bills. Red, blue, yellow and black in ascending order. Each bill had the same symbol of a beetle printed in the middle. The corners of each bill were textured in different ways. "So, if the red ones are worth five pints how much are the black ones worth?"

Jordan smiled, despite the sudden fear of answering wrong washing over him. "Five thousand?"

Dingba raised her eyebrow before smirking. "Good job. I guess we don't need to worry about math or anything.

Jordan sighed in relief.

"Thank God."

He picked up a coin, "Who made the money? I assume the beetle symbol represents something?"

Dingba wrote on the tablet then flipped it around. There in the center were two words written in Common and in Fairy.

Jordan studied it for a moment, "Collective?"

Dingba nodded, "Correct. The symbol of the beetle is the symbol of the Collective."

Jordan waited for a second. "So who are they?"

Dingba thought for a moment, "The Collective are a race of tall beetles that dominated the world before taking pity on everyone. They are all knowing and feared by the main races."

A pit grew in Jordan's stomach. "I see. Why are they feared?"

"From what Tong told me they... had a phase?"

Jordan raised an eyebrow, "What kind of phase?"

"A devouring swarm? Kind of phase."

Jordan's eyes grew wide.

"Yeah, there was a big war and a lot of races and animals went extinct. But apparently they are cool now so... yeah."

Dingba started scooping the coins back into the bag, "Anyway, just know the universal rule of the world. Never hurt a member of the Collective. It never ends well."

She secured the bag, "Alright let's go return this before Singka freaks out. We can go over more stuff tomorrow."

Jordan smiled, "Alright, let's go."

Eventually, they made it back to the hut. Both drenched in sweat, Singka came in with some drinks and a bowl filled with translucent orbs of various colors.

"Looks like you two did a lot of work today."

She gave each one a cup and set the bowl in between them. Jordan chugged his water, then looked at Singka.

"What's this?"

"I call them rainbow orbs. Just a little treat I give to the kids sometimes. Try them."

Jordan picked up a red one and held it to the light, it's hard, ruby red and in the middle, there is an object. But Jordan couldn't make it out.

"What's in the middle?"

Dingba popped one in her mouth. "A surprise."

Jordan glanced at her before popping it in his mouth. It was sweet like honey. There was a faint fruity taste, like a sweet queen, but this was sourer. His cheeks tingled as he stored the sweet orb in his cheek.

ONCE HE FELT a second texture in his mouth, he took the now shrunken orb out and studied it. Singka smiled as he did.

The object in the center was a worm. It was chubby, lifeless, and its flesh died red from the candy mixture they encased it in.

Jordan gagged and moved the candy out of his sight.

The smile on Singka's face faded away. A second later, the look of terror flashed over her face.

"I forgot. I'm so sorry." She quickly searched for a napkin or towel for him to discard the candy in.

Jordan choked down his vomit. "No, no. It's fine."

Jordan glanced at the worm. He braced himself and took a bite, tearing the whole thing out of the core. A quick shiver ran across his body as he put the rest in his mouth. He chewed slowly; the texture was slightly chewy, like a gummy worm the overall worm was sour.

"I don't hate it…"

Dingba and Singka sat wide-eyed as he swallowed the worm.

Dingba was the first to speak. "Woah."

Singka smiled faintly, "You didn't have to eat it if you didn't want to."

Jordan smiled. "It's fine. I enjoy trying new things and I hate seeing food go to waste. I actually kinda liked it." He picked up another one and popped it in his mouth.

Singka relaxed. "Well, if you say so. Help yourself."

10

THE SEARCH

ONE MORNING, before even the sun had peaked through the trees, Jordan was awake practicing his writing. He had woken up earlier, the nightmares still plagued his sleep. Once his heart stopped racing, he couldn't fall back asleep, so he tried to tire his mind out again. As he wrote, a knock came from the door.

"Come in."

Some locals stuck their head inside. "Good morning Jordan."

Above them Dingba's head came into sight, "Get- Oh. You're already up?"

Jordan nodded. "I got woken up earlier and couldn't fall back asleep."

"Oh, okay, well, get up even more. We got a long day ahead of us."

"What's going on today?"

The locals come in holding a large basket of clothes.

Dingba flew in helping Singka carry in a basket, "Today we try on clothes."

They wheeled a mirror in and laid out a bunch of clothes.

Between modeling, getting measured, and trying on clothes the hours flew by. Finally, the last outfit was tried on and accepted. Jordan was left with three complete sets of clothes. Two sets of robes, though one was closer to a skirt on him and one pair of pants with a matching shirt.

Each set of clothing was made with leaves and decorated with vines or flowers. The inside had some kind of fiber that while slightly itchy, should help keep him cool.

Singka exhaled. "Well then, I was hoping we'd have more luck but your height and frame seemed to have made things a little challenging."

Jordan chuckled. "Oh, trust me. I always had trouble finding clothes. I appreciate all the effort everyone went through. Would it be easier to do robes or something like that?"

Singka nodded, "Most likely, those seem to be the best fits for you at the moment."

Dingba groaned. "But those are so boring. He should have something he can fight in."

Singka sighed, "Yes, I suppose you have your second obligation to fulfill."

Dingba sat up. "So we can go?"

Singka sighed, "Yes, you can go."

Dingba looked at Jordan. "Jordan let's go explore."

Jordan looked at her. "Now?"

Dingba nodded, "Yes, before she changes her mind."

Dingba flew over and grabbed his hand. "Come on."

As they left the hut Singka called out, "Not too far. I want you both back before it gets dark."

Dingba stuck out her tongue and pulled Jordan faster into the forest.

Once they were a distance away, she slowed down and inhaled deeply.

"Oh, its been so long since I've left." She turned to Jordan. "I'm sure it'll be nice for you to stretch your legs more and get out of the village."

Jordan shrugged. "I didn't mind, to be honest. Everything is so new, but I will admit I have been eager to explore the forest."

"Oh really? What for?"

"Well, remember how I said I came from a different world?"

"Yeah, the... Train? I believed you called it? Brought you here."

"Yeah, I was surviving with a group of people. We got attacked by a Juk-Juk and got split up. But it chased me and not them. So I'm hoping they got away and are safe. Our survival expert was one of the people who got away, so I think they will be okay. Still, I worry."

Dingba nodded. "Well, we can head off in the mornings and try to find them. I know the forest very well so I can lead you through it safely."

"That would be great."

"Do you remember where your camp was?"

Jordan shook his head. "When I was being chased by the Juk-Juk, I took a lot of random turns then I fell into a river and got swept down it. I'm not sure how far though."

Dingba rubbed her chin. "Well, there's only one river in this forest, so if we follow it, we should be able to get back to your camp. How many days did you walk before you found Juka?"

"I think it was... three? Four days? Wait, that's not right. I don't remember how long it was. I remember up to the fourth day then waking up."

"Okay, well. Let's explore around the village for now. We aren't going too far today. Tomorrow we can go a little deeper in the morning and do some training."

Jordan nodded, "Sounds good." He glanced at Dingba who was stretching. "Who is the fairy you are looking for?"

Dingba stopped, "What do you mean?"

"When we first talked you asked me if I saw a fairy with moth wings in the forest. Since Singka said fairies don't get lost, I'm curious who is it you are looking for."

Dingba gave a sad smile, "Ah, right. The fairy I'm looking for is my big sister Tink."

Jordan shrunk in place, "Oh, I'm sorry. I didn't know, Tink said you were an only child, so I just figured... I don't know what I thought."

Dingba frowned, "Geez, did Singka tell you everything about me?"

Jordan smiled and shrugged.

Dingba sighed, "Yes I am an only child, but Tink treated me like a little sister therefore she is my older sister."

Jordan smiled, "Makes sense. But I thought fairies couldn't get lost? Did she run away from home or...?"

Dingba shrugged, "She didn't run away. She went out to check something and... never came back." She chuckled, "I'm sure she's still checking whatever she left to check."

"How long has she been gone?"

Dingba grew quiet, she squeezed her hands. "A few months now... but the forest is large and she said she was going to check it out so maybe she just isn't finished.

Jordan gave her a stern nod, "Could be that. Let's keep a look out for her as well."

Dingba turned and smiled at him. "Thanks."

They spent the rest of the afternoon walking around the very outskirts of the village; they stayed out until the sky turned a soothing golden orange color. For dinner they had some dried fish and bread, then turned in early.

THE NEXT MORNING Dingba came at the crack of dawn. To her surprise, she saw Jordan was already up and dressed. He sat on the bed with his spell circle summoned once he spotted her; he smiled.

"Morning."

Dingba smiled back. "Morning. You ready?"

Jordan stood up. "Lead the way."

By the time the sun had lightened up the forest, they were moving past the outskirts into a clearing. The area was oddly free of most nature besides grass. There was ample room to move around. Fruit trees and bushes were nearby for a quick snack. If you looked from the sky, the area probably looked like an arena. Dingba stretched with her wings spread wide. Jordan's stiff muscles hinted that it'd be a good idea for him to do the same.

While he stretched, he admired the surrounding view, "This is a nice place."

Dingba turned back and looks at him. "Thanks. Tink and I used to play here. But we need to be careful out here. I'm sure that Juk-Juk's partner has been waiting to isolate you."

Jordan touched his toes and tilted his head. "What is this about a partner?"

Dingba reached for the skies and arched her back. "Juk-Juks hunt in pairs, to surround and confuse their prey. They are partners for life, but when one dies, the other seeks revenge. Since you only killed one, their partner should be stalking you."

Jordan paused and thought for a moment. "I killed two already."

Dingba's eyes opened wide. "Two?"

"Yeah, the first one was hunting me and my friends, the second one was the one I saved... Juka...? From. I think there was a gash above its eye too."

Dingba nodded, her mouth slightly agape as she absorbed in the information. "How?"

"The first one I used my magic, the second one... I'm not sure what happened to be honest. That part is still pretty fuzzy."

"I'm impressed."

Jordan smiled.

Dingba took flight and hovered in the air. "You ready?"

Jordan completed his last stretch and bounced in place. "Yep, let's do this."

"Let's just see what you really got. Don't worry, I'll go easy on you for now."

Jordan frowned. "What? No. Fight normally."

"Last time I fought normally you ended up back in bed and I ended up getting yelled at by Tong and Singka. Not to mention I had to baby-sit you for weeks on end. So no, I will not fight as I normally do. You couldn't handle it anyway."

Jordan huffed, "Fine, but if you lose, I don't wanna hear it."

Dingba drifted towards him. Her body is stiff, her hands in a traditional boxing stance. Jordan stepped in and threw a right hook, he aimed at Dingba's face.

She swatted it away, creating a minor explosion of force as she did. The force threw Jordan off balance, causing him to stumble to the ground. He scrambled back up and put his guard back up. His cheeks burned as he stared at Dingba. He could just barely see a smirk peeking out from behind her fists.

He stepped in once more and threw another right hook, this time slower and more in control.

Dingba responded the same way and Jordan answered back by rolling his wrist mid-flight causing Dingba's swat to miss. The second he cleared her hand, he sped up his punch. Dingba's back hand sprang into action and swatted his fist back towards him. Once again a minor explosion accompanies the swat.

Jordan put some distance between them and shook the pain off his hand.

Dingba looked over her guard. "You okay?"

Jordan hugged his hand between his legs, "Yeah, I'm fine."

"*That hurts like hell.*"

"You can use your magic too, you know that, right?"

"Yeah, I know, just feeling you out."

Dingba smirked, "Okay, continue to feel."

Jordan stepped in and threw a straight punch. Dingba went for another defensive swat. Jordan's spell circle appeared before her and yanked her forward. In a panic, she adjusted her body and leapfrogged over his fist before resetting the distance between them.

It was Dingba's turn to attack; She floated forward and lightly jabbed at Jordan; she was careful not to augment her fists. Even though they were tiny, they still packed quite the punch. Each one threatened to break his guard.

He used Gao to push her back and renewed his attack. Dingba met him halfway. This went on for some time until they were both dripping with sweat. Every time Jordan felt himself breaking under Dingba's pressure, he would push her back with Gao to give himself some breathing room. After getting knocked down for the fifth time today, Jordan's body lost the ability to stand back up.

Dingba lowered herself back to the ground. She wiped the sweat from her brow. "You alright?"

Jordan sat up and nodded. "Yeah, just tired is all."

Dingba tossed him a waterskin, "I haven't had a sparring partner in so long."

Jordan raised the waterskin to his mouth, his hands trembled from fatigue and pain as he tried to drink. He managed to still his hands just long enough to get a swig. "How come you were so hesitant about training me?"

"It's a weird thing to ask someone who put you in the healer's hut, don't you think?"

"I mean, yes, but you know."

Dingba gave him a cheeky smirk, "It's a strange thing to ask." Dingba chuckled. "I thought I did brain damage."

Jordan laughed, "No, no, I just like fighting I guess."

Dingba went to some nearby bushes and picked some fruit off, then brought them to Jordan. "Eat up, then we can go searching for your friends some more."

A while later, they are approaching the river. Jordan knelt down and let the water run through his fingers. "It's like I remember. But I haven't seen this location before so I'm pretty sure we need to follow it up more."

Dingba nodded, "Well, it's a start." She grabbed a stick and stabbed it into the ground. "We can use this as a marker just in case."

After a filling lunch, they walked north a bit more. Jordan tried his best to make a mental map of the area, but with no significant markers, he found it difficult. Without Dingba he would have gotten lost already. After a while they turned back and headed towards the village. Once there, Singka greeted them with a hot meal.

Singka sat across from Jordan. "How was your first sparring session, Jordan? Was she gentle?"

Jordan chuckled. "Yeah, she took it as easy as possible on me."

Dingba leaned forward. "See? I told you I'd be gentle with him." She leaned back and took another bite of her food.

Singka chuckled. "I'm glad you proved me wrong. So, what's the plan for tomorrow?"

Jordan glanced at Dingba.

Dingba had just shoveled more food into her mouth. "Whrist-"

Singka lower her eyes, "Don't talk with your mouth full."

Dingba rolled her eyes and swallowed, "First we are going to explore some more, then train."

"And what about his studies?"

"W-We talk while sparring and exploring."

"Alright, as long as you aren't neglecting that."

They finished their food and turned in for the night. Jordan was dead asleep the second his head hit the pillow.

The next day Jordan walked around the village, his morning training put on hold due to Dingba overeating the night before and sleeping in this morning. He spotted Tong walking through the streets his head was low and his eyes focused. He's used to seeing Tong like this, he wondered if the old fairy was just naturally serious looking.

He called out to him nonetheless.

Tong stopped and his face softened, "Oh Jordan, how is it going?"

Jordan smiled, "It's going good. Do you mind if we chatted for a little while."

Tong thought for a moment, "Sure. I can make some time."

They walked a while then found a spot to sit down and rest.

Tong leaned on his cane, "Alright. What is it you wanted to talk about?"

Jordan stroked his beard, "Well I was talking to Singka the other day at the Noble Tree."

Tongs eyes lowered.

"And she mentioned how Humans went extinct. She said you would know more about it."

Tong widened his eyes and relaxed, "Oh. Yes, I can tell you about that."

Jordan smiled, "I suppose you know already that I'm not a Sel... Sel' Kree?"

Tong nodded, "I knew right away. Your eyes are too plain."

Jordan sighed.

Tong grunted in amusement, "But yes Singka told me. As for your question, it's a difficult answer."

Tong thought for a moment, "It was before my time, but I was told of two races that disappeared at roughly the same time. One was the humans, but sadly I can't remember the name of the other race."

Tong groaned as he racked his brain, "I feel like I should but I just can't think of their name at the moment."

Jordan shrugged, "That's fine, maybe you'll think of it later. One last thing if you don't mind me asking?"

Tong nodded, "Go ahead."

"When I first got here. You asked me if I saw anything weird. Was that in relation to Tink?"

Tong eyes grew wide, his fist tightened around the head of his cane. Jordan felt his hair stand on end.

Tong kept his eyes fixed on Jordan, "How do you know about Tink?"

Jordan leaned back slightly, his eyes widened slowly, his body readied itself. "Dingba told me about her yesterday. She said she ran off to check something in the forest and hasn't come back yet."

Tong calmed himself, "I see, sorry."

Jordan relaxed, "It's fine. So, I can take that as a yes?"

Tong looked off to the side, "It's nothing that concerns you."

From the center of the village Dingbas voice rung out. "Jordan!?"

Tong looked over, "Looks like Dingba is ready for you. Be safe Jordan." Tong got up and started walking away.

Jordan frowned, "Yeah. I will." He watched the old Fairy walk off.

Dingba came up to him, "What were you and Tong talking about?"

Jordan smiled, "Just some history about Humans. Nothing important I suppose."

11

RULES

AFTER MANY DAILY SESSIONS, Jordan's confidence outpaced his patience. He stretched and stared at Dingba trying to figure out the best way to get her to fight him harder.

Dingba glanced over, "What's wrong? Do you have a question or something?"

Jordan lowered his eyes.

"Ease into it Jordan."

Jordan smiled, "I'm still confused about the difference between temperance and magic."

Dingba sat up. "Well, think of magic as... the magic of the mind and temperance being the magic of the body. While practicing and training can improve both, there are some differences. Temperance requires you to have a healthy body and the limbs that use your temperance. For example, I wouldn't be able to use my abilities should I break or even worse, lose my arms. You, though, can still do magic even if you were simply a torso and a head. But if you lost control of your mind or had a mental illness..."

"I wouldn't be able to use my magic?"

"Yes, either that or you'd be unable to control it, which let's be honest is basically the same thing. There are, of course, rare temperance abilities like flying and rare magic like mind control."

"That explains it, why I couldn't use it to save Juka."

"So where does it come from?"

Dingba scratched her head, "From the Primordials. But Singka would know more about that. Maybe if we get back in time you can attend story time."

Jordan puckered his lips in excitement, "Oh... story time?"

Dingba nodded, "Yeah she does it every so often with the young ones. I'm not sure what she was planning on talking about tonight, but you can probably ask her about them and she'll tell you. She likes sharing knowledge."

Jordan bounced in place, "Sounds fun." He shakes his limbs loose, "Alright one last question or more like a request."

Dingba raised an eyebrow, "Hmm?"

Jordan smirked, "Go al--"

Dingba gave him a disinterested look and quickly cut him off, "No."

Jordan deflated, "Come on..."

Dingba turned her back to him and floated away, "Nope."

Jordan followed her like a lost puppy, "Dingba..."

She refused to look at him, "Nope."

He ran around to have her look at him, "It's just one time."

She snapped her body away from him, "One time is all it takes."

Jordan groaned, "I promise you I can handle it. And you know you want to, think of how much fun we'd have if we could really just brawl with each other."

Dingba looked over her shoulder, "Singka will get mad."

Jordan smiled, "Only if something bad happens. Come on, just one round where you go all out. It'll be so fun."

Dingba rolled her eyes, "If I go all out, you might die."

Jordan beamed with joy. "And that's okay Dingba."

Dingba glared, "Thats not okay."

Jordan laughed, "Okay, okay, what about? Fifty percent?"

Dingba raised an eyebrow, "What?"

Jordan smirked.

"Gotcha."

He angled his hand then lowered it slightly, "Fight me at about half your strength. It'll be low enough that you don't kill me but high enough that I can really see how good I've gotten."

Dingba sighed, "Fine."

Jordan pumped his fist. "Yes."

Dingba frowned, "Just one round. And if something hurts, we stop, okay?"

Jordan pranced in place, "Oh, it'll be fine, let's just start."

Dingba smirked, "Alright, don't blame me if you get hurt."

They took their starting positions. At first no one moved, they took their time staring each other down. Dingba was the first to act. Like promised, she took the fight more seriously. Her wings quickly sped her towards Jordan as she prepped her right hand for a right hook.

Jordan's eyes widened as they took in the information, then lowered as he focused.

"Dodge right."

He shifted his stance to evade to the right as he did; he used Gao to push Dingba off center.

Dingba's swing went wide, causing her to expose her back. Jordan seized the moment and pulled her towards him with Ver as he swung his fist. Dingba blocked, but the strike threw her off balance.

"Push her down, keep her off balance."

Jordan unleashed a powerful blast of Gao, shoving Dingba towards the ground. He pounced, Dingba hit him with an uppercut, and an explosion rang out in the forest. The force shoved Jordan into the air and back towards the bushes.

His left arm landed inside of a bush and besides the aching pain in his stomach he felt fine.

Dingba lost sight of him. "You alright?"

Jordan sat up, "Yeah." He tried to stand up but felt multiple stabbing pains in his arm. He screamed as he fell back down.

Dingba came bursting through the bushes in a panic.

Jordan looked over and saw thorny vines tangled his arm. He went to pull his arm out and felt more thorns pierce into his flesh.

Dingba gasped, "No. Don't move."

Jordan looked at his arm, then looked at her. "What's wrong?"

Dingba kept her hands out, "That's a clingy thorn."

Jordan glanced at the plant, "A what?"

"It's a type of plant that ensnares things that touch it. The thorns are... kind of... poisonous."

Jordan felt his heart race. He could feel panic induced sickness creeping through his body. "How do I get out?"

Dingba dropped and inspected his arm, "Very carefully."

She looked around and found some tall grass. After grabbing a handful, she quickly twisted it into a rope, then wrapped it around Jordan's bicep before tying it tight. "We need to slow the poison and make it think you are dead."

She grabbed two sticks, "We need to get these thorns out of your skin too."

She got close but hesitated to touch the bush, after steadying her hands she tried to lift some thorns out, but for every thorn she removed two more found its way into Jordan's flesh.

"You're tangled up pretty bad."

Jordan could feel his arm going numb. "How bad is the poison?"

"What do you mean?"

"Like is it treatable? Will my arm melt? Will I die?"

"Yes, no, yes if it spreads too much."

"Alright fuck it. Move."

Dingba stepped back.

He charged up Gao and with one swift motion yanked his arm and some unfortunate vines free from the bush.

Dingba jumped, "Woah. Are you crazy?"

Jordan inhaled through his teeth. "It'll be fine." The pain made his legs tremble from the sensation. Once his mind worked through the pain, he took out the thorns, then took off his shirt and wrapped his arm in it. He compressed down on it, hoping to slow the bleeding.

He smiled, "Welp, let's go say hi to Singka."

Dingba groaned and led them back to the hut.

Jordan walked in first. He clutched his throbbing arm as he saw Singka.

"Hey, Singka. It's my fault, can you fix this?" He offered his arm.

Singka looked over and saw him clutching his arm. "What happened?" She rushed over and peeked underneath the shirt and saw the bloody mess.

Dingba stepped forward. "I accidentally knocked him into a clingy thorn." She kept her head low.

Jordan nodded. "It's my fault to be honest."

Singka sighed, "Go sit on the bed while I get some supplies."

After cleaning and rubbing a medical paste onto his wounds, Singka wrapped his arm with a thick leaf bandage. She pulled it tight, causing Jordan to wince and tap his foot in pain. Dingba had long since left the hut. She wanted to go explore a little more before the sun went down.

"I told her to be gentle with you."

Jordan winced in pain as she finished bandaging his arm.

"So, what happened?"

"It's not entirely her fault. I told her to go all out. She said no, the first five days but you know what they say sixth time is the charm."

Singka glanced up, "What does that mean?"

"It's a joke of a popular human saying 'Third times the charm.' basically the third time you attempt the same thing you succeed."

Singka smiled and rolled her eyes, "Ah, well if this is what a success looks like."

Jordan watched her put up her supplies. "So, I was wondering…"

Singka looks up, her eyes softer now that she bandaged Jordan's wounds. "What is it?"

Jordan's cheeks warmed up, "Dingba said you were going to do a story time thing tonight and I was wondering if I could stay and listen."

Singka beamed, "Of course. Was there something you had in mind?"

Jordan nodded, "She told me magic came from Primordials? I

wanted to hear more about them, and she said you were the best one to ask."

Singka nodded, "Sure I'll tell you the story of them, why don't you relax until the others get here?" She hands him a vial filled with some amber liquid. "Drink some of this if your arm starts hurting."

Jordan took the vial, he held it up to his eyes and shook it gently watching the amber liquid slosh around. "Thanks."

A FEW HOURS GO BY, and the hut is filled with little fairies and some older ones. Bowls of fruit and nuts are placed in the center for easy snacking. Jordan sat in the back, so he didn't block anyone's sight. Dingba sat nearby, her mouth already filled with a snack. A small fairy with white hair and butterfly wings walked up and hugged him tightly.

"Thank you for saving me, mister." Her big butterfly wings flapped gently.

Jordan looked down wide-eyed then looked at Singka.

Singka chuckled, "Jordan… This is Juka, the fairy you saved."

Jordan grinned, "Ah. You're welcome." He patted Juka's head.

Juka looked up and pouted, "You were always running out with Dingba so I couldn't see you."

Jordan chuckled, "Sorry, blame Dingba for wanting to sneak out all the time."

Juka turned and glared at Dingba, who responded by looking away.

Singka smiled, "Alright everyone. Today we had a special request from our guest Jordan." She motioned to him, "So tonight we will talk about The Primordials."

The kids murmur in excitement.

Singka smirked. "Long ago, when the world was new. A group of beings appeared. Each one embodied an element. We called them The Primordials, they breathed magic into the world and taught others how to use it."

135

A child rose their hand, "You said they 'appeared,' how did they appear?"

Singka looked at them, "There's a lot of theories and myths. Like summoning gone wrong, they were always there, but showed themselves randomly. But the most common one states that a giant serpent appeared shortly before they did, after which the serpent left."

Jordan could feel his mind tingle.

"Serpent? So maybe The Train and this Serpent are the same thing?"

Singka continued, "When The Primordials showed up they taught animals, plants and people alike magic, the world exploded with wonder and quickly dived into the period known as the purging."

Singka made a scary face by scrunching her face and showing her teeth, she growled at the children who giggled in response. "One race in particular went into a phase... can anyone tell me what that race was?"

A child rose their hand, "The Collectors?"

Singka nodded, "Almost right, The Collective turned into a..."

Jordan mumbled, "A devouring swarm."

Singka looked at him in surprise, "That's correct. Very good Jordan."

She turned her attention back to the kids, "The Collective declared war on the entire world moving through it in frightening speed. Those that could, scattered throughout the world trying to get away. Eventually they came upon the first forest of the fairies during the reign of the first pix fairy queen, Jaya The Victorious."

Singka stood up and gave her best body builder pose, flexing her muscles as much as she could.

The kids "Ooh'd" and "Ahh'd". Singka laughed and sat down.

She cleared her throat, "Under Jaya's commands, we fairies held on, but we were slowly slipping into the void of extinction. So Jaya made a deal with The Bright Liar and The Void King. The Primordials of light and dark, respectively. She was the first fairy to have her wings change. Some say this is why our wings change, but I disagree."

Jordan tilted his head, "Why do you disagree?"

Singka held up her finger, "Because other races have similar stories and to my knowledge, they experience no physical changes as a result of making deals with Primordials."

She motioned to her wings, "Some even said she could change her wings colors at a whim. This is also something I have never heard of another fairy doing. Though it was taxing on her body, the power she gained was worth it. After leading her people in many victories against The Collective. She held out until the Collective decided extermination wasn't the best thing for the world. We were officially the second race acknowledge by them. The first being the Aphami's."

A child groaned, "So we all learn the same spells?"

Singka shook her head. "It depends on who teaches you magic. Since Jaya's time there's been a lot of development in terms of magic and of course temperance. A lot of mixing of 'bloods' so to speak. For instance, the healer fairy I learned magic from had more offensive magic, so while I learned a spell or two from her, I ended up learning magic mainly from someone who knew more defensive magic. The theory being not everyone needs to be a fighter, but someone needs to pick the fighters up."

Singka continued her story about Jaya and The Primordials. Before long the sun had set, and the village darkened.

Singka looked over at a window sighed, "Time flies when you're having fun. Alright everyone that's the end of story time for tonight."

The children groaned in protest.

Singka chuckled, "I know, I know. But I promise we will have another one soon."

The parents collected their children some of which had fallen asleep and took them home for the night.

Jordan and Dingba helped Singka clean up the hut.

Singka placed a brown book on the table and looked over at Jordan, who was carrying a few empty bowls. "How was your first story night?"

Jordan nodded repeatedly, "It was fun. I learned quite a bit."

Singka smiled, "I'm glad."

Jordan scratched his head, "So, would it be possible for me to learn fairy magic?"

Singka wiggled her head as she thought, "Well first we have to see if you can even learn magic th--"

"Oh, I already have magic."

Singka cut him a confused look. "You have magic?"

Jordan tilted his head, "You didn't know?"

Singka shook her head, "I don't think I've ever seen you use magic. Well, there was that one moment when you had that break, but I wasn't sure if that was magic or temperance then."

Jordan looked at Dingba who shrugged.

Singka waved off her confusion," Anyway, the answer kind of depends on a variety of things like which of the Primordials you are 'aligned' with. Show me your magic."

Jordan nodded and summoned his spell circle. Singka leaned back, her eyes wide with shock.

He pulled a book over to him with Ver, then launched it into the air with Gao. He turned to Singka who stared at him, confused and shocked.

Jordan glanced around, "What's wrong?"

She looked at him. "Who taught you magic?"

Jordan tilted his head, "A burning lady?"

Singka scrunched her face up, "A what?"

Jordan grabbed a wooden tablet and drew a rough sketch, "She was tall and had long flowing hair, but she was on fire, like she was made of fire. She told me these words and now I can do what I just did. Why?"

Singka took the tablet and inspected the drawing, "Mm, that sounds like The Burning Queen." She placed her hand on her chin. "No one uses spell circles anymore. The Primordials used to use them, but history just randomly stopped talking about people who used spell circles. After that point there are fewer mentions of circle users until eventually there is none."

"Why did everyone swap over?"

Singka shrugged. "No one knows, it just kind of happened. Some think it was because someone figured out how to skip the circle requirement."

Jordan frowned, "So does that mean I can't learn fairy magic?"

Singka gave him an apologetic smile, "Well, yes. In theory. The problem is even if you were aligned with the right Primordial, your magic core is locked with circle usage. Which requires you to know the base word for the spell. Since we don't use words to cast our magic, we can't teach you the words you would need. Plus, because circle users disappeared randomly in history there's no text that I know of that can help you."

Jordan deflated in his spot. "Oh, okay. No worries I guess." His heart sunk.

"Aw… man."

Singka patted his head, "But it's not that bad. If a Primordial taught you directly, then you should be able to learn lots of magic. That's pretty special if I say so myself."

Jordan smiled.

Singka smiled, "I hope that answered some of your questions."

"It does." He looked down and remembered the book he pulled earlier, "Do you want this back?"

"Ah, you can use it for study material. You might find it interesting."

He thumbed over the pages. "What is it?"

"It's a bounty book. It might be a little outdated, but you can still find some interesting things in there."

Jordan looked down his eyes glowed with curiosity.

"Oh, that sounds fun."

On the front cover was the symbol of the Collective. He flipped open the book to the first page that acted as a glossary. It listed hundreds of names with their page number. Jordan flipped the pages until someone caught his eye.

A man not bound by the past nor the laws of the present. His power does not follow a straight path but follows his whims by leaps and bounds, for he is Unbounded.

Wanted: Noritaibu The Unbounded

HT: 7' 8" WT: 251 Race: Abomination Color of soul: Pitch Black
Leader of the Reclaimers, wanted for:
3206 counts of murder
The Assassination of Arch Ruler Weilio of the CloudSide Empire
Theft and destruction of numerous caravans from various nations
And much more.
A Reward of 85,235,783 Pints
Dead or Alive
Noritaibu The Unbounded

A drawing of a man with dark skin, a wild look on his face. A braided ponytail could be seen in the middle of his head.

"Woah, he bad..."

Singka looked over at the book. "Ah yes, he's one of the highest bounties."

"Damn I want a bounty too."

Singka gently popped his hand, "Don't aspire to do bad things."

Jordan chuckled. "It just sounds cool. You get an awesome name, a big ass bounty."

"You only get a bounty if you make people mad enough to pay for you to be killed."

"Fine... I'll be good."

Singka giggled, "You better."

Jordan kept looking through the book, "How did you get this?"

Singka thought for a moment, "Ah, a while back the Collective flew over and gave them out. That was a while ago, they normally come once every year or so to check up on us. My sister used to bring the bounty books back whenever she went traveling. She said she liked reading them."

She let out a deep yawn. "Alright, it's getting late. I'll leave you alone to gush over bad people. Goodnight Jordan."

Jordan grinned, "Night."

Once Singka left, Jordan bounced in place. His cheeks ached from smiling. This world set his brain on fire he wanted to learn more. He wanted to explore, learn more spells, and try new combinations.

Somewhere deep in his heart he hoped The Burning Queen would teach him fire magic. He was always a fan of that element; hopefully if he kept practicing, she would reach out to him again. He just had to keep practicing.

TRICKED

JORDAN DUSTED HIMSELF OFF, his brow sweaty from his latest sparring session with Dingba. Another lost, another failed move experiment.

Dingba floated over, her face glistened with sweat, an improvement compared to the days she could fight him for hours and leave with barely a drop of sweat. "You alright?"

Jordan nodded, "Yeah, I already got a few new moves to test on you."

Dingba laughed, "Alright, well let's call it here for today. You wanted to go exploring deeper in the forest, right?"

"Yeah, I'm still hoping to find my friends."

Dingba nodded. "Well, it's still early and there will be two of us so it shouldn't be an issue if we go deeper."

Jordan tilted his head. "Why would it be an issue?"

Dingba frowned. "Well, lately some fairies have gone missing, and we don't know why. So, Tong suggested no one stray too far from the village and not go out alone. Since then, disappearances have gone down."

"So why was Juka by herself?"

Dingba sighed. "She was with a group and for some reason

wandered off and accidentally went deeper into the forest without realizing it. But if we hurry, we can be in and out before anyone notices."

Jordan stood up, dusting his pants off. "Lead the way."

A while later, they were back in a familiar spot.

Jordan gasped as he entered the clearing. "This is it."

Dingba looked around. "Your camp was here?"

"No, this is where I saved Juka. I think. It looks familiar."

"Oh. Well, let's look around and see if we can find anything useful."

Jordan nodded and walked to the center of the clearing, even though his mind wasn't in the best of states. He felt a familiar rush as he scanned the area. He remembered seeing Juka struggling in a web, then the fight with the Juk-Juk.

As he reached the center of the clearing, he saw a small crater in the ground; he knelt down and gently ran his fingers in the crater.

"Did I do this?"

Dingba's head popped out of some nearby bushes to the left. "I found a body."

Jordan rushed over to see what she found.

On the ground there laid a decomposing corpse of a Juk-Juk. Jordan knelt down and poked at it with a stick. He noticed a few stab wounds, which his knife could have caused. What concerned him the most was the gaping hole in the beast's chest.

"This is weird."

Dingba held her nose as she got closer. "What is?"

"If this is the spot, then this is the Juk-Juk I killed. Well, the second one. But I never hit its chest and there's a crater in the ground that I don't remember being there."

"It's been a while since you were here so who knows what happened while you were gone."

Jordan frowned has he tried to remember, "Well, I remember the Juk-Juk acting strange before I killed it."

"*Never figured out why.*"

"Strange how?"

Jordan stood up, "Well, it acted like it forgot I existed or simply couldn't see me. It's fuzzy and hard to explain. I remember it missed its pounce on me even though I wasn't moving."

Dingba hovered into the air, "That's not... impossible. Maybe it just rushed to take you down?"

Jordan shrugged, "True, but I don't know... it was weird. Anyway, this looks like the place. And if it is." Jordan pointed off into the distance. "I came from the north."

Dingba tilted her head. "That's East."

Jordan cut a look at her. "I came from that way."

Dingba giggled. "Alright, well, let's go that way. We still have some time so if we hurry, we can cover some good distance."

Dingba led them deeper into the forest. Jordan took the time to appreciate the nature that he missed the first time. They had walked for what felt like hours until Dingba suddenly stopped. "This isn't right."

Jordan stepped beside her and looked at her. "What's wrong?"

Dingba stared ahead, her face twisted, as if trying to figure out a puzzle. She scrunched the bridge between her eyes together as she looked around. "Do you know where we are?"

"Why would I...?"

Jordan looked around, and his eyes widened. The area before them was the same area they left a while back. Expect this time the Juk-Juk's body was to the right and not the left. "We are back where I saved Juka?"

Dingba nodded, "But that can't be right." She stepped forward and went to the bushes.

She spread them and saw the decaying body of the Juk-Juk.

"This is the spot."

Jordan walked up behind her. "Did we take a wrong turn somewhere?"

"Maybe, but I can't remember a time I got turned around in this forest."

Jordan placed his hand to his chin as he thought.

"Is there something about this area that confuses people?"

He looked at Dingba, "Want to try again?"

Dingba looked up at the sky. "We have awhile before the sun gets low. Let's explore a little more."

Once again Dingba led the way. She made sure they took no turns while walking. The only time they would deviate from their path was to go around a tree, a clingy thorn or some other obstacle. As Jordan's legs ached, they came upon another clearing.

Jordan was hopeful until he saw the same crater in the ground. The smell of the rotting Juk-Juk was directly to his right.

"Something is very wrong here."

Dingba sighed, "What? How is that even possible?"

The hairs on Jordan's neck stood on edge, he's felt this before like the world was changing around him. He scanned the area, but wasn't sure what he was looking for.

Dingba scratched her head as she paced back and forth. "I don't understand. I never get lost." She stopped walking and looked around. Her eyes were focused as she scanned the area.

The feeling of unease grew stronger.

"This is worst then the Juk-Juk. Much worst."

Jordan looked around, "We should leave."

Dingba glanced at him, "What about your friends?"

Jordan shook his head. "It's getting late, we can try again later. Plus something feels off."

Dingba clenched her fist, "I feel it too. Lets head back to the village."

Jordan nodded, "Lead the way."

They walked back in silence. Jordan stayed close to Dingba and didn't take his eyes off of her. Dingba seemed lost in thought as she moved through the forest with an instinctive grace the kind you develop when you have walked the same path numerous times.

Jordan's unease continued to grow, even though he tried to distract himself his mind would always lead back to the problem at hand.

"Fairies don't get lost. Right?"

His eyes narrowed as he watched Dingba lead him back to the

village effortlessly, even while seemingly lost in her thoughts. He couldn't shake off his suspicion.

"Either they lied about never being lost or something is interfering with her ability to navigate past a certain point."

They made it back to the village a little after it got dark. As they entered the hut, Singka greeted them. "Where were you guys? It's late."

Dingba snapped out of it, "We were training and lost track of time."

Singka smiled in relief, "I got worried and asked a few people to go to your normal spot and they said you weren't there."

Dingba wore a blank expression on her face, "We went for a walk after training."

Singka frowned. "Alright, well, I made some fish tonight. I figured you would be hungry."

On the table a plate of baked fish rested, a little steam wafted off of them.

Dingba smiled. "They look good." She flew over to the table and patted a chair next to her. "Come on, let's eat."

Singka patted Jordan on the back. "Come on. Let's eat."

Jordan sat next to Dingba. While Singka filled his plate with fish.

She slides his plate to him. "Careful, the bones are still in there."

Dingba took a large bite and scraped the meat off the bones.

Jordan chuckled. "I thought it had bones?"

Singka sighed as Dingba looked up. "You can just hold the bones and scrape the meat off with your teeth. Like this." She turned and demonstrated the technique.

Sure enough, she pulled all the meat off the bone; she looked up at Jordan and nodded.

"I'll stick to being careful, for now."

Singka smiled, "So how's training?"

Dingba sat up, "Oh. Jordan is learning a new move."

Singka glanced at Jordan, "Oh? What kind of move?"

Jordan's cheeks got warm as he smiled. "It's nothing special I just grab my opponent and use magic to throw them really hard."

Dingba nods, "He likes to go for the face."

Singka raised an eyebrow. "Is that so? That sounds like a very useful move to learn."

Jordan beamed. "I try. Dingba helps me experiment a lot."

It's Dingba's turn to beam with joy.

After they finish dinner. Singka left Dingba and Jordan to talk for a little while before bed. Jordan flipped through the bounty book. He lifted his eyebrows and showed Dingba the book.

"What's this word?"

Dingba, who had been staring off into the distance for the past couple of minutes, comes to and leans forward to look. "Kubwa. It's a race."

Jordan nodded and wrote the word down, "Thanks."

Dingba rubbed her chin as she looked at the ceiling. After a few moments, she spoke. "It still bothers me."

Jordan looked up from the bounty book. "What does?"

"I don't understand how I got lost today. It's one thing to get turned around while searching in random areas, but to get turned around going in basically a straight line. It doesn't make sense."

Jordan slides a leaf into the page he was looking at, "So the first time, we were exploring aimlessly but still heading east, right?"

"Correct."

"But the second time we simple walked directly east, only adjusting our path to avoid trees, right?"

"Right, we never changed directions. We just scooted over."

Jordan stroked his chin. "Are we sure?"

"What do you mean?"

"Are we sure we never took a turn while we were walking? Cause we reentered the clearing twice from different spots."

Dingba raised an eyebrow as Jordan grabbed a tablet and started drawing.

He drew a square, in the middle he placed a circle and to the left of the circle he drew a stick figure of a cat with Xs for eyes. He then labeled each direction with east at the top and north to the left.

After showing the drawing to Dingba, He drew a line from the west, entering the square. Together they mapped out the routes they took and how they reentered the clearing. They went over every attempt trying to remember if there was anything they noticed while walking. Though so far nothing of note came up, fatigue started to set in as they discussed the last attempt.

Jordan erased the previous lines, "So we exited through the east side again and this time we entered from the north side, right next to the Juk-Juk. Which means if we truly walked straight, we shouldn't have entered from that side. To do that, we would have had to make three left turns to reach that location."

Dingba scratched her head. "R-Right."

Jordan leaned back and tapped the ink stick on his chin, "So if you really didn't get lost then somehow, we took three turns and didn't realize it."

Dingba stared at the tablet in silence. Her body rocked slowly back and forth as she did.

Jordan thought for a moment, "Is there some kind of plant or animal that can cause confusion or mislead people?"

Dingba shook her head. "Not that I know of."

Jordan snapped his fingers, "Ah. What about some kind of magic? Like illusion magic?"

Dingba's eyes widen. A bolt of fear flashed over her face. She calmed herself, "illusion magic is possible."

Jordan tilted his head slightly. "Is there someone who can use illusion magic?"

Dingba shook her head. "No one in the village knows that kind of magic."

Jordan lowered his eyes. "Maybe Tong or Singka knows of someone?"

Her head shot up, her eyes wide almost pleading. "No one knows illusion magic here.", her eyes gave a hint of truth to her statement, but the look of fear told him it wasn't the whole truth.

"*You're lying but okay.*"

She looked away and quickly erased the board, "We should figure out if something is actually tricking people, then that would explain all the missing fairies." She smiled softly, "Maybe we can find them."

Jordan nodded, "Alright, so we need to test this."

Dingba looked up, "How?"

Jordan started drawing on the table again, "We go back to the same spot and travel east again. Then randomly we split up and head different directions. If something is preventing us from traveling east, we can test how well it can track things."

Dingba nodded, "But, what happens if we both end up back there?"

Jordan shrugged, "If both of us end up there, it means whatever is messing with us can keep track of both of us. So, it's either an area of effect or has some other way of watching us. But if only one of us makes it back then we know it can only focus on one person or group."

Dingba smiled, "Then the other person can continue exploring?"

Jordan nodded, "That's right."

Dingba nodded with a smile, "Let's do it."

THE NEXT MORNING, they skip training and rush to the clearing. They stood on the eastern edge, staring into the bushes. Dingba turned to Jordan.

"Ready?"

Jordan nodded.

They entered the trees and proceeded forward. As they made small talk, their eyes darted around, looking for anything strange. After a few moments, Dingba floated in front and turned around.

"Okay bye."

She darted off in a different direction, Jordan took off running in a straight line. He ran hard to put some distance in between them, and eventually he felt alone.

13

FOLLOW ME

DINGBA FLEW THROUGH THE TREES, zig and zagging away from Jordan. After a moment, she stopped and took a breath. She glanced around, trying to get her bearings. She floated up to the tree line but a rustling of some bushes stopped her.

She raised her fists. "Who's there?"

Jordan stumbled out of the bushes, his clothes ripped and his arm bleeding. He looked up at Dingba.

"Dingba, we gotta go now. It's not safe here."

Dingba lowered her fist. "Jordan?"

Jordan looked around and started stumbling away from the bushes he just left. "Dingba, we gotta go. It's bad very bad. We need to warn Tong and the others."

Dingba landed and inspected Jordan's wounds. "What happened?"

"How did he get in front of me? I'm faster."

"After we split, I ran, then got attacked by... some kind of monster. I barely got away, but I think it's right behind me. We gotta go."

Dingba looked behind him but saw no movement in the forest. When she looked back at Jordan, he gave her a wary smile.

"Come on, we gotta go before it catches up."

Dingba nodded. "Okay, let's get going. Follow me."

She grabbed his arm and started leading him back to the village.

But as they walked, she couldn't shake this feeling that something was wrong.

She slowed down. "Hey? What did you see?"

Jordan shook his head. "It's hard to describe it was green and had these whips on it that really, really hurt."

"How did you get away?"

"I ran. After days of chasing you through the woods and sparring with you, it was easy to get away once I got some distance. It had a long reach though."

"We should go back and capture it."

A flash of panic washed over Jordan's face. "No, no, it's not safe. We will die. We should tell Tong and Singka."

Dingba frowned, "But we'd have to show them proof of what we found or else we'd have to bring them back and that could be dangerous too."

Jordan groaned. "But we'd have more people. We'd have help. It'd be safer. Now come on we gotta get moving."

Dingba continued to float, the feeling of unease still lingered in the back of her mind.

———

THEY MADE slow progress through the forest. Jordan's injuries made it hard for him to move fast. He eventually asked to stop talking so he could conserve his strength. Dingba respected his request, but still had more questions to ask.

Her eyes widened as she stared at Jordan's back.

"Why am I following him?"

She looked around and realized she didn't recognize where they were.

"How does he know which way the village is?"

She bit her lip, her eyes lowered.

"I have to try."

"Hey Jordan. Do you know what an orange is?"

Jordan sighed and turned towards her, annoyed at the question. "What?"

"An orange, do you know what it is?"

His eyes dart around. "Why are you asking?"

Dingba lowered her eyes but kept a smile on her face. "I know you are in pain so I figured we can have a quick lesson to take your mind off of it."

Jordan rolled his eyes, "I don't real—"

Dingba gave him a stern look, "It'll be fine. Trust me."

Jordan sighed and rolled his eyes. "Fine, what was the question again?"

"What. Is. A. Orange?"

Jordan thought for a moment, and her fists tightened.

Jordan shrugged. "I don't know. Let's keep going." He turned around and her heart dropped.

"Why don't you know?"

"W-Well, what about a criti? Bonus points if you get it right."

Jordan groaned, "It's a fruit, there's plenty in the village I can show you them when we get there."

"Why don't you know?"

She glared, "Correct." Her wings flicked up, and she dashed as fast as she could towards him.

"Reach him before he turns around. You have to."

She clenched her right fist tightly and cocked her arm as she took aim at the small of his back.

She saw Jordan turning towards her; she angled her body to avoid seeing his face and to keep her eyes on her target.

She threw her punch; the world shook as the explosion rang out. The force cut Jordan in half, as his torso flew over her body a black smoke rose from his halves.

Dingba could feel tears welling up.

"It's fine, you were right. This isn't Jordan. You were right."

As Jordan's body dissipates into strands of smoke, the world shimmered around her, changing by the second until it finally stopped.

"Where am I?"

She glanced down and saw the crater surrounding her feet. "No."

She ran to the left and saw the Juk-Juk's body.

"No, no, no."

She took off at top speed.

"How far did we get separated? How long have we've been separated?"

She zoomed to the spot where they split up, hoping to catch up with Jordan.

"Don't die, I can't lose anyone else."

14

PROOF

JORDAN STOMPED the ground as he continued his run through the forest. After the rush of running aimlessly wore off he placed his hand on a nearby tree.

He panted as he caught his breath. "I'm out of shape."

He surveyed the area, trying to locate anything memorable. To help him navigate in the forest.

"Now that I really think about it. This was a stupid idea. How am I supposed to get back?"

He snapped his finger as an idea came to his head.

"The river, if I find it I can follow it down."

He turned to the right and kept moving. Eventually he heard running water. His skin tingled with excitement, and he hurried to the river. When he arrived, he saw a large creature standing next to it.

Its body resembled a pitcher plant in both shape and color. Its lid currently open and accepting any visitors. Jordan is taller than it but judging by its size someone like Dingba could fit inside its fluid filled body. The plant had tendrils dipped into the water, its 'back' turned to him.

Jordan stood still as he watched it, curious to what it was doing. In the center of the plant was a large, dark spot. Something wiggled inside.

His eyes widened as he watched it wiggle.

"Could that be a fairy?"

To his side a long stick laid, mostly straight with a somewhat pointy end. Perfect for throwing.

"Might be able to use this."

As he reached for it, his mind flashed back to Cindy and her death. The memory froze his hand, and he lost himself for a moment. His chest tightened, and his breathing grew harder.

The plant turned and made a guttural sound as it shambled towards him. Crushing a twig on its way.

The snapping sound snapped Jordan out of his thoughts. He turned to see the plant rushing towards him. One of the tendrils raises into the air and strikes at him.

He rolled out of the way just as the tendril whipped the ground, cracking the air with force. Jordan stood up and braced for a fight.

The plant attacked again, this time sending a flurry of whips as Jordan kept his distance. The sound each tendril made when it slapped the ground made him sure he didn't want to get hit. He continued to dance around it, looking for an opening. But he could find none. It never took its sights off of him, and the tendrils that weren't being used to attack mindlessly were hanging back, most likely for defense.

He bent down and scooped up a handful of dirt.

"Let's see if it really has eyes."

With a flick of the wrist, a cloud of dust wafts over to the plant. Undeterred by the useless attack, it continued its advance. Jordan sucked his teeth and looked around for some other inspiration. He's used to the range by now and how slowly it moved. The only concerning thing is those tendrils and what happens if they catch him.

He picked up the stick from earlier and tossed it. He wasn't sure what he expected to happen, but after seeing the plant attack it and some tendrils wrap around it before they freed themselves, he felt a spark of inspiration.

He glanced at the branches of some nearby trees and smiled.

He bent down and picked up a small rock. "Hey follow me." He tossed the rock, and it bounced off its body.

The plant shambled a little faster towards Jordan as he led it into the brush. Once he put some distance between the plant and him. He tore off a healthy branch from a nearby tree and pointed the leafy end at the plant.

He rushed it and like he expected, its tendrils touched the branch and attacked with all their might. Jordan twisted and rotated the branch, hoping to tangle its weapons like violent spaghetti. Once he felt the plant tug, he shifted his footing and pulled up to lock the knots in.

The plant tugged against the branch more, Jordan swelled his Circle and with a mighty Gao threw the plant beast into the air tearing its tendrils off. It landed loudly. When it moved again Jordan rushed over and stepped on its lid.

"Alright, let's get you open."

He grabbed the rim of the plant and pulled in different directions until it tore open. Once the initial resistance faded, he ripped the plant completely open. The juices and contents of its stomach spilled out onto the ground. The air filled with a sickly-sweet smell. Inside the stomach were a few large fishes, some of the fish had their flesh melted, one flopped in the mess in search of water.

"Alright, little one. Let's get you back into the river."

He found two sticks and used them to pinch and lift the fish carefully. Once he got it near the water, he launched it with Gao. It flew and landed in the middle of the river. He could see the trail of dirt and pitcher fluids as it swam off somewhere.

Walking back, he spots another pitcher plant shambling towards him. Picking up his trusty branch, he rushed that one before it got too comfortable. As he reached it and started tangling its tendrils up, a jolt of pain shot up his arm.

He looked to the left and saw another one moving in; he tried to move away, but it wrapped his leg and yanked him off his feet. Luckily, he threw his hand back behind his head to protect it as he slapped the ground. The plant unleashed a volley of whips onto his chest. The leaf clothing provided enough protection for the moment.

He growled at the plant, "Get off and wait your turn."

He lifted his leg and stomped on the tendril smashing and breaking it off. After he scrambled back to his feet, he checked his arm and saw blood.

He smirked, "Alright, I can take two of you at once."

From the bushes more rustling can be heard. He looked over and saw a horde of them coming over.

"Okay... nevermind."

He turned on his heels and took off running as fast as he could. With no clue where he was, he followed the river down. The sound of the plant monsters soon faded into the distance. Knowing the clearing where he saved Juka wasn't too far from the river he slowly drifted to the side hoping to run into the clearing. Instead, he crashed into something else and tumbled to the ground.

After shaking the pain off, Jordan looked to see what he ran into.

Dingba pushed herself up and shook her head. "Ow."

Jordan beamed with joy. "Dingba. You okay?"

She looked over and glared.

"Listen, we gotta go. It's not safe here."

Dingba huffed, "Another trick." She lifted herself into the air.

Jordan raised an eyebrow. "What are you talking about?"

Dingba rushed at Jordan and swung at him.

Jordan rolled away and scrambled to his feet.

"Dingba its me."

She raised her hands and attacked once more. Jordan put his guard up. This time she connected, her tiny fist crushed through Jordan's guard before the explosion went off and staggered him.

She reared back, eyes watering up as she glared at Jordan.

"Now or never."

In an act of desperation, Jordan pulled her head forward with Ver and clutched her face in his hand. Quickly, he followed up with a Gao empowered throw, launching her towards a nearby tree, at dangerous speeds.

Jordan gasped, "Shit, Dingba."

Before Dingba touched the tree, an explosion went off before obliterating the small tree trunk, giving Dingba enough time to recover.

She looked at her fist. "How did I do that?" Then she looked at Jordan, her face softer and a little confused. "What's an orange?"

Jordan shook off the confusion and slightly lowered his guard. "What?"

Dingba groaned, "What is an orange."

"A color and a type of fruit from my world. Why?"

Dingba grinned and zoomed into Jordan's chest. "It is you." She hugged tightly.

"Who else would it be?"

She hugged him tighter. "I was worried I'd have to kill you again."

Jordan pulled her off. "What?"

She giggled. "Nothing, I'll explain later. Let's head back to the village."

Together they rushed back to the village, on the way they gave each other a rundown on what happened while they were split up. Once they were back into the hut, they were finally able to take a break and rest their aching bodies. A box of bandages sat between them. Jordan grabbed one and started tending to his wounds.

Jordan thought for a moment. "So, the things that attacked me were large plant creatures. Well, monsters I guess." He grabbed a wooden tablet and drew a rough sketch. "They looked like pitcher plants and behaved pretty similarly. I killed one, and it had a bunch of fish in its stomach. Shortly afterwards, a bunch came from the bushes. They attacked me but they were slow, so I got away."

Dingba looked at the drawing. "I've never seen those before. They aren't native to this forest. At least, I don't think they are. Maybe this is why something is trying to keep us from going too far east?"

"Is it for our protection? Or to stall while those creatures breed?"

"Well, we should find out for sure. But we can't stay together, or we will get turned around. We can't split up because we might attack each other."

Jordan rubbed his chin. "Well, if we had some way to identify each other than we can."

Dingba's wings flicked out, "I have an idea." She flew off to the back of the hut.

THE NEXT MORNING, they stood at the edge of the clearing. It had rained last night, the ground was soft and damp. Puddles darted the terrain in various places, a slight fog slithered between the trees, discouraging further progress.

"You ready?"

Dingba nodded, "Ready."

They took off into the woods, crashing through the foggy barrier. Slowly they separated until the buzzing of Dingba's wings no longer accompanied the thumping of Jordan's shoes.

Once his chest got heavy, he stopped and took a swig of water.

The fog danced around him, pulling his attention in every direction. The forest was oddly quiet, no rustling of bushes, no birds chirping. It was just him and this chilling fog that obscured his vision. Looking down, he could barely see his feet. He continued forward.

The bushes rustle, and he braces himself for a fight.

"Who's there?"

A few explosions sound off in the distance. His eyes widen and he ran towards the sound.

By the time he makes it to the location, his shoes are soaked and caked in mud. In the fog, he saw a figure standing still. He approached slowly until the fog gave way and revealed Dingba. She turned around and raised her fist, ready to strike him down.

"Woah Dingba it's me."

Dingba sighed, "Oh good, I was worried it was another one of these things."

She motioned to the corpse of a plant monster; it had chunks of flesh missing from its body. Likely caused by the explosive force of her punches.

"I guess whatever is going on, doesn't want us to separate."

Jordan kept his guard up as he inspected Dingba.

"It's okay. I took care of this one, but I think I made too much noise. We should head somewhere else in case more are coming."

Jordan nodded. "That's a good idea. That was pretty loud."

Dingba laughed. "Yeah, sorry. I thought they would be tougher, so I didn't hold back. Here, follow me I'll take us somewhere safe." She floated back into the tree line, "Come on, this way."

Jordan lowered his head, "Sure, but first. Lift your shirt."

Dingba stopped, "What?"

Jordan lowered his eyes. "Lift your shirt."

15

THE REVEAL

DINGBA COVERED HER CHEST. Her cheeks turned a soft rosy color. "So sudden." She looked Jordan up and down before shaking her head. "We should be looking for clues not fooling around."

Jordan smirked. "We've known each other for a while now, so it's not that sudden. Plus..." He looked her up and down "You're the biggest clue I want to look at right now."

She covered her face and kicked her feet. "Jordan..." She giggled while slowly rolling in the air.

"I'm serious. Aren't you even the slightest bit curious? After all those intimate fights we've had?"

Dingba's face burned bright red. Jordan could hear her breathing heavily between her hands.

She peeked through her fingers. "We have to find clues."

"We have all day to find some clues, what's the harm in having a little fun while we do?"

Dingba turned around and inhaled deeply. "Okay, fine. I'll admit I was curious about you. Just. Don't look."

Jordan chuckled, "It'll be more exciting if I do."

Dingba's legs wiggled as she laughed. "Alright. You win."

Jordan lowered his eyes and placed his hand on his hip. "Yay."

Dingba grabbed her shirt and took a few more breaths.

Jordan swelled his spell circle. "Do it slowly."

She giggled and dragged up her shirt. Her hips came into view, then her lower back. Once her shirt was halfway off, Jordan glared.

"Alright you can stop."

Dingba froze. "What's wrong?"

"You can drop the act; I had no interest in seeing you topless from the start."

Dingba's head snapped around she wore an ugly glare. "Huh?"

"I know you're not Dingba. You can stop pretending."

Dingba laughed, eventually it turned into a cackle. Her voice grew deeper and sharper but kept its feminine qualities. After she finished laughing, she sighed, "Man, I was really hoping I'd get to see a naked human."

Jordan chuckled, "I mean you still can, it's just a little weird since you're in Dingba's body. Maybe if you changed into your real body, we could keep the show going." He twitched his eyebrows up suggestively.

The Impostor smirked. "Nice try."

Jordan smiled and shrugged.

The impostor walked around and continue to inspect Jordan. "I figured you be more worried about this situation."

Jordan scrunched up his lips as he shook his head, "Nah."

"Oh?" She floated up and got closer to Jordan's face. "Why not?"

"If you really wanted me dead, I'd be dead. After all, you went through a lot of effort to pretend to be Dingba."

She smirked, "Maybe I just wanted to give you a happy memory before I killed you."

Jordan shrugged, "A lot of effort just to kill someone who can't see past your illusions."

The imposter leaned in and looked him in the eyes, "Maybe I wanted to humiliate a pervert before killing him."

Jordan matched her gaze, "Who's the real pervert? The one testing an impostor or the impostor pretending to be someone else and will strip for the person she's trying to trick?"

She chuckled, "I feel you know the answer to that question."

Jordan shrugged.

She leaned back. "So how did you know I wasn't Dingba?"

"We drew a mark on our backs, you didn't have it."

She raised an eyebrow. "What would you have done, if I kept facing you while lifting my shirt?"

"Asked you to turn around."

"How come you didn't attack me once you realized I was a fake?"

"Didn't seem like the best option. Since I could just talk to you instead."

She huffed, "Maybe it was worth saving you after all."

Jordan lifted his head. "You saved me? From the Juk-Juk?"

She nodded, "Yep, you weren't doing so hot, so I figured I'd lend my assistance."

Jordan crossed his arms, "But why?"

She tilted her head, "Why did I save you?"

Jordan nodded, "Yeah, why go through the effort of saving me?"

"I suppose there are a lot of reasons. But you saved Juka, even if you didn't mean to. I guess I was paying it back."

"Why would you care if I saved Juka or not?"

She shrugged. "She reminded me of someone I suppose."

"Who?"

"Don't worry about it."

Jordan frowned. "So why are you getting in the way now?"

She frowned back. "I'm just tired of seeing death."

"What do you mean?"

She looked up; her gaze weakened, and a pained smile crossed her face. "I jus-"

The ground rumbled. Her eyes opened wide.

"What are you doing up?" She looked at the sky. "You shouldn't be up yet. What are you doing?"

She turned to Jordan; her face riddled with dread. "Leave now." The ground shook more.

An orb appeared in front of Jordan. "Follow that to Dingba, I'll tell her to run, you have to go now."

Jordan could only see her illusions. If it wasn't for the ground shaking beneath his feet, he would be unaware anything was going on.

"Go. Now. Saving your life means nothing if she catches you now. Find Dingba and run back to the village. Don't stop for anything."

Jordan couldn't see it, but he could feel it deep inside. Fear too big to swallow, he felt surrounded.

She slapped him across the face, shocking his mind back to reality. "Go!"

He turned on his heels and ran as hard as he could. The orb shined brightly, guiding his retreat. It's fast. Even running at full speed, he had trouble keeping up with it. His chest burned. He was having trouble breathing. He wanted to stop and catch his breath, but the ground continued to tremble.

"Don't stop. You're running for your life."

Eventually adrenaline kicked in fully and fatigue melted away. He knew if he kept moving, he'd be fine, but the second he stopped. He wouldn't have it in him to run anymore. Moments later, Dingba came into sight.

"Oh, thank god."

She turned towards Jordan and put her fist up.

"Lift your shirt."

Jordan snatched her up and continued running. "No time, we're in danger."

The orb faded from sight.

"Shit, Dingba where are we? We need to get to the village."

"Not before you prove who you are."

Jordan reached under his shirt and ripped a red ribbon off before handing it to her. "There, now tell me where we are, we have to get back to the village."

"Ok, follow me." She wiggled out of his arms and pushed ahead.

As they passed the Juk-Juk clearing, a loud scream rang out in the forest.

"Dingba. No, we can't stop."

She looked back, "That didn't sound far, we need to go help."

"Dingba no...."

"Come on." She took a sharp turn towards the screaming.

"God damn it."

Jordan followed on foot.

As they rushed towards the direction of the scream, the sound of struggle got louder. More tiny screams rang out, causing them to double their efforts. Busting through the bushes, they saw two fairies on the ground near an overturned basket of fruit. They had straight lashes on their backs. A few feet away, another tinier fairy was being dragged by her foot towards a group of giant pitcher plants. While they restrained another one in a mess of tendrils, two plants fight over the meal, pulling her back and forth.

The fairy reached out for them, "Help."

Dingba and Jordan sprang into action, rushing towards the plants. Dingba went for the fairy being restrained while Jordan focused on the plant dragging the fairy.

He ran past the fairy; the plant raised its tendrils at him; he clenched his fist.

"Don't stop."

He threw a Gao empowered punch that cleanly swept through the body of the plant. He winced as he felt a twinge of pain radiate around his wrist. The plant was still moving; he kept running. After circling around, he instigated another joust. When Jordan got close enough, a vine shot from the mouth of the plant at high speeds. Jordan barely dodged it by leaning to the left at the last second. He could feel the vine cut his cheek as it passed by. He threw his punch and missed as his fist flew through the hole he already created.

He could hear multiple explosions coming from Dingba's side as a quick glance showed her on the defensive. He took a deep breath and pushed his body to run faster. After circling the plant monster again, he rushed it. This time he aimed for the right side.

"Keep moving. Don't stop until its over."

The plant monster met his challenge by sending out a volley of vines. Jordan dropped to his knees, sliding forward underneath the attack. As he reared back and swelled his circle, three vines he didn't notice sunk into his thighs and chest. He groaned through the pain and finished his attacked by slamming his fist into the center of the plant monster's body. It exploded, spraying digestive juices all over Jordan and the surrounding area. Jordan clutched his body as the stinging acid seeped into his wounds.

"Get up and move."

He tried to stand up. His legs wobbled uncontrollably. He could feel it coming.

"Hurry and move."

He took a step and crumbled to the ground. Fatigued consumed him whole. He couldn't breathe. Stars danced in his vision as darkness lingered at the edges. The leafy fabric clung annoyingly to his skin. He tried to peel it off but couldn't get a good grip.

"Damn it. How long was I running for?"

He propped his body up with his elbow. His eyes followed a lone vine that was outstretched away from the main body. The fairy that was being dragged is missing, the end of the vine undone and limp on the ground.

"Okay, we just need to hold out."

He looked back at Dingba and saw her guard breaking, her forearms bloody from repeated blocks.

"I have to help."

He tried to move his body; jolts of pain mixed with waves of fatigue threatened to knock him unconscious. His eyes grew heavier by the second. He forced them open to watch Dingba fight. He could barely hear her explosions over the sound of his heart drumming.

Despite seeing various objects on the ground, Jordan was hesitant to launch those willy-nilly into the fight. The fear of striking Dingba overwhelmed him. In the middle of the fear, a new idea formed.

"Can I just… sustain a spell?"

He focused on one of the plant monsters. His circle appeared in the center of its body.

"Gao."

The plant monster gets thrown back away from Dingba. Jordan continued to focus and little by little the monster slid backwards until he pinned it to a tree. It struggled to move forward.

Now that it was a one-on-one fight, Dingba went on the offensive. She ignored her wounds and rushed to end the fight. Three punches into the fat belly of the plant and it fell over limp. She rushed towards the one Jordan pinned to the tree. The spell circle was fading as darkness continued to consume Jordan's vision.

Dingba threw a right hook right in the middle of the circle. An explosive wave crashed through the area, destroying a row of trees and evaporating the plant monster. The sound of the explosion rang their ears.

Jordan sighed and closed his eyes. He could feel himself drifting off. A small hand touched his shoulder and shook him back awake.

Dingba cupped his face and gently slapped his cheek, "Hey, stay with me."

Jordan smiled.

"Don't worry, I'm right here."

Dingba smiled. "I guess humans can fight."

Jordan took a deep breath. "Oh, please, my race lived for killing each other, I'm just glad---" He stopped to catch his breath again. "... You can throw a punch."

Dingba flexed her biceps. "Best puncher in the whole village."

A deep, feminine voice echoed around them. "And here I was worried. Guess I shouldn't have been."

Dingba froze in place as her eyes grew wide. The voice had replaced the pride and ego from earlier with fear and confusion.

Jordan looked into Dingba's eyes.

"That voice."

Dingba looked around, searching for the owner of the voice. Jordan mirrored her. In a tree sat a Pix fairy, her orange-colored eyes scanned the two plant slayers. Her hair was short and spiky, like daggers to the sky. It had a similar shade and color to Dingba's.

Dingba gasped. "Tink..."

Tink smiled and hopped out of the tree, her onyx black moth wings stretched out as she flapped only enough to keep herself hovered in the air. "Hello Dingba." She glanced at Jordan. "I see you're still alive. But didn't I tell you to run and not stop?"

Dingba looked back at Jordan before returning her gaze to Tink. "You know each other?"

Tink smirked, "Of course, I saved his life. Twice now I believe." She angled her head, noticing the bloodied soil around Jordan. "Though it looks like, it didn't matter. This is what happens when you don't listen Jordan."

Jordan glanced at Tink. Her onyx black wings stood out against her sun-kissed skin and pearl white hair. He wanted to respond, but he just focused on surviving his wounds.

"So, this is Tink."

Tink shrugged. "Just focus on surviving. I won't be here for long."

Dingba instinctively took a step forward. "What happened to you?" She reached out towards her. "What happened to your wings?"

Tink looked back at her wings with a surprised look. "Oh, these?" She turned back and smiled. "I got an upgrade." Her eyes grew focused. "I have a message for you both."

First, she glanced at Jordan, "You, Jordan, leave the village. What happens next doesn't concern you. Or don't, you might be useful, who knows." She looked at Dingba. "And you... Tell Tong that the fairies need to leave the woods, or my mistress will have her way with everyone. Failure to leave will result in--" Tink paused and conjured two large black orbs in both her hands as a crazed smile took over her face. "Purging..."

Dingba choked on tears. "What are you talking about? Tink. Come back... I miss you..."

Tink just smiled. "I miss you too Dingba, now either you all leave the forest, or you suffer. Although I think mistress will accept submission as well...", She put her chin in her hand and thought. "She does love obedience..." She cackled. "You have five days to leave. On the sixth day, we will spill blood."

With her threat issued, Tink's wings glowed and clones of Tink appeared around her. before they all scattered in different directions.

Dingba floated up. "Tink." She tried to give chase, but Jordan grabbed her leg stopping her.

He shook his head, "We gotta go, it's not safe here." He inhaled sharply. "I can't fight like this, and I can barely move." Though Jordan could not see any threats, the sense of malice was present. "Plus, those two, need help getting back to the village." Jordan nodded towards the other injured fairies.

Dingba bit her lip before nodding in agreement. Together, the two made their way back to the village, carrying the injured with them. Thankfully, a small militia of fairies met them halfway. Easing the trip and getting Jordan some desperately needed medical attention.

When they arrived, they took the injured to the healer's hut while Dingba explained the situation to Tong. The old fairy's face grew to a level of seriousness Jordan hadn't seen.

"So, Tink reappears with a threat of death."

Jordan felt Singka tighten his bandages around his stomach. He winced in pain.

Singka looked up. "Are you alright?"

Jordan nodded, "Yeah thanks."

Dingba scowled at Tong, "She's being controlled or something. There's no way she would hurt us."

Tong frowned, "It still doesn't change the fact that after missing for months on end she now turns up out of the blue threatening the village."

Dingba clenched her fist, "She's my big sister. We need to help her. She'd help you if you were in danger."

Their arguing grew louder as their voices crashed into each other. They stumbled over each other for dominance of the conversation. Singka had moved in between them to attempt to keep the peace. Jordan sat on the outside, his hands clasped together and his chin resting on his thumbs as he thinks.

"Dingba was definitely the reason *she saved Juka. But why me?*"

He thought back to Tink's words.

"*'Tired of seeing death'. 'Might be useful'. Is she hoping I can help with the missing fairies? Why not just ask...unless she can't?*"

Jordan glanced up, Dingba is red in the face with tears welling in her eyes. Tong on the other hand is stone faced, his face just as red as

Dingba's. Singka seemed lost in the conversation, not sure how to calm the two down.

"First I gotta help here."

Tong clutched his cane, "If her wings are black, it means she's been corrupted Dingba. Whatever happened in those months she's been gone has changed her."

Dingba stomped her foot, "Her wings have always been a darker color then most. That doesn't mean she's a bad person."

Tong sighed, "That's not what I'm saying Dingba, and you know it. You said her wings are black. Obviously, something is going on that we don't know about. Whoever this Mistress is must have corrupted her."

Jordan looked up; he projected his voice to dominate the conversation. "Actually, she might not be fully corrupted."

It worked, the two looked over as Jordan dangled the allure of hope in front of them.

Tong cleared his throat," And what makes you say that?"

Jordan picked his words carefully, "After talking to her I realized a few things. One she saved me because I was saving Juka. Who probably reminded her of Dingba. She also had some plan for me, or at least she thought it'd be useful to save me. She could have killed me and Dingba multiple times over, but instead led us back towards the village. Even when I probably got closer to whatever she's keeping us away from, she risked talking to me and even risked leading me away when something, I'm assuming her mistress woke up."

Jordan thought for a second, "At the bare minimum She still loves Dingba and seems to have been going through an awful lot of trouble to keep her and probably the village safe. Plus why give us a warning with such a large window."

Jordan looked at Singka, "You said fairies don't get lost so what's stopping her from leading those monsters back to the village?"

Dingba's eyes lit up. "She could have easily attacked us after we fought those plant things. Jordan couldn't move and... I didn't want to fight her."

Jordan smiled. "I think she's been working hard to keep the village safe."

Tong scratched his beard. "So, what changed?"

Dingba deflated, her eyes sunk in as a sad realization seeped into her mind. "She got caught helping us. We kept going back and trying to push deeper into the woods, and this time we got very close. And we got caught by her Mistress... Now she has no choice but to act."

Singka soothed Dingba's hair and brought her in for a hug. "You should have told us what was going on."

Dingba clenched her fist, "We... I was worried it was really Tink who is to blame. I wanted to find her first."

Singka looked at Dingba, "Why did you assume Tink was to blame Dingba?"

"We would get tricked by illusions and led back to the village. She's the only one I know who has that kind of magic."

Jordan looked around. "So, what are you going to do?"

Tong inhaled deeply and thought for a moment. He looked up sternly, "Leaving now, risks leaving the unborn children in the Noble Tree. I will not condemn them to that fate." He looked sternly at Jordan. "I am sorry Jordan, but it would be best if you left. This doesn't concern you."

Jordan opened his mouth to say something but all that came out was a sigh. He looked down and swallowed his hurt.

"He might be right. I might end up causing more harm than good."

His mind drifted back to Cindy and Jason. He squeezed his hands thinking back to the misuse of his magic. His mind flooded with various ways his magic can get people killed should he stay and help.

Tong sighed, "I'll do a speech tomorrow. Let's get some rest I must think about this. I-I need to plan."

Dingba floated up into the air, her face covered by her bangs. Without a word she flew out of the hut.

Tong inhaled deeply, "Goodnight Singka, young Jordan. I'll see you two tomorrow."

Singka stood in the center of the hut she squeezed her hands together as Tong started to leave. "Goodnight Tong."

Once he left, she relaxed.

Jordan waited a moment then spoke, "You alright?"

Singka turned and smiled, her eyes were closed as she did, "Yeah. Sorry about that, those two can get very stubborn at times." She chuckled, "I guess I should take stock of the medicines we have; things are about to get rowdy it seems."

Jordan could see the faintest glimmer of a tear pushing its way past her eyelids.

She carefully opened her eyes; the outer edges are already turning a pink hue. "Anyway, get some sleep, there's some things I need to take care of before I head to bed."

Jordan nodded, "Alright goodnight Singka."

She smiled, "Goodnight."

Once she left Jordan's stare turned into a fiery glare.

"After all of this? 'It doesn't concern me?' Nah Tong it does."

His knuckles were white as he continued to glare into space.

"If I left now what would Kyle say? Oh god what would my mom say…"

He could already hear the disappointed "Bruh…" from Kyle. The thought of leaving the fairies to their doom filled him with a shameful rage. A nagging voice of his mother stormed into his mind next, and he groaned in annoyance. He shook it off and gave a stern nod to himself.

"I refuse to run away. Not again, not with two failures under my belt. I won't live with it."

He clenched his fist before snapping it open. His spell circle hovered over his fingertips; its purple brilliance illuminated the hut.

"Third times the charm."

16

CONNECTIONS

THE NEXT DAY, Tong called for a gathering.

Jordan walked up to him, "Morning Tong."

He glanced up at Jordan, "Good morning young Jordan."

Jordan glanced out to the crowd then looked at Tong, "Why don't you stand on my shoulders so everyone can see you better? This is important so it might be better for everyone."

Tong thought for a moment, "If you wouldn't mind, that would help an old fairy out."

Jordan lifted him up and placed him on his shoulder.

Tong wobbled as he tried to find his balance, he chuckled and looked around at the world from his new height. He could see the whole crowd from this height.

He patted Jordan on the head, "Goodness, you're tall."

Jordan laughed, "Thanks."

Once the village finished gathering, Tong cleared his throat. "As you all know. Yesterday we received a troubling message from one of our very own. Leave, submit, or die. Someone is forcing our poor Tink to ask something so terrible of her family."

He paused for a moment. "I don't agree with those choices. I believe we have a fourth one. Fight. I won't force you to join me. But I ask for your help and to bear with your selfish elder. We have several lost children who are scared and held prisoner. I want to bring them home."

Jordan lifted his head, "And I will help you all bring them home."

Tong's head snapped towards him, he went to say something, but Jordan looked at him with the strongest gaze he could muster. "You don't have a choice Tong. You guys have helped me so much, I'm helping whether you want me to or not."

Tong laughed then smiled, "Are all humans like this?"

Jordan stared with a blank face, "No."

Tong raised his eyebrows then glanced at the crowd before looking back at Jordan.

Jordan smiled, "But the good ones I know will be very disappointed in me if I didn't help y'all."

Tong patted Jordan on the head then with a smile on his face turned to the crowd. "Young Jordan has agreed to lend me his strength. Now I am asking you. I understand if there are those who wish to flee, I will not hold it against you. But I ask you please fight to save our home."

Silence overtook the village. No one moved. No one even looked around. Jordan could see Singka sneaking around the group as she headed towards the back.

She cupped her hands around her mouth and shouted, "Tell us what to do!"

A wave of energy rushed through the crowd, and they let out a roar.

Jordan felt Tong's hand tighten around his hair. He glanced up to see the old fairy's chin quiver.

He smiled and with a whisper said, "Thank you."

He steeled himself and returned his gaze to the crowd. "We must act fast, those who can and wish to fight step forward. We need to start patrols and we need you all to be ready for a battle."

Two handfuls of fairies stepped forward, all different ages and sizes.

Tong nodded. "Those who do not wish to fight or can't, we need your help to prepare the village. We need to prepare armor, medicine, weapons. Also, we need to secure a few huts for you all to hide during the battle."

Tong scanned the crowd. "Let's get to work." Tong hopped off Jordan's shoulder and glided to the ground.

The crowd dispersed to prepare. Dingba floated up to Jordan.

"Are you fighting?"

"Of course, I want to fight. After all you trained me, it'd be a waste if I didn't show off for you."

Dingba smirked. "Then let's train harder. I won't go easy on you this time. We don't have time for that."

Jordan grinned. "Don't threaten me with a good time."

JORDAN SAT ON A NEARBY ROCK, watching Dingba's shadow box as a warmup. To his left was a small slab of stone that he kept launching a few feet into the air before slowing its descent with Gao.

He took a breather, "So, what do you want to work on?"

Dingba wiped the sweat from her brow. "I wanted to try something. But I'm not sure how to explain it."

Jordan raised an eyebrow, "Oh?"

Dingba rubbed her chin, "Remember when I thought you were an impostor, and I attacked you? You grabbed me and threw me towards a tree. Remember?"

Jordan nodded.

"Well, before I hit the tree I threw a punch, but I miss timed it and I didn't touch it."

Jordan raised an eyebrow. "But it broke before you hit it?"

"Right, I think because I threw the punch while moving so fast, I could launch the explosion outwards. Then when I hit your spell circle it also launched my explosion away from me."

Jordan smiled. "Oh... that sounds pretty cool."

Dingba nodded. "Do you think I can punch your spell circle a few times?"

Jordan conjured the circle in front of her. "Hit it as much as you'd like. I'll dial it back though; we don't want to scare the village."

Dingba smiled and assumed her stance. She threw a slow punch just to test how her punch interacts with the circle. The resulting explosion is what she expected. It only covered the area she finished her punch in and nothing else.

Dingba groaned while she thought for a moment. She adjusted her stance and threw a quicker jab. The explosion traveled a bit further before dissipating into the air. She tried a quick three hit combo which yielded roughly the same results. She cocked her arm and threw a heavy punch; the explosion was large but still centered around her fist.

Jordan sat on a nearby rock and watched Dingba continue to strike his circle. Each time he could feel a bit of stress wash through his mind, he watched the air deform from the constant explosions.

Needing a quick mental break Jordan sat up. "Maybe it's a speed thing?"

Dingba looked over. "Hmm?"

Jordan could feel the stress slowly seeping away by the second, "To make it travel maybe you need more speed or to hit it faster?"

Dingba hovered backwards, then dashed and threw a sharp right hook. A wave of force shot from the circle into the trunk of a nearby tree.

The two fighters "Oh…" in excitement.

Dingba turned to Jordan, her little legs kicking in the air. "Did you see that? We did it."

Jordan nodded. "Our own little combo attack."

She floated backwards, "Let's try it again."

Jordan re-summoned his circle, bigger than the last time. Once again, she dashed and hit the center, causing another larger wave of force to shoot forward. Jordan kept re-summoning his circle further away, allowing Dingba to chase it around the forest. Nearby birds scattered from the sounds of danger emanating from these two.

Jordan felt dizzy after a moment and stopped summoning his circle. Dingba, losing her target, flew back towards him.

"You alright?"

"Yeah, just a little dizzy. I probably started overdoing it a bit, so I stopped."

"Well, we can't have you passing out two days in a row. Singka will yell at us."

"Yeah, we don't want that now, do we? How are you feeling?"

"I'm good. I'm happy we nailed down this attack." Dingba clutched her fist. "I think... I know I'll be able to bring Tink back."

"Good, and I'll help in any way I can."

Dingba sat next to him. She took a bite out of a Queen's drip. The spicy sweet juice dripped down the side of her mouth. A greedy tongue quickly caught and licked it up.

Jordan bit into his piece of fruit. Spiteful. His third one in a row. He was feeling unlucky. He glanced at Dingba, "Tell me about her."

She looked up, "Who?"

"Tink. I feel like I've interacted with her a bunch, but I know nothing about her."

Dingba smiled. "Well, she's nice. When I was younger, she used to make illusions to help me sleep... or to tease me. She would always sneak off and I'd try to follow but back then I didn't know how to fly fast." She flicked her wings up. "It didn't take long for me to figure it out, eventually, when she really didn't want me following her. She would create an illusion and have me mindlessly chase it around the village. It was one of those days where I met Master Jul'. They actually fought when they first met."

Jordan raised an eyebrow, "Tink fought Jul? Why?"

She giggled, "She had heard what happened and after beating up the bullies she rushed to find me in the forest." With a soft sigh, she finished her fruit. "Jul' had knocked me down while teaching me. She only saw the part where he knocked me down and sprang into action. Like any good big sister would."

TINK

EIGHT YEARS BEFORE THE ARRIVAL OF HUMANS.

DINGBA WALKED into a clearing just north of the village, her eyes blurry with tears. Once she got to the center she wailed as loud as her little lungs would allow her and fell to her knees. She rose her fist and slammed it on the ground.

"Why?"

She slammed her fist harder.

"Why do they hate me? I'm not a freak…" She sniffled, "I'm just a little different…"

She continued to pound the ground, the sides of her hand turning red with every slam. From the corner of her eye, she saw it, the thing everyone hated, the thing she was born with. Her black wing, her rage refocused.

"Stupid, ugly wing." She reached up and clutched it.

Pain shot from her wing to her back causing her to yelp.

"I should just tear it off."

She squeezed harder.

"Tear it off."

She braced herself, she shut her eyes and jerked her arm as she yanked on the wing. It didn't move, not the wing nor her arm. Something had grabbed it. She opened her eyes and saw a large furry hand grabbing her arm.

She followed it up and saw a large goat man staring at her, his oak brown eyes stared into hers. At least she thinks it was, his pupils were long lines instead of a dot which made it hard to see what he was looking at.

He smiled, "Looks like I made it in time."

Dingba sniffled as she looked at him.

He loosened his grip, "You shouldn't tear off your wings. I'm sure your parents wouldn't be happy about that. I'm going to let go now, promise you won't rip your wing off?"

Dingba nodded.

The man let go and as promised Dingba let go of her wing. She then wiped her tears away.

The man smiled, "There's a good girl." He reached into his pocket and pulled out a rag. "Here use this, it's softer."

Dingba took it and wiped her eyes and nose. "Thank you…"

The man smiled, "You are quite welcome. Now why were you about to do something so bad to yourself?"

Dingba shrugged and looked away.

The man smoothed her black hair back, "Come on, it's okay you can tell me."

Dingba glanced at the man, "Everyone hates my wings."

The man tilted his head, "Well that's not true. I certainly don't hate your wings and I'm sure I'm not the only one either."

Dingba looked up, "But they all say it's weird and make fun of me for it. Plus, I can't even use magic like everyone else so I can't even stand up for myself or else I'll get beat up."

The man smiled softly, "We are two peas in a pod."

Dingba tilted her head, "What does that mean?"

He smiled, "It means we are alike. My eyes are weird too and I can't use magic either. But do you want to see something cool?"

Dingba nodded.

The man stared straight, then did a handstand. "Watch my pupils." With an expert display of athleticism, he leaned back and forth and while he did his eyes stayed perfectly still as if they were rotating in his head.

Dingba tried to mimic it but had no success in making her eyes stay still.

The man hopped up. "See? Weird. I remember getting made fun of for my eyes but once I realized I can always watch my surroundings I grew to love them. Cool right?"

Dingba smiled, "Yeah it's really cool."

He smiled, "Now as for that nonsense about not knowing magic. Did you know there are two types of magic?"

Dingba's eyes opened wide, "Two?"

He nodded, "Yes, magic and temperance which is the magic of the body. If you can't learn magic, you can learn temperance. Shall I show you mine?"

Dingba nodded excitedly.

The man turned and flicked the air causing a small explosion of air.

Dingba frowned, "That's it?"

He laughed, "Well, if I punch it'll be larger." He looks up into the sky, "I have some time, how about I teach you somethings to defend yourself?"

Dingba beamed, "Yes please."

The man helped her up, "Well then my little student. My name is Jul'Cur'Drl but you can just call me Jul. What's your name little one?"

Dingba dusted herself off and smiled, "Dingba."

Jul smiled and lifted his head, "Well Dingba there's something I want you to remember. If you can't be a normal fairy, become an extraordinary fairy."

Dingba stared at him wide eyed, her heart thumped in her chest. She felt... elevated almost unbelievably light. She could only nod and smile. "I will."

Jul' nodded, "Alright let's do some warm ups."

DINGBA STOOD IN FRONT OF JUL' her fist clenched, sweat dripped from her forehead. Jul stared at her with his hands up palm facing her. She stepped in and threw a sloppy jab, it landed softly in Jul's palm.

He nodded, "Okay you're getting better. But you want to use your hips more not your whole body. Here put your guard up and I'll show you the difference."

Dingba put her guard up and braced herself. Jul' gave her a similar sloppy jab then let her reset her posture before giving her a proper jab. The force of which knocked her off her feet.

Jul' gasped, "Whoops." He reached out to catch her but a scream from the bushes snatched his attention.

"Dingba!"

Dingba turned and saw Tink rushing out of the bushes, she conjured onyx black orbs and threw them at Jul'. Jul' turned, and with a straight jab struck the ball. An explosion dispelled the ball. Dust filled the air. Tink used this to her advantage and scooped up Dingba.

Dingba sat on the ground coughing, her face covered in dirt, Tink wiped off her face and moved Dingba's hair out of her eyes. "You alright?"

Dingba's eyes widened. "Tink?"

Tink nodded, "It's fine I'm here now." She noticed the damaged black wing. She scowled at it. A fire raged in her eyes. "Did he do that?" She turned and conjured two more balls.

Dingba looked at her wing then back at Tink. "Tink wait."

Tink glared at Jul'. "Stay here Dingba. I'll be quick."

Tink leapt from the bushes and took flight before launching her orbs. Jul' punched these two out of the air as well.

He looked up at Tink. "Oh my. I didn't mean to cause trouble today."

Tink raised her right hand and conjured an even bigger orb, "Shut it sapsucker."

Numerous clones spread out from Tink's body surrounding Jul', each one holding up their own orb. "Catch." They all threw their balls,

Jul' ran for cover as the orbs peppered the ground, rending it as they do.

Tink rushed him, her hand clawed, a dark energy surrounded it, she swiped.

Dingba's eyes grew wide.

"Tink no."

Jul' dodged, letting a nearby tree take the brunt of the attack. Its bark clawed off in an instant.

Jul' let out an interested bleat. He responded to the attack with an open palm strike and an explosion of force engulfed Tink's body.

Fear washed over Dingba for a brief second, but she relaxed when she saw Tink's body had shattered into a swarm of phantom moths that fluttered into nothingness. Jul's eyes widened for a moment as his pupil rotated to adjust for his dodge.

When Jul' reached the end of his dodge, Tink was there to greet him. Her hand glowed with pure malice. Jul' brought his arm to block and Tink gripped it tightly sinking her nails into his flesh. The malice ignited and grew in intensity.

But something is wrong. Jul' seemed unphased by the attack. In between Tink's nails and his flesh, a steely blue aura coated his arm. The Color of Gentle Calmness.

"Woah..."

He moved his arm to get a better look at Tink and strikes the air in front of her with another open palm. This time the wave of force engulfs her.

Tink staggered backwards, her wings fluttered trying to keep her upright.

Dingba leaned forward.

"What happened?"

Tink stayed on her feet. She panted heavily while staring at Jul'. With no sign that her attack did anything. She growled. "Fine." and flapped her wings, beating the air and spreading her wing dust.

Dark energy swirled around her. The air trembled as the sky filled with a massive black sphere. It grew to the size of a boulder, easily dwarfing Tink.

Jul' sighed, "Young lady, I think we're getting a little wild."

Tink continued to swell the black boulder over her head, "Anyone who hurts Dingba will answer to me."

Dingba leaped out of the bushes and ran in between them. "Tink stop."

Tink relaxed, causing the orb to shrink in size. "Dingba move."

Dingba shook her head, "No, you have to stop. He didn't hurt me."

Tink scrunched her face in confusion, "He was attacking you and your wing is bent."

Dingba frowned. "He was teaching me how to defend myself and I bent it. He stopped me before I tore it off."

Tink gasped. The orb blinked out of existence. She rushed to Dingba and cupped her face. "Why would you do that?" She hugged Dingba tightly. Tears formed. "Why would you try to tear your wing off?"

Dingba clutched Tink's sides. "Everyone hates my wings."

Tink hugged her tighter. "I don't hate your wings, Dingba. I love them." She kissed Dingba's head, "Don't let anyone tell you your wings aren't beautiful. Everyone's wings are different, and everyone has beautiful wings, no matter the color. You understand?"

Dingba nodded, then buried her face into Tink's stomach. Tink could feel her shirt become wetter by the second. She held Dingba until the sniffling stopped.

She smoothed Dingba's hair. "It's fine Dingba, I'm not mad." She picked up Dingba and kissed her right cheek. "I'm just a big worrywart." She crinkled her nose and rubbed it against Dingba's nose.

Dingba slowly stopped crying.

"There's a big girl. Let's head back to the village."

Jul' cleared his throat, Tink leaned her head over and gave him a disinterested look. "Oh, right. You."

He smiled. "My name is Jul'Cur'Drl."

Tink raised an eyebrow, "Jul' Cu… Gul' Kurd…"

"Jul'Cur'Drl."

Tink blinked, "I'm just going to call you Jul'."

Jul' smiled, "That works too."

"So, Jul' what are you doing beating up on children?"

He chuckled. "Yes, Young Dingba was about to make a horrible mistake. Luckily I happened across her and stopped her."

Dingba nodded, "That's right. Then he said he'd teach me how to be extra ordinary."

Tink leaned back, "I think you mean extraordinary."

Dingba giggled, "Yeah that."

Tink frowned, "Haven't I told you not to talk to strangers?"

Dingba shook her head.

Tink sighed, "Well… Nevermind. No one comes out here anyway."

Tink turned back to Jul', "So we are leaving."

Jul' nodded, "Understandable, let me escort you two back home. After all, I injured you."

Tink cut him a look, "I'm fine."

Jul' motioned to her legs, "Your legs are wobbling."

Tink looked down, and sure enough, she couldn't keep her legs still. She looked up and glared weakly, "I'm a fairy I can fly." She floated up into the air. Once her feet left the ground, her world spun as she lost balance. She came crashing back to the ground headfirst. Luckily, she curled her body around Dingba to protect her.

Dingba closed her eyes as they slammed into the ground, after a moment she opened them. She could feel Tink's hand on the back of her head protecting it from the ground. "Tink?"

She groaned and sat up, "I'm fine." She returned her glare to Jul', "What did you do?"

He smiled, "Messed with your sense of balance, fighting flying opponents is hard when you don't really want to fight."

He reached out his hand. "Let me escort you home. I'd feel bad if something happened to you two."

She ignored his hand and forced her body up. "Fine. No funny business."

A WHILE later they sat in Singka's hut, a soft light shined as Singka repaired her Dingba's damaged wing.

Tink sat crossed leg on the ground with Dingba in her cradle. Tink kept her arms up while Singka worked. Dingba looked over her shoulder and watched Singka work.

Singka glanced up at Tink, then looked at Dingba. "You should be more careful with your wings. They take a long time to repair themselves and if you lose one it might not grow back correctly."

Dingba nodded, "I know… I'm sorry."

Singka rubbed Dingba's head. "Alright, I'm sure Tink already gave you an earful already."

Once Singka finished up with Dingba. Tink leaned forward and crossed her arms across Dingba's chest. She held her close while she watched Tong and Jul' talk. Dingba smiled and nuzzled herself deeper into her arms.

Tong slid a bowl of fruit towards Jul'. "So, what brings you to our forest, let alone our village Jul'?"

Jul' took a piece. "Thank you. I was just wandering around the world when I stumbled into the forest and explored. Then I came upon Dingba hurting herself and luckily, I managed to stop her. I also met her lovely protective sister." He turned and smiled at Tink, who huffed in response. She instinctively tightened her hold on Dingba.

Tong stroked his beard, "You have my thanks for intervening in that. It would have broken my heart to see her missing a wing."

Jul' stroked his in response, "No need to thank me. The youth must blossom if the world is to keep moving."

Tong nodded, "I agree."

Jul, glanced over at Dingba, "I was thinking, she seemed interested in learning to box. How about I stay for a few days to teach her? After all, if she can't learn magic then she can learn temperance. If that's okay with you."

Tong nodded, then looked at Singka. "What do you think?"

Singka shrugged, "Learning a temperance wouldn't hurt, but it is up to Dingba."

Dingba beamed with joy and leaned forward. "Yeah. I wanna learn."

Tink softly pulled her back and glared at Jul'. "Why are you so eager to teach her?"

Jul' smiled. "Uh oh, looks like I have to convince the big sister. Like I said, the youth must blossom, so the world keeps moving. You're more than welcome to supervise us, if it'll put your mind at ease and if you feel like I'm a bad teacher, you can put an end to it at any time."

Dingba looked up. "Please… Tink? I want to learn."

Tink sighed, "Alright, but if I don't like what I'm seeing I'll put an end to this."

Dingba smiled and wiggled with joy.

Tong stood up. "That settles it. Let me show you where you'll be sleeping at Jul'."

He led Jul' out of the hut. Eventually Singka left to make some house calls leaving the sisters alone.

After a few minutes Dingba looked up, "You can let me go now."

Tink loosened her hold but kept hugging her. "Let me hug you for a little longer. I won't be able to do this when you get older."

Dingba frowned. "Won't you still be my big sister?"

Tink smiled, "Of course, but eventually you'll be taller than me." She nuzzled her head before kissing her right cheek.

Dingba groaned. "Why do you always kiss my right cheek?"

Tink giggled, "Right cheeks are for kissing while the left is for pinching." She punctuated her point by pinching Dingba's left cheek, causing Dingba to fuss in her arms.

Dingba continued to fuss as Tink teased her until eventually she fell asleep in Tink's arms.

THE NEXT MORNING, a surge of energy filled Dingba.

She sat up and glanced at the window, the sky was still dark. She turned to Tink who was sleeping beside her.

"I can't wait..."

She wiggled in excitement.

"Oh, wait that's right."

She reached over and gently shook Tink awake, "Tink... Tink..."

Tink groaned and pried one of her eyes open, just enough to see who was disturbing her. Dingba greeted her with a loveable grin. Tink glanced at a window and saw it was still dark out; she turned her gaze back to Dingba.

"What's wrong? You have a terror sleep?"

Dingba shook her head. "I woke up cause I'm so excited."

Tink's sleep filled head failed to see why someone would be excited this early in the morning. "Excited for what?"

Dingba frowned, "You remember Jul' is going to teach me tem... prance?"

Tink blinked, "Temperance. And that isn't for a few more hours. Go back to sleep."

Tink closed her eyes and rolled over but Dingba shook her again.

"Wait, I wanted to ask something."

Tink sighed, "What?"

Dingba smiled. "Can you turn my hair white?"

Tink turned towards her and blinked. A moment passed before she spoke, "Turn your? Your hair white?"

Dingba nodded, "Like yours."

Tink raised an eyebrow, "Why? Your hair is fine the way it is."

"But I want it like yours."

Dingba stared intently at Tink, her desire oozed from her.

"Don't say no. Don't say no. Don't say no."

Tink shook her head, "Singka would get mad."

Dingba tilted her head, her face scrunched up. "Why would she get mad? Does she not like your hair?"

Tink smiled, "No, she likes my hair, she also likes your hair too."

Dingba frowned, "Then why would she get mad?"

Tink sighed, "Its complicated."

Dingba crawled on top of Tink's belly, her hands drummed on her stomach, "That's not an answer."

Tink groaned, "It's totally an answer."

Dingba pouted, "Come on, please…"

Tink stared into Dingba's pleading, round eyes. "By the Wilt, I spoil you."

Dingba giggled.

Tink sat up, "Fine, go get two big bowls. This will take a while so I don't want to hear any fussing."

A FEW MOMENTS later they are in a clearing with Jul'. He laughed loudly seeing the new Dingba. "Well, this is a surprise. I was worried you weren't coming."

Dingba stood with a heroic pose, her hands on her hips. Her head held high, pristine white hair spiked and wings outstretched. "Of course I'd come."

Tink covered her mouth and yawned, "Yep, we're here."

Jul' smiled. "Shall we start?"

Dingba nodded, and Tink walked away.

"You two have fun. I'll be over here watching."

THIS QUICKLY BECAME the norm for them. They would wake up, go meet Jul', Tink would watch from a nearby rock while snacking sometimes she'd make monsters for Dingba to fight and beat up. This went on for months on end. As Dingba got better, her confidence grew.

One morning Tink sat on a rock watching Dingba warm up in the nearby grass. They had arrived a little early this morning. Tink cracked open a Lasnut with her canines. She tossed the soft insides in her mouth.

Dingba walked up, the excitement on her face slowly draining away as time passes without Jul' showing up.

Tink offered a Lasnut, "You want one?"

Dingba stared at the deep brown shell. It was two inches long and about an inch thick. Tink held the fat part towards her. She nodded.

Tink wiggled it, "You have to bite it open."

Dingba bit the shell and tried to crack it open, but couldn't get the power she needed. She bit it from multiple angles before she could feel Tink tugging on the nut.

"It's hard..."

Tink pulled the nut out of her mouth. "Your teeth aren't strong enough. Here, I open them like this." She turned the nut on its side, lining up the edges with the points of her canines. She carefully bit down and cracked the shell. She took the nut out of her mouth and opened it up handing Dingba the meat inside.

Dingba took the snack. "Thank you."

Tink smiled, "Alright, let's go to his hut. Maybe he overslept or something."

THEY STOOD in Jul's hut, it's clean. Perfectly clean. The blankets are folded, bowls stacked, cushions stacked neatly in the corner. If they hadn't spent the last few months coming here, they wouldn't have known anyone had stayed here recently.

Dingba looked up at Tink. "Where is he?"

Tink clenched her fist. On the bed, on top of the folded sheets she could see a note, held down by a small rock. "I'm not sure." She floated over to the note and picked it up. Before hovering back to the ground. Dingba floated up and looked over her shoulder to read.

Dear Young Dingba,

It has been a pleasure to know you and train you. Unfortunately, our days of training in the forest must end. I had never expected to find a student while traveling, definitely not one with such bright eyes like you. I wish I could say goodbye in person, but I've tried for five days now, and each time failed to find the strength...

Tink's breath got heavier.

So please forgive this old goat for taking such a cowardly way out, but there is something I still need to take care of. Keep training and one day when your older come find me and I'll treat you to something delicious from my childhood. Bring Tink too, though I'm sure she'd follow you regardless.

Your teacher.

Jul'Cur'Drl

Dingba's heart twisted as it sunk into her stomach. She sunk back to the ground.

"Why do they always leave me? Why doesn't anyone stay? Is it cause I'm bad?"

She started to breathe harder, tears swelled in her eyes her vision blurred. She could feel it, the heartache, the snapping of the heart strings.

"I'm sorry I'm a --"

The air trembled around her, halting her tears. A wicked aura swirled around Tink. Dingba looked up at Tink her mouth agape.

Tink grip tightened around the letter crumbling it in her rage. She could hear Tink breathing heavily.

Dingba touched Tink's hand, "Tink?"

Her voice snapped Tink out of it. She slowed her breathing and stared at Dingba.

Dingba moved her hand away, "Are you okay?"

Tink's chin quivered. She inhaled deeply and steeled her nerves. "Come on." She grabbed her hand.

Dingba looked around as Tink dragged her towards the door, "Where are we going?"

Tink squeezed her hand, "To go train."

Dingba smiled, "Okay."

As they walked, Tink kept looking ahead. "Hey, I'll never leave you. Okay?"

Dingba smiled with tears in her eyes, "Okay."

Five months before Jordan arrived.

Dingba raced towards the edge of the village with a frown on her face.

"Can't believe she would sneak out while I slept."

Up ahead she spotted Tink standing on the edge of the village, staring deep into the forest.

Dingba flew down behind her, "Tink, where are you going?"

Tink turned and smiled. "Hey, I'm going to explore the forest a bit. Something's bothering me."

Dingba smiled, "Oh, I'll come with you."

Tink shook her head. "No, it's fine. It might be dangerous, so I'll go by myself, okay?"

Dingba frowned. "I'm not little anymore you know."

Tink crinkled her nose and wiggled her head, "But you're still my baby sister." She fixed her face. "So do me a favor today. Stay in the village, okay?"

Dingba smiled softly, "Okay, just be back before it gets dark."

Tink nodded, "I will. Oh, and I love you, speedy dragonfly."

Dingba grinned. "I love you too, pretty moth."

Tink lifted herself into the air and flew off into the forest.

18

FINAL PREPARATIONS

DINGBA SMILED SOFTLY, "And that was the last time I saw Tink. Until a couple of days ago."

Jordan patted her on the back, "She sounds like a great big sister."

Dingba chuckled, "She could be mean at times."

Jordan nodded, "I think all big sisters can be mean at times."

Dingba looked over and smiled, "How's your injuries?"

Joran shrugged, "Hurts like hell. But considering the alternative I suppose I can't complain." Jordan finished his food. "What do you want to do? Head back for the day?"

Dingba stood up, dusting off her butt. "If it's okay with you. I want to train for a little longer."

Jordan nodded, "Go for it, we can train all day."

She looked over. "So how does your spell work?"

Jordan scratched his head, "Well, from what I've noticed. The circle determines the effect area of the spell. Gao, which is my pushing spell, pushes objects depending on how hard I focus on the spell."

He swelled the circle, causing it to grow. "If I swell it, I can push things harder."

Dingba punched the bigger circle the same way, and it caused a larger explosion. "Oh, I see. How big can you make it?"

Jordan thought for a moment, then frowned. "I... I don't know."

Dingba beamed, "Do you want to see how large you can make it?"

Jordan stood up and re-summoned his circle above their heads, "Let's see how big it gets." He focused.

The circle widened, eventually becoming the size of a standard area rug. Jordan could feel the strain of having it that large, "I wonder what happens if I use Gao right now."

"Go for it."

He could feel the magic swell in him, it's going to be big.

"*Gao.*"

HE WOKE up a few hours later. Looking to his left, he saw Dingba sleeping in a chair next to him.

"*What happened?*"

His head hurt, and his brain felt empty. He reached out and tapped Dingba on the shin; She shot back to life.

"You're awake."

Jordan blinked, "What happened?"

Dingba beamed, "It was amazing. You made your spell circle huge then you cast your spell and a tremendous gust of wind and, and–"

"You went into Mind Down." Singka said, coming into the room.

Jordan looked at her as she approached the bed, "Mind down?"

Singka nodded. "The effect of using too much magic in a day. Your mind shuts down and you pass out. Luckily for you, you were nearby, and it doesn't appear that you went too far over your limit."

"What happens if I go too far over my limit?"

Singka thought for a moment, "Various things, depending on how far you go. I've read of people losing the ability to use magic for days, some for months, others fall asleep and don't wake up, some die. But the worst I've heard is when you go over your limit by so much you 'crack' your magical core. It's like crippling yourself. You won't be able to do magic like you once could or ever again if you're unlucky enough."

Jordan sat up, "How do you increase your limit?"

Singka shook her head, "You don't. You just train until your magic is more efficient. Everyone's limit is different, but what really makes the difference is how you practice and how you developed your magic. Can I ask, what did you focus on whenever you practiced?"

"I wanted to lift heavier things and use it more often. So, I would just constantly use it until I felt tired, or I'd push and pull heavier things."

Singka nodded, "So you focused on strengthening your base spells while also trying to squeeze more out in a day. Given your situation that's about all you can do to be honest. Remember magic is mental, strengthen your mind and everything else will follow. Makes sense?"

Jordan nodded. "It does."

Singka felt Jordan's forehead. "Once you get a deeper pool of spells, you can try casting them faster or maintaining them but what you are doing is fine for now. You should also try getting into contact with the Burning Queen. Meditation might help you or however you encountered her before."

Jordan watched her as she checked his wounds, "Got it thanks."

Singka smiled. "Your wounds are still healing, so for now, it's the best you can do. No physical stuff until your wounds are healed all the way."

Jordan pouted. "Can't you just use healing magic?"

Singka nodded, "Yes. I can use healing magic to close your wounds, but you lost a lot of blood, and your body needs time to recover. When you have time to let your body naturally recover, it's best to use medicine and natural healing over healing magic. Forcing your body to suddenly heal puts a strain on the body."

Jordan sighed, "I see, that's fair."

Singka smiled, "If you haven't fully healed the day before the attack, I will heal you. But for now, we will let your body recover normally."

"Can I still go train with Dingba?"

Singka smiled, "Of course, just don't push yourself and reopen your wounds. Nothing physical, focus on your magic only."

Singka looked outside. "It's late. I know you just woke up but try to get some rest. You too Dingba."

Jordan nodded. "I'll try meditating then I'll get some rest."

Singka smiled, "Alright, if you meet the Burning Queen ask her to teach you healing magic. It's quite useful to have."

After they left, Jordan got comfortable and closed his eyes. His rowdy mind took a moment to settle down. His breathing slowed. He didn't know what to do, so he tried picturing the Burning Queen. In the dark void, shapeless figures danced. He could see a large woman and a horde of small beings about the size of pix fairies hovering around.

He could hear a guttural sound reverberate in the darkness. It shook his concentration until it broke. Disappointed and exhausted, he sighed and went to bed.

———

THE FOLLOWING days were a blur of training and fortifying. With his body still injured, Jordan couldn't do much besides train his magic and try to contact the Burning Queen. Despite his best efforts, he could produce no results. His spell circle contained the same two spells, though his control and comfort with them has increased significantly.

Two nights before the battle, Jordan paced back and forth in the hut. He stroked his chin while he sunk deeper into his thoughts.

"So, what am I missing?"

He closed his eyes and tried to remember the time's he met the Burning Queen.

"A few days after I came here, she reached out. Then with the fight with the Juk-Juk..."

Jordan stopped walking as he opened his eyes. His face scrunched up, "Do I have to be in danger?"

He shook his head, "Then that would mean I was in danger the first time. Was I? It did help us survive but then... Why is she silent now?"

"I've tried different times of day, different mental states. I'm missing something important."

He glanced at the window, the dark of night lingered outside.

With a sad groan he sat on the ground, for another attempt.

"I want more spells…"

He sighed and calmed himself down.

The night before the battle Jordan sat on the bed and watched Singka heal his wounds the rest of the way.

She glanced up at him. "So did you ever get in contact with the Burning Queen?"

Jordan pouted softly, "Nah, every time I felt close, like I was right outside the hut. But it was like I couldn't go inside. I think I can see them in the void but not as well as I did the first time."

Singka tittered, "Hmm, I suppose that's why she's also known as the 'Fickle Queen.'"

Jordan rose an eyebrow, "Is she really called that?"

Singka smiled and nodded, "Mhm, I remember reading stories of her teaching random people magic, then just disappearing and leaving them to figure it out. Kind of like you I guess." She laughed at the realization.

Jordan chuckled, "Yikes. But I gotta admit, I'm happy she at least took the time to teach me something before ghosting me."

Singka looked up. "Ghosting?"

"It's when you vanish from someone's life without telling them why and never contact again."

"Ah, sounds sad."

Jordan nodded.

As Singka closed the last wound, she sat up and sighed. "Alright, you're all set. I made sure some of the weavers made thick clothes for you. It should protect you from those vines."

"Thanks, I'll try not to get hit too much."

Singka smiled, "Thank you again for helping us."

Jordan shook his head. "There's no need to thank me. I wouldn't be able to live with myself if I left y'all."

Singka patted his leg, "Well, thank you all the same." She stood up. "What about your night terrors? Still having those?"

Jordan wiggled his hand, "Some nights, but since I've been spending time with Dingba they don't come as frequent. I can go through most if not the entire day without thinking about so it helps. Talking to you about it helps as well."

Singka smiled, "I'm glad you're getting better. I need to go check on everyone else make sure they are in tip-top shape. Try to get some rest, have a good night."

Jordan nodded as she flew off.

After she left, he summoned his circle and stared as it spun slowly in his hand. The same two symbols sat at the top of the circle. They looked so lonely there, like a single house in a culdesac with no neighbors. He was disappointed and nervous. Could he really make do with just these two spells?

He sighed. His mind knew the answer before he even thought about the question. He had no choice but to make do.

He laid down and calmed himself; he wanted to get the best sleep possible. For tomorrow, blood will flow.

19

THE START

THE DAY of the promised purging had arrived. The village was quiet, huts boarded up. In the middle stood the militia, about twenty people strong. They stood defiantly, waiting for their enemies to appear. Some stood with weapons, while others stood unarmed, hoping their magic would keep them safe. Tong stood at the very front of the pack, Singka was in the rear, Dingba and Jordan sandwiched in between.

From beyond the tree line, they could hear shambling creatures, bushes rustling and twigs snapping as monstrous silhouettes appeared, varying in size and shape. They all had that pitcher plant shape, all but one. The shape of a fairy with moth-like wings led the mob. Once she was in full view, she spoke.

"I thought you were smarter than this elder."

Tong stepped forward. "Tink. End this, there is no need for bloodshed. Tell us who is forcing you to do this, we can help you."

"No one can help me now Tong." She blinked slowly, then turned her attention towards Jordan. "Still here? It matters not, Mistress could use a new plaything."

Dingba stepped forward, clutching her hands close to her chest. "Tink, please…"

Tink glared softly, "I don't remember you being this weak Dingba."

With a flick of the wrist, she caused the horde of plant monsters to waddle forward. "Try not to die."

Wiping her tears away, Dingba glared at Tink. Her wings flicked open and buzzed. Her body lifted off the ground. "I will bring you back..." She clenched her fist and made herself a smaller target.

The two groups charged at each other. A volley of tendrils shot from the plants, the fairies responded with a mixture of magic and projectiles. Their opening gambits slam into the opposition, both sides trade kills. Jordan and Dingba survived the opening volley and joined the vanguard in the initial slamming of the hordes.

Jordan reached out and grabbed the lid of the nearest plant, he yanked the plant down to the ground then stomped a hole into its body. Digestive fluid leaked on the ground coating the bottom of his shoes. Next to him Dingba's punch caused one to explode. Coating nearby combatants in its mess.

The mobs continued to mingle until a mosh pit of bodies were formed. Jordan focused on punching and kicking the nearest plant while trying to move forward. He used his larger body to push the plants back and give the fairies a stronger foothold on the front lines.

Soon the armies were at a standstill, Jordan's arms were decorated with welts from successful blocks. His knuckles red from bashing in various plants.

"Be careful, don't get greedy."

He carefully selected his next opponent but from the corner of his eye he saw a streak of green coming towards him. His attention snapped to the attack and his body quickly dodged out of the way.

Another attack forced him to dodge backwards evading a whipping from a sneaky plant-based opponent.

"I can't get surrounded."

He glanced around looking for an ally.

To his right he saw a Nix with a Blood Leaf sword hacking away at a pitcher plant. He maneuvered closer then attacked.

"Stay close to someone at all times."

He pulled the plant closer via its vines, then kicked it backwards ripping its tendrils off. He heard a yelp behind him. The sword fairy was on the ground covering her body as a group of pitchers merci-lessly whipped her. Her armor barely holding together as they tear into it and eventually her flesh.

Jordan saw her sword on the ground, he yanked it towards him with Ver, catching it by the handle. He stepped forward and slashed at the plants horizontally.

"Careful, not to wild."

He managed to cut enough tendrils to lunge over the fairy covering her body with his. He swung the blade harder lopping off the tops of the plants. The plants continued to flail at him, lashing him in various angles.

"This is fine. You can win this."

Jordan responded with a blade flourish, he kept himself over the fairy hoping to absorb the blows while he finished off the plants. Though outnumbered his body was more durable and he outlasted the plants.

He bent down and scooped up the fairy. "You alright?"

She grasped her arm to stop the bleeding, "Yeah, just got to stop the bleeding."

Jordan nodded, "Let's get you to Singka."

He shoved his way out of the mosh pit, slashing down a few more plants as he did. Once he got a clear line of sight on Singka, he booked it. He ran over, past the rear guard that was protecting her and the other healers.

Jordan knelt and placed the Nix next to Singka, "Got another one."

Singka turned with bandages in hand, "How's it going out there?" She started wrapping the Nix's arm.

Jordan glanced back, he groaned as he analyzed the chaos. "I think we are winning. There's a lot of them but they are pretty weak. Nothing but fodder. Plus, we have you and the other healers picking us back up. We should be able to out sustain them."

Singka nodded, "Alright. Keep up the good work. Bring me back any others who need help."

Jordan nodded, he placed the sword by the Nix and turned to leave when she called out to him.

"Wait. Take my sword, you know how to use one right?"

Jordan nodded, "I do but… it'll be better if I don't have one. Plus, you'll need it when you get back up."

He smiled then ran back to join the fray. As he ran, he saw Dingba floating into the air.

"Ah there she is."

He noticed she was looking at Tink. Tink seemed to notice and as the plant horde thinned out, Tink retreated into the forest.

Dingba shouted, "Hey! Get back here!" She dashed after her.

Jordan tried to grab her arm but she slipped his reach.

He called out to her, "Dingba." But she flew off, seeing red.

A sharp whip lashed at his back, refocusing his attention. He growled and turned to his new opponent. Before he could engage with it, it's body turned pale as ice encased it. A pix leaped into the air and slammed a small spiked hammer into its body cracking and shattering the plant.

He looked up and gave Jordan a thumbs up.

Jordan chuckled and gave him one back. They stood next to each other as another horde came from the forest.

20

DRAGONFLY VS MOTH

DINGBA CHASED Tink deep into the forest. Her eyes rubbed raw. The sounds of the battle she left behind die as the trees get thicker. Up ahead, there is a clearing, their clearing. Dingba bursts through the bushes to see Tink floating in the air, her eyes were cold and her face emotionless.

Dingba took a deep breath. "Tin-"

Tink held up her small hand. "No words."

Her eyes lowered. She took a deep breath. With an exhale she summoned and threw two black orbs, Dingba dodged out of the way, the orbs strike the ground, leaving sizable dents in the earth. She knew if words wouldn't reach her, she would have to use her fists instead.

Dodging another round of orbs, Dingba sprang into action, closing the gap. She reared back and threw a mighty left hook. Tink's eyes grew wide as she tried to dodge. Those warm, deep orange eyes were now cold and shallow. This sight caused Dingba to stop her attack.

Tink sucked her teeth and glared. She responded to Dingba's hesitation with a powerful slap in the face, augmented with dark magic, sending Dingba crashing into the ground.

"Why are you stopping?" She summoned six more black orbs.

Dingba shook her head, "I... I don't want to hur--"

Tink's barrage silenced her.

Tink continued throwing more balls at Dingba, though these throws seemed off target. They exploded around her, but never directly on top of her.

Tink's voice cracked. "Come on... Fight me..."

"Tink..." Dingba swallowed her emotions and forced herself to stand.

She fought back tears as she stared at her corrupted sister. Once again, she dashed towards her and threw a left hook. This time, she connected. Tink shimmered out of existence as her voice appeared behind Dingba.

"Good." Tink rewarded her with another dark slap to Dingba's back, sending her crashing into the ground.

This went on for some time, Dingba would close distance and attack. Tink would replace herself with an illusion to help her avoid the attack and follow up with a counterattack of her own. Her counters were lackluster compared to the attacks she tossed haphazardly at Dingba.

Dingba's wings gave her an advantage to fly speed, and her size allowed her to take more punishment. She knew this, and so did Tink. Tink's wings, while not giving her much in terms of speed, gave benefits to Tink's magic, mainly her illusion spells. Spreading her tiny scales, she distorted the air around Dingba, making it easier to switch places with her clone.

This was a delicate game. If Tink stayed out of Dingba's range she won, the second Dingba landed a successful hit she wins. They focused all their senses on securing their win. The duel ruined the surrounding area.

Dingba used her superior speed to dodge and strike from Tink's blind spots, hoping to bring an end to this strife. While Tink opted for a constant barrage of orbs, destroying all the cover Dingba might have used.

Moments passed since the fight started. Both fighters were showing signs of exhaustion and fatigue.

"I'm losing this fight."

She covers her face as another barrage of orbs slammed into the surrounding area. The shock waves rattle her bloodied and bruised body. She could feel her knees wobbling again. With a sharp inhale, she forced her body to move once again.

"I need to get closer... or I need to strike her at range. But I don't have Jordan, I can't do our combo."

An orb explodes in front of her, knocking her down as another one lands on top of her.

She groaned loudly as her mind raced as she tried to figure out a solution.

A bolt of inspiration struck.

"I got it..."

She took flight once more, she bobbed in the air while trying to catch her breath.

Tink tilted her head. "Given up?" She tossed more orbs. "Didn't think you were such a disappointment...".

Dingba watched the orbs close in.

"They won't hit me."

She held her ground as the orbs exploded around her.

"Move."

Gritting her teeth, Dingba flew around wildly.

"Increase your speed."

She moved as fast as possible, gaining as much speed as she could.

"Faster."

She eventually moved so fast, Tink could barely keep up. She clenched her fist tightly.

"I can do this."

From ten feet away, Dingba threw a punch with all her might, the force of the explosion stopping her.

Confused, Tink opened her mouth to chastise the crazed Dingba. Unaware of the distortion in the air moving towards her. Dingba watched the wave engulf her, much like Jul's wave did. Tink's face distorted in pain, her body tightens up, then she falls. Not wasting time, Dingba strafed to the side and launched another shock wave from her fist, stunning Tink for a moment longer.

Dingba could see the flood of panic racing through Tink as she closed in on her. The force of the attack scattered her wing dust, cleansing the air of their distorting effects. She couldn't swap out with a clone without Dingba seeing it.

She reared back and delivered a solid right jab to the stomach that sent Tink flying into a nearby tree, which halted her flight. Dingba followed up with a lunging jab to her chest, breaking the tree behind Tink.

Tink laid on the ground, gasping and coughing for air. "Wh... Where did you learn that?" She fought to stay conscious.

Dingba fell to her knees beside Tink. The floodgates breaking as she saw her sister beaten half to death. "I tested something similar with Jordan..." she panted, "But this is the first time I did it myself."

"Well, look at you..." Tink praised, spitting up blood as she rubbed Dingba's leg. She smiled softly. "That old goat taught you well."

Dingba choked back tears, refusing to look Tink in the face. "Why?" Was all she could ask. Anything else was too painful.

"I wanted to get everyone out of the village..." Tink's tiny hands scratched at the earth. Tink wore a fake smile, but her eyes betrayed her, displaying her shame and anger. "That wilt... Melrose. Did things and made me this way."

Tink reached over and placed her hand on top of Dingba's hand. "I tried... I tried to fight her." She squeezed Dingba's hand.

"But I couldn't beat her, her ugly plants and —" She suddenly squints in pain and inhaled sharply.

"Tink?"

Tink panted for a moment, then smiled. "It's nothing, don't worry about it."

"Why didn't you come home? I could have helped."

Tink lifted her shirt. On her ribs, just slightly under her breasts, a black mark encircled her body. The mark resembled a crown of thorns.

Dingba traced the mark with her fingers. It was smooth, as if tattooed into her flesh.

Tink smiled. "She cursed me. I'm not sure if I understand it completely but one thing I know for sure, she can use it to track me. It also hurts me if I say too much. Luckily, I figured it out before I made it back to the village. I tried to show Jordan but..." she chuckled, "He wasn't as interested in seeing you topless as I hoped."

Dingba leaned back. "What?"

Tink smiled. "Nothing, don't worry about it."

Dingba frowned. "You still should have come back and let us help you."

Tink shook her head. "She was still being babysat. Unfortunately for her, I shrouded the village and a large area around it in an illusion, making it harder to find. I think she wanted the Noble Tree so she could grow stronger."

She inhaled deeply and cleared her throat. "I thought Jordan was strong since he just walked through it with no issues, then he saved Juka and I hoped... I hoped he could save the village."

She chuckled, "Turns out he was out of his mind."

Tink blinked, her breathing grew shallow. Dingba lightly slapped her cheeks. "Tink?" Her heart twisted in her chest.

Tink inhaled sharply as her eyes shot open. She looked at Dingba and smiled. A moment passed, and she took a deep breath.

"Hey, did you know dragonflies eat moths?"

Dingba bit her lip in anger. Her bloody fists balled up. She diverted her eyes from Tink.

"What was the point in telling me that?"

Tink chuckled. "They also eat mosquitos, butterflies. And other dragonflies, if you can believe it."

"Tink..."

Tink eyes started watering as she rambled on. "Oh, do be wary of agile birds, spiders and frogs."

Dingba snapped her teary eyes towards Tink. "Tink."

Tink jumped in place and stared back at Dingba. "Oh, and be wary of yellow jackets, it's kind of a tossup with them. But if it's you, I know you'll be fine."

Dingba scooped Tink into her arms and embraced her tightly. Tears poured forth. She had so much to tell her sister, but her words died in her throat.

Tink found no difficulty talking. "Hey, I kinda like that Jordan fellow. After you beat Melrose, why don't you... go traveling with him. Didn't you want to go around the world and beat up one of every race?" A laugh soon followed, but a pained cough interrupted.

Dingba nodded, her tears soaking Tink's back by the second.

"I saw you beating him up when you guys were training. You should do it again once he gets strong."

Dingba nodded once more.

"Plus, you need to find that old goat... what was his name again?"

Dingba choked out a response, "Jul'... Jul'Cur'Drl"

Tink smiled, "Ah yes, Master Jul, always had a hard name to pronounce." Tink grew silent for a moment as her breathing softened.

"Tink...?" Dingba slowly went to look at her face, but Tink suddenly embraced her.

Tink forced her raspy voice out of her tattered throat. Her hands clutched Dingba's back as her arms tightened like a snake seizing its prey. "Promise me... promise me you will never let someone turn your wings black."

Dingba nodded and buried her face in Tink's neck. "I promise..." The last of her will broke, and she unleashed an ugly wail.

Tink chuckled, "Always were a big cry baby..." She soothed Dingba's hair. "This. This will hurt a bit, okay?" Her hand gripped Dingba's hair, holding her head in place while her other hand wraps around Dingba's body.

Quickly she chanted dark and arcane words. Her wings shined as miasma flowed out of her body. She leaned close to Dingba's ear, who froze in fear. "Please remember... that I love you... my dear speedy dragonfly." She leaned in and kissed Dingba on the right cheek.

The Miasma flowed into the spot like it was a vacuum, sucking up the filth of the world. Dingba roared in pain. Her eyes rolled back in her head. Tink's body glowed as it dissipated into the air.

Tink's last words floated into the air, "A Midnight Farewell."

Dingba rolled on the ground, her hands holding her face while she prayed the pain fades.

21

SICK GARDEN

WHILE DINGBA CHASED TINK. Tong, Singka and Jordan, along with the remaining members of the fairy militia, fought to protect the village.

Jordan smashed open a pitcher plant, he covered his face as its juices splashed on him. With no time to relax he felt something snag is ankle and yank him off his feet. He landed roughly and turned to his opponent.

Stars danced in his eyes, but he shook off his daze and glared as the plant yanked him closer, "Get off." He rose his foot and tried to kick it, but another tendril snagged his foot and pulled his leg in a different direction. Soon another tendril from a different plant yanked one of his arms towards it.

Jordan yelped as his muscles strained from the tension. A chunk of ice flew from the crowd, it caved in the plant holding Jordan's arm.

Seeing a moment of opportunity Jordan pulled the chunk with Ver, before relaunching it at one of the plants holding his legs.

He sighed in relief as it crashed into the plant and stayed there without harming anyone else. He turned his attention to the last of the trio and rushed it with a Gao empowered backhand.

His hand stung from the digestive fluids and force of his slap. He paused to catch his breath and shake the pain from his hands.

"Punching shit all the time is not as easy as the movies make it seem."

As he caught his breath, he attempted to survey the battle, a mistake. A tendril wrapped around his neck and yanked him back to the ground. His hands shot up and tried to free his neck. He pulled his body forward tightening the choke, suddenly he fell forward as the tendril went limp.

After ripping off the tendril he turned around. Behind him the sword nix from earlier is cutting the plant down to size.

"Oh shit, you go girl."

He regained his footing and regrouped with his battle buddies.

The nix hovered close to him, "Are you alright?"

Jordan smiled, "See? Told you, you would need that sword."

She huffed, "Let's keep going."

Another ball of ice is launched from the hammer pix, and they jump back into the fray.

As they pushed forward, slowly edging the plants back to the forest. They spotted Tong in the middle of a protective formation around him. While a small group was dedicated to protecting him, Tong was far from a liability. From inside the circle, he was firing bolts of energy so bright and so fast it'd make a roman candle jealous. When a tendril got too close, he would charge the top of his staff with magic and bash it away.

Plants had holes shot into their stomach and were falling in quick succession. Jordan and his two partners made it to the circle and joined it.

Tong floated near Jordan after batting off a handsy tendril. "So many... there must be a place they are coming from."

Jordan punted one away from him. "We need to find that before we go help Dingba. Otherwise, we will get overran."

Tong fired a bolt of energy, killing another pitcher plant, "Agreed."

From the forest a fresh batch of plants came shambling out.

Jordan sighed.

"Really?"

This new wave crashed into the front lines and started mowing them down. Jordan prepared himself for another round. His heart was thumping in his chest as the plants grew closer, he summoned his Spell Circle.

"Bring it on."

Jordan glanced down at the hammer Pix; he could see him breathing heavily. "You alright?"

He nodded, "I'm getting close to my limit. I'll try to open up a path for us." He flew into the air.

The air chilled around the Pix then it spread throughout the fight. Air froze in Jordan's throat. With a burst of magic large spikes of frozen stomach acid erupted from the pitcher plants mouths and bodies.

The Pix dizzily fell out of the sky, Jordan caught him.

The Pix sat in his hands panting while Jordan beamed at him.

Jordan looked around at the carnage. "Holy shit that was awesome."

The Pix laughed, "Gotta do something to help the efforts."

Jordan nodded, "That was one hell of a something, let's get you back to Singka. God, what a fucking play."

"God I wish I had more spells."

With a lull in the battle Tong flew into the air, holding his staff high. A brilliant light shined from its tip. "Everyone. We advance. Find their breeding ground and we win this fight."

The militia erupted in a battle cry before charging into the forest, mowing down any remaining plant monsters. Following the direction, the plant monsters were coming from proved to be a bloody struggle. The constant river of plant monsters never ended. Fatigue slowly spread among the ranks.

A voice rang out from the front lines, "I think I found it!"

Everyone gathered around. Hearts jumped as an unnatural sight greeted them; many pods sat rooted into the ground, they pulsated letting off sounds of viscous fluid being squeezed through thin holes with each breath. They were as big as a medium-sized boulder. Their roots stretched and mingled with each other. Every so often a new plant monster would emerge from a pod and shamble its way forward before being cut down.

Tong broke the silence. "Seems like we found it."

Singka opened a bag and started pulling out supplies. "Anyone who is badly injured, come to me, everyone else destroy the pods."

Jordan walked up to the nearest pod.

"Why are these so big?"

He picked up a thick stick and stabbed into the pod. After tearing a small hole, he noticed something hard inside the pod.

His mind went back to the pitcher plant grabbing fish from the river, he then remembered the missing fairies.

"I swear to god..."

He took a deep breath and forced his hand into the thick green gunk. His skin crawled as he felt the inside. Thick and sticky, like a runny nose, the smell is that of wet fertilizer. The creepiest part of the situation was the feeling of a body inside the pod. Jordan braced himself as he gripped it, dragging it out. A fragile fairy came out with his arm, malnourished and barely breathing.

He turned to the militia, gagged, got himself together then called out. "Careful! The pods have fairies in them!"

Every able-bodied person carefully cut open the pods, pulling out both nixies and pixies. Some looked as if they were fresh, while others looked as if they were already decomposing. Out of the twenty-two fairies, only four could move on their own, twelve were on the verge of death and six were dead. That was a small number compared to the amount of animal remains they found.

Jordan laid down the last fairy with the others, its body heavily decomposed. "That's all of them."

Singka looked at Tong, "I have to take care of the injured, they can't move."

Tong nodded and looked at the four able-bodied survivors. "You four need to go to the village and get help. We will go find Tink and Dingba."

"Sir, about that." One of the rescued fairies spoke up. "Tink isn't responsible. She's being controlled by a giant plant woman named

Melrose. She put us in those pods. Tink begged her not to, but she almost killed Tink. Please Tong, save her." The other fairies nodded in unison.

A scream echoed out in the middle of the forest.

Tong's head snapped towards the scream. "Dingba?" His old worn-out wings flapped as hard as they can, lifting him into the air and pulling him towards the scream. Jordan ran after him before scooping him up in his arms and running as hard as he could. As they reached the edge of the clearing the ground trembled knocking Jordan down, while the fairies instinctively took flight. Jordan stayed low to the ground.

"This feels… familiar?"

2 2

MY FAO

FROM THE CENTER of the clearing an enormous stalk covered in large bumps arose from the ground. A cloud of dust obscured his vision while a cacophony of screams and destruction rung his ears.

When it cleared, a two-story tall flower greeted him. A deep green stalk rose from the ground, covered in outward protrusions. At the top, a burst of vibrant orange and yellow petals surrounded a green woman in the center. Her "hair" was slicked back, her pouty lips teased her playful side while her bloodlust shone in her eyes.

Jordan looked around, as he tried to assess the situation.

Underneath him was Tong, on the ground in front of the woman, Singka held up her hands as a barrage of tendrils slammed the surrounding air. With each hit, a bubble shimmered around her and the injured fairies. Some of the militias are still standing; they roared, charging towards the flanks, clashing with more tendrils. Some of the rescued fairies grabbed weapons while others stayed back to assist Singka.

Jordan looked at the woman.

"Who's this skank?"

From behind him someone roared in anger, "Melrose!"

Jordan turned around and saw Dingba mid-dash towards her.

"Oh shit."

Tong pushed himself up from underneath Jordan, "Was that Dingba?"

Jordan nodded, "Why yes it was, and she's very pissed off."

Dingba reached her top speed, her fists clenched, prepping for the solid right hook she was going to throw. The woman paid her no mind as she approached. When Dingba threw her punch, a petal snapped up and blocked the woman. Tendrils wrapped around Dingba's waist, holding her in place.

The woman looked at her slowly. "Do I know you, fairy?"

Dingba clawed at the tendrils holding her in place. "I'll kill you. How dare you do that to Tink."

"Oh?" A vile smirk creeped over her face. "You're Dingba..." She brought Dingba within whisper range. "She always became more obedient when I threatened to hurt you."

"You wilted—"

Dingba screamed as Melrose flicked her towards the ground at high speeds.

"Shit." Jordan dashed behind Dingba. "Gao." Jordan held his hands out. His spell circle formed around Dingba and like rubber it stretched as he pushed her away, slowing her descent, allowing her to recover and hover.

Melrose cooed, noticing Jordan's trick. "What an interesting toy. Might need to save you for later."

"Shit... it never did that before." Jordan gasped, hunching over, sucking in wind, unaware that a tendril was cleaving towards him.

The air by Jordan shook as a tendril slammed into another barrier that shimmered, halting the attack. Jordan looked around and saw Tong holding up his staff. Quickly, he fell back to catch his breath. "Thanks..." He said in between breaths.

Tong simply nodded and turned back to Melrose, who was busy defending from attacks from all sides.

"Be careful. You have been using a lot of magic today. We can't have you going into Mind Down."

Jordan nodded. "Right, I'll be careful, but you should too. We need you more than me." He noticed Melrose's stalk had a bunch of bulges on it.

He crouched down, whispering, "Hey Tong. You think those bulges have more fairies?"

Tong narrowed his eyes. "Only one way to find out. I will protect you. Go." He raised up his staff.

Jordan nodded and rushed forward as Tong readied his staff to intercept any attacks. Melrose quickly refocused on the human rushing toward her. She launched a focused bombardment of tendrils. Each crashed into the barrier Tong erected. Jordan focused on his task of ripping apart the bulge. Thick green pus spilled onto the ground, and in the mess sat a fairy bound by small vines.

Jordan glared, "Piece of shit..." He reached in and ripped the fairy out.

Melrose screeched as three of the tendrils she was using to defend herself withered and died, allowing the militia to strike at her flesh. Jordan rushed back to Tong. "The pods have fairies in them! The pods have fairies in them!"

The others took note and formed small teams. One would rush a pod and start cutting it open. Two would hang back and provide defense, covering the retriever's back. Dingba, still lost in rage, had her own plans. Every time Melrose looked away, she would attack with all she had.

From the outside, the plan looked reckless. But by forcing Melrose to monitor her, Dingba was successfully supporting those who were trying to cut open the pods. As time went on, more and more fairies were being freed at a quicken pace.

Melrose slowed, her horde of tendrils purging with each successful rescue. Dingba's battle fever was sustaining her. She was slowly getting closer to Melrose and her strikes were hitting significantly harder, forcing Melrose to use more of her petals to block. While she continued to harass Melrose, Singka snuck off into a hiding place and was slowly reviving fairies. The pressure on Melrose was cracking her defense. This renewed vigor and morale was too much. She had to derail this train before they overtook her. Her eyes spotted a familiar troublemaker, Jordan. He was rushing to another pod, taking the long way to perform a hard flank. When Jordan changed his path and bee-lined to a pod, Melrose saw her chance.

Jordan smirked as he approached. He had been eyeing this particularly large pod for quite some time. The thought of the number of tendrils she'd lose if he popped that pimple. It tunneled his vision. From the very edges of his vision a sharp vine stood out. It was closer than it should be. Jordan stopped running and leaned back to dodge the attack. It cut his cheek as it passed.

He looked back, "Tong?"

In the distance, he saw Tong defending himself from a group of tendrils. A few feet away from Tong, Dingba laid on the ground. His eyes widened.

"Dingba's down? Since when?"

Something wrapped around his ankle; he looked down just as a tendril yanked him off his feet. He felt himself get dragged before it lifted him into the air. In a panic, he wrapped his arms around the front and back of his head and shut his eyes. A second later he felt his body slam into the ground.

He gasped as the shock paralyzed him; he felt himself get dragged again before being lifted into the air. His grip tightened around his head as a jolt of fear shot through him. He kept his head covered as his body met the ground. After reuniting with the air and quickly slammed onto the ground for a third time, his grip around his head weakened. His arms limply let go, his body shook with panic.

He's dragged once more and lifted into the air. This time, he felt the tendril release from his leg. He forced his eyes open and saw the world spin as the ground shrunk away from him.

Jordan was losing consciousness as he tumbled up to the heavens, though his armor protected his life from the rag-dolling. The blows did significant damage to his body. As he floated up, his visage stunned the entire group. Melrose surrounded herself in tendrils, forming a gaping maw. He could feel the fight ending.

He could see Dingba struggle on the ground and look up at him. She couldn't move.

Melrose opened her maw wider as if shouting, "Fall."

The world deafened around Jordan as he slowly reached his peak altitude, a slurry of voices flooded his mind. Each spoke with a different message. They began spreading doubt, fear, anger, and sadness in his mind. Some mocked him, others pitied him, while others said he did his best.

"Is this what it's like to be at death's door?"

He felt his will slowly slip away.

"Fuck, I'm tired."

His eyes slowly closed; his mind started to drift away.

He clenched his hand then slapped himself awake.

"No. Wake up."

He forced his eyes open.

"You said you'll win. You promised them."

He summoned his circle.

"I can still fight. Think Jordan, think."

He reached his peak and felt his body start falling back to earth; he looked around the battlefield. His mind searching for the best option in this situation.

"Nothing to pull, bad angle for pushing anything."

His eyes spot Dingba still on the ground.

"I could give the circle to Dingba, do our combo attack? No, she can't do it without moving. Still, it's our best option."

He glanced over the circle, then snapped his vision back.

Underneath the symbols for Gao and Ver, sat a second ring and in the middle of that ring...

"A third symbol?"

He scanned it repeatedly.

"When did I get this? I can't read it, what does it do?"

Underneath the symbol, in bright orange letters, a word shimmered into view.

Fao

The ground continued to get close.

"What do I do? Use it raw? No, it's on a level by itself maybe I need to augment it? With what though? What does this even do?"

He was running out of time. Soon he'd be within reach of Melrose's jaws.

"Gao is my strongest spell, I have to use it."

He swelled his circle and cocked his arm back.

"I'll take her head off with Gao."

A jolt of panic flushed in his mind.

"Why give this to me now? What if I need it to win? Fuck it, I'll use both."

He waited until he was closer; he swelled his circle as large as he could.

"Even if I pass out the spell with still go off, so I just need to make sure I hit."

His mind throbbed. It was reaching its breaking point.

He finally got into range. Melrose shot her tendrils up as he threw his punch. The tendrils reached him first, skewering deep into his body, some going clean through. His Circle blinked out, he clutched one of the tendrils in his body.

"Fuck."

2 3

THE END

Dingba watched in horror as Jordan hung in the air like a piece of meat dangling from meat hooks. Her heart ripped itself in two.

"No, no, no, no, no, no, no."

Melrose cackled as she dangled Jordan in the air, shaking his body like a limp puppet. She shook his body a few times, "Oh no... he might be dead." She shook him once more, "Looks like I broke my toy."

Her tendrils lifted Jordan higher into the air so all the fairies can see. "Now what shall I do with you all?" She rose even more tendrils into the air and aimed them at the stunned fairies.

Dingba dug her nails into her arms as she choked on heartache. Her body trembled with agony. The world around her deafened.

"I can't lose you too... please I don't want to lose anyone else."

Her body rocked back and forth as she continued to choke on the pain of it all.

"Please don't... please don't leave... don't..."

It was too much, the agony forced her mouth opened and she wailed, "Don't die!"

Her words hung in the air as she glared at Jordan.

He answered by swelling his Spell Circle to its maximum size.

Melrose flinched from the light, panic danced on her face as the light illuminated her.

With the last bit of his will, Jordan finished his attack.

A wave of purple fire erupted from him, coating his arm in their royal appearance, roasting his flesh. His head rolled back, and his body went limp as the flames rushed towards Melrose.

Melrose gasped, "Why do you have your Colors?"

The flames continued their descent as Jordan went limp once more.

They crashed into Melrose, and she let out a pained screech. She writhed in flames, her arms slapped against her flesh, desperate to put herself out.

She screamed as the flames devoured her. "Help me, please." She looked to the sky, "Sister please..." She clutched her body and wailed, "Mistress save me!"

Dingba looked to the sky, but only saw what appeared to be a bird flying off into the distance.

Melrose wailed louder, "No. Come back. Please..." Her body began collapsing under its own weight, the remaining pods bursting open and with it her tendrils wilted.

The ones holding Jordan dropped him onto the ground with a thud.

Dingba forced herself up and ran over, "Jordan."

Melrose groaned weakly. Her remaining tendrils lifted into the air. Jordan's fire had started to devour those as well. Melrose let out a demonic groan and launched the tendrils towards Jordan's unmoving body. Dingba threw herself in front.

She glared as the tendrils closed in on her. "Back off."

Dingba threw a flurry of blows that blew her tendrils back onto the pyre. Melrose struggled to push herself back up but collapsed, eventually she stopped moving, leaving only the sound of crackling purple flames as they continued to consume her mountain of a corpse.

The fight was over.

Dingba reached Jordan. She knelt down and panicked at the multitude of holes in his body. "No, no, no." She placed her hands on the biggest of the wounds, one in his stomach to the right of his belly-button and one that hit a little under his left pectoral. She pushed down and applied pressure. Blood seeped through her fingers, Dingba pressed down harder.

"I'm sorry, I'm sorry."

She turned her head. "Singka help."

She looked at his arm; the flesh bubbled and cracked. Beneath the blackened skin, his muscles shined with an inflamed crimson. Small flames danced on top of his flesh.

"What happened to your arm Jordan?"

She leaned in and blew on the flames extinguishing them one by one. Her eyes kept darting to a new flame which she proceeded to promptly blow out.

She turned and called again, "Singka."

"Where is she?"

A wet warmth embraced her kneecaps, she glanced down and saw the sticky crimson soaking into the ground and coating her knees.

Tears dropped from her face and mixed in with Jordan's blood.

"Come on Jordan stop bleeding."

She applied more weight on Jordan's wounds. Her hands were sticky from the mess. She looked around and saw the carnage of the fight. So many fairies were on the ground some in similar conditions to Jordan. The healers scrambled to the nearest injured they could find. In the distance she spotted Singka throwing out orders and passing out medical supplies.

She inhaled deeply and shouted.

"Singka!"

24

RECOVERY

SINGKA CAME RUSHING OVER, medicine bag in hand. When she arrived, she recoiled from the sight of Jordan's body.

Her hands leaped to her face, covering her mouth, "Oh no."

Dingba's face distorted from sadness, "Help him."

Her eyes scanned the various injuries as her mind worked through a diagnosis. She leaned down and placed a hand near Dingba's.

"Let me see, let me see."

Dingba slowly moved her hands to show the wounds. Blood bubbled forth, now freed to flow once more.

"Okay, push down on those hard. Don't worry about hurting him, we need to slow his bleeding."

She watched as Dingba shifted her weight to press down; she nodded. "Good, just like that."

She took out these fibrous balls of puff and stuffed them into Jordan's wounds.

A voice shouted from behind, "Singka we need help over here!"

She turned, "I know, almost finished here!"

She turned to Dingba. "Move your hands again. I have to see which one is bleeding the most."

Dingba moved her hands once more.

Singka held another puffball in her hand, and a soft light shined from the other.

Dingba held her breath as she watched, the urge to cover the wounds were causing her hands to creep forward.

Before she could, Singka stuffed the puff ball into his stomach and healed the wound on his chest.

Once the wound was closed, she stood up and grabbed her bag. "He's good to move, but we need to get him back to the village and I need to help others." She thought for a moment, "Can you fly?"

Dingba looked back at her wings, they were stiff in their movement. "A little."

Singka nodded, "If you can't fly, run back to the village. Fly when you can but if it hurts, don't push it. Get help from the villagers and bring them here. We need people to move the injured quickly. Do you understand?"

A wave of fear crashed over Dingba. She shook her head, "I don't want to leave him."

Singka crouched, "I know but I need you Dingba, you are the fastest and I know you can handle yourself."

Dingba glanced at Jordan's body, blood continued to flow from smaller wounds. Her eyes grew wider with panic. "But he--"

Singka grabbed her face and looked her in the eyes, "Look at me."

Dingba's eyes went to look back at Jordan, but Singka turned her head more.

Singka intensified her stare, "Look at me. I know he is bleeding, so are a bunch of others. But he is fine at the moment. This is a time issue, the faster we get him back to the village the better chance we have of saving him. No one is faster than you, you are his best hope of surviving. Do you understand?"

Dingba blinked away her tears and nodded.

"Good, be careful." She kissed Dingba on the forehead.

Dingba took off running. "I'll be back."

When she reached the bushes, she leapt high into the air before landing and running back to the village.

Her feet stomped the ground as she ran, she tested her wings.

"I can do this."

She leapt into the air, her wings buzzed but the rhythm was off, she could feel them stuttering and every so often one will fail to flap throwing her balance off.

She landed and ran some more. With her body being used to flying instead of running, her fatigue quickly grew. Her legs slowed as it did.

"I can't stop... I got to do something."

Once more she leapt into the air. Her wings ached as she forced them to flap. She gritted her teeth as she pushed past the pain. Once the pain got too much her body forced her to stop. For a moment she was weightless and, in that moment, she had an idea.

She threw her arm backwards and created an explosion behind her, the force pushed her forward. Her eyes opened wide from awe.

She threw another punch and once again the force pushed her forward. Her ears tingled from the air rushing by them.

"I can do this. I can make it."

She continued striking the air, picking up more and more speed as she went. She would time the explosions to get the biggest boost, every so often she would flap her wings to change direction and gain more speed.

As she soared through the forest she came upon a lone pitcher plant, seemingly lost from the rest of its group.

Dingba growled.

"Are you joking?"

She flew directly at it. It attacked with a volley of tendrils. She punched the air in front of her while angling herself down with her wings. The force propelled her up and over the tendrils just over the pitcher's body. As she fell behind it, she threw a punch backwards exploding the pitcher plant and sending her forward once more.

"I never realized how much push-back these punches had. Guess I just got used to it."

A few seconds later Dingba made it to the village, she skidded across the ground before stopping fully.

She inhaled deeply and shouted. "Everyone! The fight is over, but the militia needs help moving the injured!"

Heads poked out of the huts.

"Dingba? Where's Tong and Singka?"

Dingba frowned, "Where do you think? They are tending to the injured. Now grab medicine and let's go this is a time issue."

The able-bodied villagers flooded the streets holding supplies.

Dingba looked them all over, "Good, now follow me."

She turned, rose both of her hands above her head and slammed her fists into the ground launching herself back towards the forest.

She turned around, "Keep up." Then she blasted herself forward. She took the shortest route back to the battle. Her arms throbbed painfully from overuse, but she forced herself to go faster. Not wanting anyone to get lost she laid out a path of destruction by mowing down trees, bushes and the like.

Every so often she would check back on the villagers struggling to keep up with her.

"Come on, move faster."

She sped up and continued carving the path back to Singka and Jordan.

———

MOMENTS LATER, faster than the last time. Dingba saw the bush line of the clearing.

"I got back here so fast…"

She grinned and blasted through the bushes into the war-torn clearing.

"Singka we're back." She skidded past Singka on her way towards Jordan.

Singka looked at her before looking for the other fairies, "Dingba? You're back fast."

Dingba smiled, "I'm the fastest remember?"

Singka smiled back, "Yes you are… where's everyone else?"

Dingba glanced at the bushes she just busted through, "They should be here…"

The rest of the group came through the bushes panting.

Dingba smiled, "Now. I left a path of destruction towards the village, so it'll be easy to follow."

Singka nodded, "Good girl. Take a break and look over Jordan while we clean up here."

Dingba clutched Jordan's hand, "Hold on Jordan you'll be fine."

Tong floated down to her, "How is he?"

Dingba shook her head, "I don't know, he's not moving but Singka said he's stable." She looked around, "We have to get him back to the village."

Tong nodded," The others are here. Stay with him, I'm going back to set up another healing hut."

He flew off towards Singka to relay the plan to her before flying off towards the village.

Together they bandaged the injured as best as they could and rushed back to the village. Upon their return to the village, they were greeted by the gasps of the villagers who stayed behind; Out of twenty militia members, only about ten could barely walk on their own. Tong had come back earlier to help set up the healer's hut. They hadn't expected the number of injured they'd have.

Once Singka was back, it was all hands-on deck with her in charge. Those nearby helped with bandaging and cleaning of wounds while Singka buzzed around, checking on as many people as she could before she turned to Jordan. Dingba stood by him motionless and in a daze.

Singka landed next to her and leaned in, this snapped Dingba out of her daze.

Dingba looked over, "What do you need me to do? What can I do?"

Singka motioned for her to relax while she studied Jordan's wounds.

Though the battle was long over, the smell of smoldering flesh and the sound of crackling of skin still lingered. Underneath the flaky charred skin and sticky scarlet flesh, she could see its light. The light of traitorous embers clinging to life, devouring more of their master's flesh. Singka's hand hovered over various cutting instruments and medicinal salves. Each option tempting, but nothing standing out as the best option.

Dingba watched in horror, "You're not thinking of..."

Singka nodded, "We have to save what we can..."

Singka grabbed a scalpel and started removing unsalvageable flesh. She carefully snuffed out the remaining embers before they could do anymore damage. A few more cuts here and there and Jordan's bones showed. Singka flinched at the sight.

"What in the seven...?" She leaned in closer.

Dingba leaned in, "What's wrong with his leg? Is that normal?"

Singka slowly shook her head, "No."

Jordan's bones are cracked but not fully broken, even stranger instead of being smooth. They were bumpy and had thick lines criscrossing throughout.

Singka's face scrunched up in confusion, "Boneworms?" She looked at Jordan. "When did you come in contact with boneworms, little one?"

Dingba looked at her, "What's boneworms?"

Singka placed her arm on Dingba stomach moving her back, "I need you to stand back." She handed Dingba a random bundle of bandages. "Hold this for me while I do this."

Singka refocused on salvaging his arm, she examined the flesh even more. What muscles Jordan didn't tear; his flames burnt.

She bit her lip in frustration, "I can't save this arm..."

Dingba walked closer, "Can't you use your healing magic?"

Singka shook her head, "This would require a level of healing I simply can't do or a treatment I don't have the materials for."

She looked at Dingba with tears in her eyes, "I'm sorry Dingba but..."

She reached for her bone saw. "This is the best for him."

Taking a deep breath, she steadied her hands and prepared to start. "I'm so sorry, little one." At the first cut, a bright orange light engulfed Jordan's arm, knocking them both back.

It silenced the hut that was buzzing with orders and requests as it lifted Jordan into the air, ethereal energies caressed and teased the injured arm. These hands peeled his skin and flesh back like a thick banana, exposing the muscle underneath. They dusted off burnt matter while realigning and resetting any parts out of place.

Singka sat back on her hands, wide eyed.

"No stop."

Dingba in a panic stumbled towards him but Singka jumped on her and pulled her back. Singka squeezed her tight to calm her, "It's okay this is good. This... This is good for him."

Dingba clutched Singka's arm, her voice wavered, "What's happening?"

Singka soothed Dingba's hair and continued to watch. The way these fingers danced over death and decay, rejuvenating flesh as it went. She wanted to learn this godly healing spell, she wanted to learn it all, but she just sat and stared like a child watching their parent play the harp.

Singka smiled, "Something is healing him... This level of healing magic is... extraordinary. It's at a level I've never seen or heard of before."

After some time, the hands pulled the skin forward, taking great care not to tear it any further. A fluffy cloud like substance filled in the spots where muscle was burnt away and missing. Once they laid the skin in place, bright sparks appeared and crept down the edges where they peeled the skin, welding the arm like the side of a ship. More of that fluffy cloud surrounded the arm before they lowered Jordan onto the mat.

Singka walked over to inspect Jordan and waved her hand over the cloud. It was hot, but when she touched it; It didn't burn, but warmed her hand. She noticed it was hard instead of soft like she had been expecting. She decided it was best to treat the minor wounds and leave Jordan be.

Singka lifted his shirt to check his stomach wounds and saw they were still open. She chuckled, "A Fickle Queen indeed." She held out her hand, "Hand me those bandages please."

25

BONEWORMS

TWO WEEKS LATER, Jordan regained consciousness. He heard childlike giggling nearby. Slowly he turned his head and saw Dingba playing with some kids. Sitting next to him was a smiling Singka.

"Good. We won."

Singka smiled, "And the last one wakes up."

The kids turned their heads. "He's awake." They cheered and rushed towards him.

"Hey. Brats. No." Dingba tried to grab them all, but one white-haired pix slipped by and made it to Jordan.

Jordan chuckled, "Hi Juka."

Juka looked up and smiled at him, "Hi Jordan."

The other kids broke away from Dingba and bombarded Jordan with their excited ramblings. Jordan sat there with a smile on his face nodding along to a conversation he could barely follow. Eventually Singka rescued him and shooed out the kids.

They groaned at her and started to whine.

Singka sighed, "I know, I know. You've been wanting to play with him for a while now, but I have to talk to him... alone." She kept shooing them away.

The kids pouted but slowly funneled out of the hut. Dingba got up to leave but Singka called out to her.

"Not you Dingba, I need you to stay."

Dingba raised an eyebrow, "Okay?"

After a moment, Singka turned to Jordan. "I have a question. If you don't mind. Well, a few questions actually." She was tense.

"How's your arm, little one?"

The cloud that surrounded Jordan's arm had dissipated over time, leaving no evidence. Compared to his left arm, his right arm looks brand new, somewhat hairless and blemish free.

Jordan looked down and wiggled his fingers. He tried to bend his arm but found the skin to be tight and his muscles rigid. "It's a little tight, but nothing some stretches can't fix. Thanks for fixing it."

"What happened to my arm?"

"That's the thing. I never fixed your arm. It was a mess when we got you back. I had opted to just cut it off before something healed your arm. It was beautiful but strange." Singka paused, her eyes seemed to look for something on Jordan's face.

Jordan looked at the two, then nodded with an understanding look on his face. He was curious about a lot of things, but he only asked one question. "What was strange about it?"

Dingba leapt forward, "It was like some awesome magic and it--"

Singka placed a hand on Dingba's shoulder.

Dingba deflated, "Oh, sorry."

Singka sighed and looked around. "Like everything, the sight, the magic, the effects. It was all unusual." She regained her composure. "Healing magic is very simple. It is used to close wounds, that is all. But what healed you not only closed your wounds, but it also repaired your arm to a better state than it was. You had a chunk of muscle destroyed due to what I am assuming was your first-time using fire magic."

Jordan's eyes lit up. "I have fire magic?"

Singka blinked twice in shock. "You... don't remember the fight?"

"I remember helping then I remember Melrose grabbing me, pain, blackness and now I'm here. I had assumed we won when I woke up and everyone was still here."

Singka nodded and took a seat. She recounted what Jordan had missed the past few weeks and how Melrose died. She then explained how his arm was injured and then healed. Then followed it up with one more question.

"How did you get infected with boneworms?"

Jordan replied with a question of his own. "What are boneworms?" His eyes and face proved his ignorance on the subject.

Singka got up, grabbed a medical book and shifted through pages until she found what she was looking for. She turned the book, so Jordan could see. On the page a chubby white worm was depicted. It was like the ones he threw up before passing out back on Earth. He reminded Singka of his departure from Earth, including the messy details.

Singka sighed in relief, then cleared her throat. "Boneworms are highly illegal; the major races have banned their usage and cultivation. If someone finds out they infected you, they will stop at nothing to retrieve them. Do you understand?"

Jordan nodded slowly. "But why? And what are they?"

"Boneworms are a beneficial parasite. When they infect a host, they spread throughout the host's body and increase bone density and strength. When they finish, the excess worms get violently expelled from the body and shortly die afterwards." She glanced around once more to make sure no one was eavesdropping. "After they strengthen the bones, they leave behind eggs. The eggs lie dormant waiting for the host to die and those bones to get ingested so they could spread to more hosts." She let it soak in. "Questions?" She asked, scanning his face and eyes.

Jordan nodded, "But why were they made illegal? It seems like they are very helpful to people."

Singka nodded, "They can be. But they cause extreme pain, and if the host moves too much, it weakens the effects. The more movement the worms detect, the slower they go until they eventually stop. But the main issue was the Maiti." Singka's eyes lowered.

"Maiti? Is that some kind of race?"

"Correct. The Maiti weren't an official race until shortly before the great war. In their ranks there is a group of magic users who specialize in reviving the dead for their armies. They called themselves Wazimu Maiti's. A Wazimu Maiti by the name of Yaga got her hands on some bone worms. She theorized corpses can get the maximum benefit from the boneworms because they won't move due to the pain. So, they raised a few undead and tried it out."

"She was right. Even the most fragile bones became strong enough that they could break a sword made of star metal. Of course after enough movement the worms stopped strengthening, so they left their armies still until they needed them. She passed this technique onto the four grand houses, causing their armies to grow out of control. Thousands of undead enhanced with magic and boneworms invaded every nation, coupled with the fact that some Wazimu Maiti nobles had corpses of magnificent beasts under their control. But we can save that war for another time." She sighed, fatigued from lecturing.

Jordan's head was spinning so many questions. But he was so hungry, and all this recent information fried his brain. He looked at Singka, who was expecting another question.

He smiled, "When's dinner?"

Singka stared before giving into a warm chuckle. "Well, now that our hero is up, we can start the feast. In the meantime, I will get you some fruit. How's tomorrow's sound for a feast?"

Jordan nodded greedily. "Tomorrow sounds great."

"Then it's settled. Remember though... no one must know about your bones and tell any humans you meet. I doubt you were the only one infected."

Jordan nodded.

Singka turned to Dingba, "That goes for you too. You have to keep that secret as well."

Dingba nodded, "I know it's bad if anyone knew."

She smiled. "Good, one last question before I go. I know you're tired but, how are you?"

Jordan tilted his head in confusion. "I'm fine?"

She frowned softly. "How are you really?"

He glanced around. "I'm fine."

"Jordan. You almost died. Twice now if we don't count the incidents with Dingba. That's very serious and I understand if it is a lot."

"*Ah.*"

Jordan smiled. "Yeah. I see what you mean. I guess I'm okay because where I came from, my generation had no future. Most of us would have spent our entire lives working to pay off a never-ending debt. While doing something we really didn't care about. Some got lucky and followed their dreams to success, but a vast majority of us were… unhappy. Very unhappy."

He looked down, and his smile faded a bit. "So, for the first time in a long time. I feel like I have a future, I feel like I'm doing what I want to do and I'm happy. We didn't have magic or temperance where we came from. There were no adventures to be had. Just sadness and no escape."

He looked back up and grinned at her. "So yeah. I'm fine. These past few months I've been here have had more value than my past six years on Earth." He chuckled. "I'm not dead and I'm free. So, I'm fine."

Singka's lip trembled. She grabbed Jordan's hand and stared sternly in his eyes. "Your life has value. It always did. So don't throw it away in a new world. I want to see you grow old. I'm not sure if your mother or father are here too. But if not, I'll claim you as mine. That way you'll always have a family and a home to come back to."

Jordan could feel his eyes watering. He sniffled, then nodded. "Alright. I'll be more careful."

Singka patted his hand. "Good." She wiped a tear from her eyes. "By the wilt I've been crying so much lately. Let me go get you something to eat, you just keep resting."

Jordan chuckled. "Thank you."

Singka smiled. "No need dear."

When Singka left, Jordan felt a wave of exhaustion wash over him. He passed out before the food arrived.

2 6

SCARS

THE LIGHT of an early morning sun crept in behind a dashing Dingba. "Jordan." She dive-bombed into his stomach.

Jordan's body collapsed around her. "Fuck." He exhaled, awakened by the sudden attack. He glared at the intruder. Only for his fury to die from the smiling face of Dingba. He sighed, looked at her, and cocked his head slightly to the right. "Yes?"

"Get up. It's time for the celebration."

Jordan yawned and glanced at the window. "This early? We haven't even had breakfast."

"Of course. It's an all-day thing. I've been told to get you ready." Dingba jumped up and strikes a heroic pose. "As for breakfast... the faster we get you ready, the faster you can eat. Now get up."

Stifling a hearty chuckle, Jordan blinked quickly, staring at her. "Sure, let's do it." He swiftly removed his bed sheets.

Dingba cheered and zoomed out of the tent, then returned with multiple vials, each filled with colorful liquids. Singka and another fairy entered shortly after, carrying a thick wicker basket that over-flowed with clothes.

Dingba waved as they left. "Thanks guys."

Singka waved as she left. "Have fun you two."

"First, let's get you cleaned up and we also need to pick out an outfit for you." Dingba shifted through clothes, handing Jordan some undergarments and a towel.

"Go bathe while I get everything ready. Also." She handed Jordan a vial of greyish liquid. "Rub this all over your body when you get out. It will make your body all smooth." Her eyes are bright, an untamed smile was plastered on her face.

Jordan nodded slowly, carrying the stuff to the backroom.

While he soaked, he called forth his spell circle. Staring at it, he had confirmed what Singka said. On his circle sat the symbols for push and pull, underneath it sat a new circle, carrying what Jordan assumed is the symbol for fire. He tried to remember how to pronounce the symbol. His mind was still hazy, his brain throbbed as he kept trying to recall.

Dingba's voice pierced the silence. "Did you drown in there?"

He looked back, "Just about to get out. Sorry."

Once he's dried off, he turned his attention to the vial. Holding it up to the light, he found it hard to see through it. Uncorking the vial, he tipped it. The thickness is very reminiscent of ketchup. It bubbled forward. The goop took its sweet time to reach the mouth of the bottle before stretching down to meet his hand.

With a soft plop, a generous drop of goop landed in Jordan's hand. Setting the vial down, he spread it in his hands like he would lotion.

"Smooth…"

It was very much like lotion. His skin sucked it up greedily, after months of not having any forms of skin care. After rubbing himself from head to toe, he even put some in his hair. Much to his pleasure, it worked well. His scalp felt renewed. With that, he got dressed and exited.

While he was bathing, Dingba had arranged various outfits, all with different styles and colors. Jordan stood wide eyed at the vast options in front of him. "About time. I was worried you fell asleep." She motioned towards the clothes. "Pick something you like."

Jordan stepped up, glancing a little closer at the clothes. As he picked them up, he noticed how delightfully and unexpectedly soft they were. He also noted how revealing and small they were.

Dingba caught the look on his face and smiled. "Don't worry about how small they look. Singka measured you thoroughly, so they fit. As for all the skin that will show. Well... you'll see why later." She winked.

Dingba walked over to a red and orange outfit and held it up. "May I suggest trying this one?"

Jordan smiled, "Sure, I'll put it on."

Dingba assisted Jordan in putting the clothes on, ensuring he doesn't rip them. Once on, she turned him to a mirror.

Jordan soaked in his image. On his feet were his filthy tennis shoes, holes from battle still shown in the leather. The pants he wore are asymmetrical. Thick orange leaves covered his left leg. His right leg was bare to his upper thigh. There was a slight gap showing off his midsection before it continued into an open short-sleeve shirt that revealed the center of his chest.

Dingba's head was low, and her hands were behind her back. "Well...?"

Jordan took the hint and smirked. "I like it a lot."

Dingba's eyes lit up once more. "Really?" She lifted herself up with her wings.

He chuckled, "Yeah, it makes me feel cool."

Dingba fist pumped. "Yes. Okay, onto the next part. Sit down, this will take a while." She grabbed different brushes and vials.

Jordan watched as she shook various color filled vials and one opaque vial that is filled with a mucus like liquid.

She had dipped the tip of a paintbrush in a black vial, tainting the white fibers of the brush.

She brought the paintbrush towards Jordan. "Okay, sit still."

Jordan held still and stared into her eyes as she brought the brushes tip under his. She did a quick stroke right at the edge of where his eye socket was. She then leaned in and gave it a gentle blow, causing it to dry quickly as Jordan's eyes fluttered.

"The reason the clothes are so revealing, is so we can show off our

'Scars'." She kept drawing on his flesh. "After a serious event, fairies gather in groups and paint on each other. We paint on our friends and allies." She blew some more paint dry.

"Why?"

She moved to his chest. "To turn our scars into something beautiful."

Jordan nodded then tilted his head, "So, can I paint you?"

Dingba paused for a moment. Her eyes widened, but she forced them to relax. She kept her face low to hide her smile. Her hand continued painting, albeit slower than before. She tried to keep her cool. "We're friends, aren't we?"

"The first non-human one I've made."

This stopped her hand. She inhaled slowly, catching her breath.

After a few moments she spoke, "Thanks."

Dingba groaned and frowned before clicking her tongue. She lowered the brush and snatched a nearby rag; She wiped off some paint before starting again. "Now stay still. This takes forever, and I don't want to mess up."

A few moments later, Dingba glanced up. "I always meant to ask you. What does... 'Fuck' mean? You like using it, at least when we trained you used it a lot."

Jordan's cheeks grew warm. "Ah... well. It's... a word for when two humans make babies."

"Oh. So, it's a good word?"

"Well, no, it's a rude way of saying baby making. Well, actually it has a bunch of uses, some good some bad. I'll teach you later if you want."

"Yes. Teach me all the fucks."

Jordan laughed, "Right, I will teach you all the different ways to say fuck."

"*Maybe I should watch my mouth... Nah.*"

THE PAINTING TOOK A FEW HOURS. While Dingba worked they talked about various things, including the many uses for "Fuck". Dingba splashed Jordan with a variety of colors, coating each painting with that clear mucus, making sure it was fully dry before allowing Jordan to move again.

Jordan picked up the mucus vial. "What's that mucus stuff, anyway?"

"It's a secret. Just make sure you cover every scar you paint on with it. It will be cool, trust me." She smirked as she grabbed her uniform. "My turn."

She hopped onto the edge of the bed. Dingba also chose to expose her midriff for the celebration. Her top was a simple dark green grass tank top. She wore vine bracelets around her wrist and ankles. Bright pink flowers decorated the front. Around her waist was a skirt made of thick blue leaves. Like most fairies, she was barefoot.

Jordan tested each color on a leaf before he painted on Dingba, who sat humming as she kicked her feet. Once he had some basic concepts in his head, he began drawing. Starting at Dingba's tiny feet, he drew his own little flower. A red flower surrounded by a black border. He repeated this process on her other foot and then with both her hands. Alternating the colors as he went. Red, blue, orange and green. On her hands, he drew flames surrounding the flowers.

Dingba cocked her head to the side. "Why flames?"

"Because you only use your fist to fight. So that is where you bring the heat from."

Dingba tilted her head, "The heat?"

"It's a saying for power. Like if someone jumped into a fight with an amazing sword, people would say he brought the heat." He grabbed more paint.

"Oh… cool." She bounced in place while punching her fists in the air. "I bring the heat." She declared, still punching.

Jordan looked up and frowned. "Stay still before I mess up."

Dingba replied with a giggle and went back to sitting still. Jordan eyeballed her midriff, trying to decide what design he wants to put on.

A confident nod later, he drew once more. The artistic talent buried deep within him flowed throughout his body.

On her stomach, he drew two dots with a generous distance between them. Underneath these dots he drew a three turned on its side, where the curves were pointing to her waist, and it opened towards the dots. He then drew three dashes on each side of the shifted three. Each dash was slightly longer than the previous. Finally, he finished the masterpiece with a large "V" in between the dots.

Dingba looked down, her face scrunched up. "I'm not mad, but what the fuck did you draw on me?"

Jordan broke down in a hearty laugh.

Dingba grinned, "Wait, did I use that right?"

Jordan wiped a tear from his eye and cleared his throat. "Yes, you used that correctly."

He stood up and stepped back to get a full view of his masterpiece. "It's a cat or a Juk-Juk. The mischievous version anyway."

She looked up for reassurance. "Cute?"

Jordan gave her a thumbs up, "Very cute."

His eyes caught something he almost missed. He stepped closer, grabbing a paint brush which he dipped in purple paint. He got close to Dingba's face. She blushed.

He reached up and cupped her chin, turning her head slightly. On her right cheek, a deep purple kiss mark stained her pale flesh. Jordan stared at it, confused. He knew this was a new thing. It didn't look painted on, instead it looked as if someone tattooed it into her flesh. Jordan ran his thumb over it softly. "What happened here?"

Dingba jumped out of her skin. Her hands shot up and covered the spot. Her eyes were wide with dread.

He backed away with his hands up. "Okay, okay... I just wanted to beautify it. I won't mess with it if you don't want me to."

Dingba thought for a moment before lowering her guard. "It's fine, you can do it." She looked away and placed her hands in her lap.

"You sure?"

Dingba nodded.

Jordan approached and brought the brush closer to the mark. Dingba's lip quivered as he brushed bright purple pain over the mark, as if he's applying lipstick to it. He kept quiet as he worked. He is curious, but he didn't want to pry.

Dingba's voice shook as she spoke. "Tink did that before..." She clenched her fists in her laps as she mustered the strength she needed. "Before she died.", She wore a sturdy look, but Jordan could tell she was suffering.

"Does it hurt?"

A tear rolled down her cheek. "Not physically."

Jordan used his thumb to wipe it away. He could hear Dingba sniffling. Every so often her hands would dart up and wipe away a tear. The sniffling became more frequent and the tears more abundant. Her poor hands worked tirelessly to wipe them away.

Jordan set his brush down. "Wanna take a break?"

Dingba nodded. She was at her limit. "Y-Yeah. Sorry." She dashed to the bathroom.

He could hear Dingba breaking down inside. Her cries leaked through whatever she was using to cover her mouth. "Cuss, cuss, cuss."

A while later, she exited the bathroom. Her eyes were bloodshot and puffy. She took her seat in front of Jordan. She hung her head. Her breathing calm and controlled.

He placed a hand on her knee. "Better?"

Dingba held out her right hand, showing the ruined painting. "I messed up your painting... I'm sorry."

He grabbed the rag and placed it gently on the smudged painting. "It's fine, it gives me a chance to make it better."

He redid the orange flower, then moved to finish her cheek. He also painted under her eyes, hiding that she's been crying. Once he finished, he grabbed the mucus and covered the paintings with it.

"Aright. All done."

Dingba stood up and stepped in front of the mirror. Starting at her feet, she saw Jordan had drawn a red flower and a blue flower on her right and left foot, respectively. From her ankles he drew pink and purple streaks, which ended in a band that wrapped around her thighs. The "cat" occupied her midriff. Her arms had multiple rings descending to the orange and green flowers that were on her right and left hands. On her cheek he had amplified the kiss mark. He made it pop with a fresh coat of purple paint. He then drew butterfly wings around the mark, with streaks of purple shooting from it. Underneath Dingba's eyes, he drew blue dots against a black background that exploded into strands of color at the end as it reached towards her ear.

Jordan stood behind her watching her inspect herself, "Well?"

Her wings softly buzzed. "It's… it's beautiful. Thank you."

He smiled. "I'm glad you like it."

Dingba's hand hovered over the kiss mark. Her eyes watered and her lips trembled as she soaked in the image. It wasn't a masterpiece, but it meant the world to her. "Thank you…"

Jordan put down the brush and vials, "No worries."

They stood there in silence, appreciating their artwork. Until the sound of flutes interrupted their silence.

"Oh. It's starting." She took Jordan by the hand. "Come on." She led him outside.

As they stepped outside, the decorated Queens Land welcomed them with open arms. They covered buildings with flowers and paintings along the walls. From the buildings holding little lanterns and bells, they hung painted vines that connected to the buildings. They rocked gently in the wind. The same paint that covered the walls also covered everyone's flesh. The center of town had the biggest change to it. On some tables sat a bounty of fruit, veggies, nuts and flowers. In front of those tables sat enormous barrels of some liquid. In the middle of all this stood a mighty leaf statue, thick rocks and dirt surrounded it. The statue had some resemblance to Melrose.

Dingba looked up, still dragging Jordan through the village. "Isn't it pretty?"

"Very… you guys do this after every incident?"

"Yeah, we also host one every year as an end of the year celebration type thing. This is my first crisis celebration." She scanned the area. "Oh. There's Singka."

Singka sat on a log, humming to herself while she stared at the statue in the pit.

Dingba waved and called out, "Singka..."

She looked over and smiled. Then motioned for them to come join her. Once they were in front of her, they modeled their scars.

Singka smiled, looking over at each one. "Very cute..."

Singka wore a pink tank top and a forest green skirt. Her skin was littered with squiggly lines and poorly drawn figures.

Jordan inspected a few. "Who did your scars?"

"All the kids that have been born so far. Every year I like to go around and let them scar me. I even remember what Dingba drew."

Dingba looked away as her cheeks turned red. "Let's not... talk about that."

Singka took delight in showing which child drew what; she gave a love filled praise to each one. Jordan smiled as he watched her. He felt a warmness in his chest.

Singka flew into the air. "Anyway. It's almost time."

From various buildings, the sound of music flowed. Fairies poked their heads out in excitement as music filled the air. Soon a small marching band entered the center. Drums and pan flutes created a festive melody. The rest of the village joined the center, their bodies covered in paint. The little ones buzzed around in joy while the adults greet and hug each other.

Juka saw Jordan and Dingba and rushed over to them. "Dingba."

Dingba gave her a big hug. "Hello Juka."

Juka broke away. "Oh... pretty scars."

"Thank you, Jordan did it."

Juka hugged Jordan. "Good job Jordan."

Jordan chuckled and hugged her back. "Thanks, Juka."

Juka's tiny body had drawings by her parents, they were pictures of animals and fruit with smiley faces.

Juka looked at the food table. "Come, let's go get food."

Dingba stood up. "Yes. We were just about to go."

Jordan followed them to the food table. He recognized some things on the table, like Queens Drips and carrots. But the sheer number of choices overwhelmed him. "I... I don't know what I should try."

"Well, we know you like Queen Drips." Dingba handed Jordan some.

Her hand hovered over a yellow flower. "How about... these?"

Its petals were thick, long and firm to the touch. It smelled slightly like honey.

She greedily grabbed a handful. "Tong got me hooked on those."

She turned to Jordan and took a bite out of the petals while giving him a cheerful smile. Jordan copied her, biting slowly. The petal responded with a squirt of sap. Its sweetness reminded him of syrup more than honey, it's chewy like gum. The texture felt good in his mouth.

"Well?"

Jordan responded by nodding and taking another bite.

"Those are called Sappers. When you finish eating the petals, throw the rest into the fire pit."

Jordan nodded as he continued to eat. Dingba went down the line picking out her favorites and handing samples to Jordan for him to try. She stopped in front of a bowl filled with large brown seeds. The smile on her face faded.

"These are..." She picked one up.

Jordan leaned in to look. "What are they?"

"They are Lasnuts. Tink's favorite."

"Oh, I see."

"I haven't seen them in a while. There was a poor harvest a while before she disappeared. I didn't have strong enough teeth to open these myself when I was younger."

She lifted the nut to her mouth, turning it on its side. Her mouth opened wide as she lined up the nut with her canines. She bit down steadily, applying more and more force as she went. Her jaw jumped as her teeth cracked open the shell. Her eyes widened.

"Oh.... I did it." She showed Jordan the broken shell.

She pried it open and revealed the white flesh. "I did it." She looks around, "Singka look I did it." She walked up and showed her.

Singka smiled, "Yes you did."

Dingba grabbed another one, "I'll open one for you too." She cracked open another one. "See? Just like Tink taught me."

Singka took the nut. "She taught you well. Come on, let's grab a few in her memory."

Dingba nodded and beamed with joy.

Once their arms were full; they returned to their seats to gorge themselves. Dingba also brought these gelatin balls over on a leaf.

"If you get thirsty..." She picked one up and held it to her lips. "Suck on these." She drained the ball of its fluid.

Jordan picked one up and tried it. The liquid flowed smoothly; it was sweet but not overpowering, It tasted like basic sugar water. He stopped sucking to see if it would leak. To his surprise, the thin membrane held the rest of the water in just fine.

THE VILLAGERS soon filled the air with laughter and talking. The kids were flying around playing with balls and toys, Singka sat nearby talking to random adults. Every so often she would glance towards the children before looking back at the adults. When the young ones roped Dingba into a game of tag, Jordan and Singka sat and watched for a while chatting about random things. From the back of his mind a question formed. one that had been lingering in the back of his mind.

He swallowed his snack and glanced at Singka, "Hey, how come you and Dingba have similar names? Was she named after you by her parents or what?"

Singka's face sunk a bit. "Right... you don't know. Dingba's parents disappeared shortly after they conceived her. Her mother was a scientist. She was always experimenting and studying different things. Her father was a simple weaver, always working on clothes and baskets for the village. But when his wife got the urge to go on a 'quick' expedition, he would always tag along. He loved her so much.

So, when they left most of their things, we assumed they were coming back, and her mother simply ran off on a scientific expedition like she normally does. While the father went to make sure she was safe and to make sure she remembered they have a baby waiting."

Singka chuckled and shook her head. "When Dingba was born, I tore up their house looking for any instructions left by the parents. Her mother was good at leaving some kind of note when she disappeared like that, but there was nothing. They had left Dingba without a name and it was feeling like they also left her period."

A flash of rage danced over her eyes before she wiped it away. "Dingba took a liking to my name, so I gave her a similar one. She was delighted to have a name after so long."

Jordan gave into a slight frown. "How long was she without a name?"

"It was roughly a year. I named her before the end of the year celebration."

"Why wait so long?"

"I was so sure her parents would come back, and I didn't want to take that from them. But winter came, and they sent no word to us. I grew furious, as did Tink. She told me, 'If you don't name her, I will.'. So, I named her. I had no idea what name Tink would have chosen, but I'm sure it would have been 'Blinka' or something tough sounding. The little goof." Singka smiled as a tear formed in her eye.

Jordan hesitated for a moment. "What happened to Tink's family?"

Singka stared at the sky. Rolling her tears back, she then turned to Jordan and grinned. "Well, her mother is sitting here wondering why her sister ran off and left her child behind with no word. Her father got sick. I couldn't cure him, and he died. Her little brother caught the same thing, died. Her sister got injured by a wild animal while trying to protect Tink. I couldn't save her, she died." She grew silent. She blinked, and a tear rolled down her cheek. "Tink hated me for a long time until Dingba was born."

She glanced back down to earth; She had been using a stick to draw aimlessly in the sand this entire time. "One of my biggest failures in life was failing to protect my family. By the Wilt it drives me insane."

Jordan stared in shock, he hesitated to speak, "I'm sorry, I didn't-"

Singka turned and smiled at him, even though tears sat on her eyelids. "It's fine, dear, it's better that you know. It makes me happy to have someone to talk about it with."

"So, you're Dingba's aunt?"

Singka nodded. "Yep, her mother Fooua is my sister. Technically, I'm the older sister. I came out of the tree first, but yes. I am her aunt."

Jordan smiled, his eyebrow raised, as another question popped into his mind. "What was Dingba's first drawing?"

Singka smirked and looked around to make sure no one is watching. She scooted closer and removed a folded-up paper from inside her top. Opening it carefully, she revealed a picture of three fairies holding hands. On the right was a small one with wings of a dragonfly. In the middle a taller one with wings like a bee, and finally on the left another small one with moth wings. A name hovered above each person.

Me Singka Tink

Singka sighed as she remembered. "They were so tiny back then…. I didn't want to wash this off, so I saved the picture. It keeps me strong when things get tough. I failed to save Tink and my family. But I saved her little sister. So, I'm not a complete failure." After smiling at the picture for some time, she stowed it away.

Jordan sat in silence, wearing a soft smile. He handed her his last Lasnut.

"Oh. A Lasnut. Her favorite, thank you dear."

The sun had begun to set, and darkness crept through the forest.

"Oh. Time flies when you are reminiscing." Singka leapt up. She spread her arms and legs out. "Come on, stand up Jordan, quickly."

Jordan stood copying Singka's pose. As the forest darkened, the scars glowed, and the village is lit up in a swarm of color. The villagers filled the air with "Ohs" and "Ahs". The soft giggles of the children became the chorus.

Dingba rushed back to Jordan. "Didn't I tell you it'd be cool?"

Jordan nodded, "That you did."

Dingba gave him a greedy smirk, "Now it's time for the feast. Come on, Jordan." She grabbed Jordan again.

She dragged him back to the table, which the village restocked with fresh food and blood leaf skewers. Jordan recognized various things. Like potatoes, corn, carrots, apples and chestnuts? They looked like chestnuts.

"Here, I'll make you the one Tong made for me." She went to work grabbing and stacking various things on the skewer.

She handed the finished skewer to Jordan, who examined it. In between sapper petals rested various things. At the top sat a sapper petal with a chestnut, Dingba crossed out the top, followed by another sapper. From there the pattern continued with a sapper, then some fruit, nut or veggie. Until the skewer could hold no more food. Dingba made herself the same one, and they returned to the middle.

"Are we supposed to eat them like this?" Jordan goes to take a bite.

Dingba stopped him by pushing his head away. "Nope, they are about to light the fire once everyone is ready." She pointed to the statue.

Jordan looked and saw Tong for the first time today. He was hovering over the pit; the statue reaching up towards him. His staff glowed in bright greens and blues. He waved it in the air, grabbing everyone's attention.

He cleared his throat and stuck his chest out. "For a few months someone has plagued us with the pain of our loved ones being stolen. That someone was a monster known as Melrose."

"Boo..." Some children yelled, their parents hushed and squeezed them.

"After the kidnappings had started, we had a guest appear. He saved one of our beloved children, Juka. This young man's name was Jordan." He pointed his staff at Jordan.

The crowd clapped as their focus turned towards Jordan. Jordan shyly waved back with a soft smile on his face.

"Though he arrived on the brink of death, our beloved healer

Singka brought him back from the Whither." This time he motioned towards Singka, who also received a round of applause.

"Shortly after, one of the missing returned to us with a painful warning. Leave or face death! A different elder would have fled, but I view you all as my children. Instead of seeing a traitor or an enemy, I saw a child who was afraid and alone. Who didn't know how to save her family and I wanted to bring her home." Tong calmed his cracking voice. "I failed to bring her home and even worse my decision cost the lives of some more of my children." He paused once more.

The silence gave way to sniffling and some muffled crying. Tong took out a leaf figurine and held it in his hands. He encircled the statue as he goes over the last fight with Melrose. "She had swallowed our village up with this darkness. This smothering darkness." He circled back to the top of the statue.

"But that young man, who had no reason to stay and fight, became the light that would banish that darkness." He lit the figurine's arm on fire and dropped it. "He fell from the sky like a star crashing down. Into the horrible growth that plagued this peaceful forest." The figurine crashed into the statue.

"And his light engulfed that overgrowth." The statue bursts into flames. The light was bright and almost blinding; it illuminated the area, casting away the shadows that had moved in. "And his bravery rekindled the flame that tragedy had smothered and for this. From a proud and loving father. I thank him." Tong finished as the crowd cheered.

Jordan timidly waved at the onlookers as he searched for words to say. Dingba gave him a playful nudge. Singka smiled and wiped a fresh tear away. She clapped and cheered loudly and encouraged others to do the same.

Tong fired off a magical bolt into the air. "Now. Let's eat."

The crowd cheered even louder as they move to the fire, arranging their skewers. Tong flew over to Jordan before he took his seat. "Mind if we had a brief chat?"

"Sure, I don't mind. Watch my food Dingba?"

She nodded with a mouthful of sappers.

Jordan smiled and shook his head. He followed Tong to a secluded location. "What's up?"

Tong thought for a moment, choosing his words carefully. After a moment, he turned to look at Jordan. He wore a serious expression. "First I'd like to apologize for my rudeness to you earlier."

Jordan tilted his head, "You were rude to me?"

Tong gave him a confused look, "Yes when you asked about Tink, and I so coldly replied that it doesn't concern you. Then when you offered to help us, I had the gall to tell you that again."

Jordan shrugged and chuckled, "It's fine. You were stressed out. Sorry about forcing my way into your battle plans."

Tong smiled, "Can't say I wasn't relieved to have your help even if you had to force me to accept it." He paused for a moment before looking up at Jordan, "What are your plans now that everything is said and done?"

"Well, I was planning on leaving and exploring the world. I also want to find any other humans I can. To make sure they are okay and if not, I'll help them in any way I can. I'm also hoping two of my friends made it out of the forest and to somewhere safe. I'm hoping to find them. Why do you ask?"

"I was thinking that it might be best for Dingba to leave the village. With Tink gone, she really doesn't have any friends or family here besides Singka. Plus, she always expressed a desire to find her actual parents, or at least find out what happened to them. I had always been too scared to let her go off on her own, but I would feel better if she was traveling with someone we trusted."

Jordan smiled, "Well, I—"

Tong continued to talk, "If you could." He bowed his head. "Please take Dingba with you."

"Well, I was going to ask her to come with me before I left. It is up to her though, I can't force her if she doesn't want to."

Tong looked up suddenly, his eyebrow raised high. "Oh. So, you were planning on running off with my dear little Dingba, huh?"

Jordan took a step back with a nervous smile. "I mean... running off wouldn't be the word I'd use... more like... going on an adventure with her."

This only fueled the fire in Tong's eyes. "The youth today... always running off on adventures..." He glared. "If something were to happen to her..." He shook his staff at Jordan.

Jordan chuckled as he watched him. "I would do my best to keep her safe, sir."

He shook his staff harder. "And if you hurt her... Just because I'm old doesn't mean I can't teach you a thing or two."

Jordan fought the urge to laugh as Tong grilled him. "I would never..."

Tong squinted his eyes. "Mhm.... Kids these days, always making my back hurt." He placed a hand on his lower back, rubbing tenderly.

Jordan choked down a bubbling laugh. "I apologize."

Tong lost the serious look and smiled warmly at Jordan. They talk for a while longer before Dingba shouted for them.

Tong looked over, "Apparently our food is ready."

They walk back to the party where Dingba is laying her head in Singka's lap. Singka had a soft white light coming off her hand as she rubbed Dingba's belly.

Singka continued to rub Dingba's belly, "I told you not to eat so much."

Dingba groaned, "I know..."

Singka glanced up at Jordan when she heard him approach, "What did you and Tong talk about dear?"

"Uh... nothing really. He just wanted to make sure I was feeling okay."

She smirked. "Ah, how sweet."

Jordan reached down to grab his skewer. The chestnut had burst open revealing that it was instead a flower bulb. Yellow petals reached up to the sapper that had busted open, spilling its warm syrup onto the petals.

A warm, sweet smell flooded his nose as he sniffed his meal. Dingba watched as he took his first bite. He chewed, fighting off a smile. Dingba smiled widely when he chomped on the food once more.

Syrup coated his lips while he ate. He hummed as he watched the others play around the fire. Dingba closed her eyes and smiled, her stomach soothed by the healing touch of Singka. They partied late into the night; the music eventually lulled them to sleep.

27

DEPARTURE

A FEW HOURS later the sun illuminated the forest once more, the fire burnt out; the food devoured by hungry mouths. Dingba had passed out in Singka's lap with Jordan sleeping nearby, Juka had decided his thick wool like hair made a good bed. She tangled her tiny legs up in his curls, anchoring herself down while she slept. Other pixes and nixes had also found Jordan to be a comfortable bed.

Dingba cracked her eyes open, she saw Singka hunched over her still sleeping. Dingba smiled and nestled herself in Singka's lap a little more. Glancing down she saw Singka's hand still on her stomach. She saw Jordan still decorated with fairies. Her ears twitched as she heard Tong shifting through the ashes in the firepit. He bent down and picked up three objects then took them back to his tent.

"What was he doing?"

She shrugged and closed her eyes to enjoy the warmth of the sun and the softness of Singka's lap for a while longer.

Eventually Singka stirred awake. Dingba felt her stretch her legs slowly trying not to wake her.

Dingba smiled, "Morning."

Singka rubbed Dingba's stomach, "Good morning, how's your stomach."

Dingba opened her eyes, "Better thanks to you."

They glanced at Jordan.

Dingba yawned, "Should we wake him up?"

Singka shook her head, "No let him sleep a little longer. Plus, if we wake him, we'd have to wake up all the people sleeping on him. Come on" She patted Dingba's stomach, "Let's go get cleaned up."

A FEW HOURS later Dingba stood in front of a still sleeping Jordan, the pixies and nixies sleeping on him had long woken up and cleared out.

"And I thought I slept a lot."

She reached out and shook him gently.

Jordan groaned, "What...?"

Dingba shook him a little harder, "Can't sleep all day, Jordan. Come on, get up."

Jordan started to drift back off to sleep, Dingba huffed and grabbed his arm. "Get up." She pulled him to his feet; Jordan looked around to see that most of the fairies have regained consciousness.

After a heavy yawn, Jordan wiped the sleep from his eyes. "Morning..."

Dingba handed him a small cup of juice. "Good morning."

He took a sip. "Thank you."

"Now that you're up, go wash your scars off." She pushed Jordan towards the bathing area.

Jordan stumbled over, taking careful sips of the juice as it re-energizes him.

A while later he's clean and dressed in his last remaining leaf clothes, his other outfits long worn out and tattered from all the training with Dingba, though this outfit is one sudden movement away from being torn apart. He reunited with Dingba, who gave him a disapproving look.

"That won't do, you look homeless."

Jordan gave her a pained smiled, "Well, I am homeless. Plus, this is all I have, well besides the party uniform."

"We'll... we'll figure something out. We also gotta make you a hut." Dingba looked around the village.

"Maybe some place close to me? Would make meeting up easier. He's going to need more clothes too. By the Wilt he is tall."

She stroked her chin as she continued to think.

Jordan smiled, "Oh, there's no need for that."

"What?"

Dingba looked at him, "What do you mean?"

Jordan shrugged, "Well, I'm new to this world. There's so much to see, and I should probably find other humans as well. Maybe there's a group somewhere that needs help."

Dingba deflated. "Oh. Right, of course. It'd be silly if you stayed here forever." She glanced at the ground, unsure of what to say next.

"I guess, he would have to leave too huh... there's not really a point in staying in this village is there? Or even staying with me?"

She rubbed her arm, once again the feeling of loneliness crept in.

They stood there in silence for a few moments, when she glanced at Jordan, he had this look on his face. Like he wanted to ask one of his unusual requests.

She looked up at him, "What?"

He looked around and stumbled over his words for a moment. Eventually he stopped, took a deep breath and looked her in the eyes, "I was wondering if you wanted to come? It'd be nice to travel the world with my first friend."

Dingba's heart skipped a beat.

"He wants me to come with?"

She could feel her blood rushing with excitement, her fingers danced on her bicep as her mind raced.

Jordan continued, "It's not that I want to leave. It's just... this is a brand-new world and there's so much I want to see and experience. And, well, I wanted to explore with you. I think it'd be fun, really fun."

Dingba looked up, her gaze beamed to the skies. As hard as she tried, she just couldn't lower her wide gaze. She opened her mouth to speak, she struggled to find words while her brain was firing this fast. Her mind took this opportunity to start fishing for excuses. "I uh, I don't think I should. What if something happens to the village?"

Jordan gave her a confident smile, "Then we will come running back."

Dingba's eyes darted, "I don't--"

Jordan held up his hand, "I'm not leaving right away. Take some time and think about it. If you decide you don't want to come with me, that's perfectly okay."

Her smile softened.

"It wouldn't be okay, cause then I'll be alone again."

"Where would we be going?"

"Wherever we want. It's an adventure."

"So, we would be like a team or something?"

"Of course. We'd be an adventuring crew, and you'd be my first mate."

Her eyes lit up once more. "What's a first mate?"

Jordan chuckled, "Besides being the first person in the crew, you'd be the second in command. If something happens to me, you would be the one who the crew looks towards."

Dingba looked excited and honored, but still she hesitated. "I don't know, I need to think about it." She floated up into the air.

Jordan wore a brave smile, "Take your time."

Dingba nodded before flying off.

Jordan waved her off.

THE NEXT FEW DAYS, as Jordan prepared himself to set off, Dingba avoided him. Her mind wasn't made up on whether she wanted to go with Jordan. She sat in one of her hiding places, a clearing south of the village. The sky was gold with the light of a setting sun, a soft wind rustled the leaves in the trees.

"Can I really leave the village? Leave them alone? What if something

happens and I'm gone?"

She heard some bushes rustle nearby, she glanced over and saw Singka come out holding a basket.

She sighed, "By the Wilt you have a lot of hiding places."

Dingba gave her a soft smile, "Hey."

Singka walked over, "Hi, I thought you might be hungry, so I brought you some food." She placed the basket down in between them.

Dingba looked at the basket, "Thanks but I'm not really hungry."

Singka gave her a soft smile, "Uh oh, Dingba doesn't want food? Now I'm really worried."

Dingba shrugged but stayed quiet.

Singka sat for a moment, she reached in and pulled out a snapper petal. After taking a bite she offered one to Dingba who reluctantly grabbed it.

Singka took another bite, "Did you and Jordan have a fight?"

Dingba shook her head.

Singka thought for a moment, "Is it cause of Tink?"

The mention of Tink's name brought some tears to Dingba's eyes.

Singka cooed, "Oh, Dingba..." She pulled her in close for a hug. "I know Dingba, I know." She kissed Dingba's head. "We tried our best."

Dingba sniffled, "I'm sorry. I tried to stop her bu--"

Singka softly shushed her, "There's not a reality where Tink would have wanted you to lose that fight. There's nothing to be sorry about. It was my job to protect you both and I failed."

Singka reached up and wiped a tear from her eyes, "Tink loved you a lot and nothing could change that. Understand?"

Dingba nodded.

They sat there in each other's arms letting their tears fall to the ground. After a while the tears stopped and all that was left was silence.

After a moment Singka broke the hug and rubbed Dingba's back, she gave her a warm smile, "So, anything else bothering you?"

Dingba exhaled loudly, "Jordan wants to leave the village."

Singka's smile sunk, "Ah, I see. Well, I'm sure he still wants to find those humans he got separated from. Maybe even find others."

Dingba nodded, "Yeah."

Singka patted Dingba on the head, "I know it's hard but I'm sure he's not leaving just to get away from you or anything like that."

Dingba nodded once more, "He actually asked me to come with him."

Singka jumped in surprise, "Oh. Oh. Oh, that's great you can go exploring with him."

Dingba smiled, "Yeah, he said I'd be his first mate. Which is like his right-hand person and second in command."

Singka bounced in place, "That sounds fun... so what is the problem?"

As Dingba went to speak the bushes nearby rustled again, this time Tong was the one to emerge. He walked over with a tired look on his face, "Why must you have so many hiding places?"

Singka laughed while Dingba chuckled.

Singka motioned for Tong to sit, "Dingba was just telling us Jordan asked her to come with him on his adventure."

Tong raised an eyebrow, "Oh? Sounds fun? How come she's hiding out here than?"

Dingba glanced at both of them.

"Why are they so okay with this?"

Singka frowned, "She seems worried about something."

Dingba sighed, "What if you guys need me?"

Tong frowned, "Would you really be happy here? Waiting around for something bad to happen?"

Dingba looked at him, "That's not--"

Singka chimed in, "Plus, didn't you want to go find Jul and your parents?"

Dingba looked at her, "What if they come back and I'm gone?"

Tong shook his head, "I highly doubt they intend on coming back here. I'm sorry to say it but, If they were going to come back. They would have been back already. Assuming something wasn't preventing them."

Dingba sighed.

"He's right."

Singka grabbed a Lasnut, "Dingba... Tinks gone, your parents probably aren't coming back. You should go out and follow your dreams. This is your home, but you aren't trapped here."

Dingba sunk, "But, what if I miss everyone?"

Tong chuckled as he stroked his beard. "After all those years of running through the woods for days on end."

Dingba cut him an unamused look, "Not the same."

Singka chuckled with him. "Then you come back for a visit. Tell us all about your adventures with Jordan, all the things you've seen and learned; And if you decide the adventurer life isn't for you. Come back to us, there's no shame in that."

Dingba smiled softly. "What if he gets tired of me?"

Tong scoffed, "Well, you beat him up the first time you both met. If that wasn't enough to stop him from befriending you. I honestly don't know what is."

Singka giggled, "Humans are weird."

Dingba laughed softly. Her eyes soften for the first time in days. "They make good friends though."

They sat in agreement. A small bit of fear sat in Dingba's gut. She had never left the forest before, and now she might leave with someone from an extinct race. Her eyes focused on the sapper that was still resting in her hand. After twirling it in her hand, she went to take a bite but stopped as she realized something.

"Wait a minute."

She shot an inquisitive look at Singka and Tong, "Were you guys aware of this?"

Singka nodded, "He might have mentioned it to us."

Dingba sighed, "So you're okay with me leaving?"

Singka chuckled and cracked open another Lasnut, "I am for a few reasons. The biggest one is I know Tink would have wanted you to go explore the world. She always talked about how excited she was to go on adventures with you."

Singka ate her Lasnut and smiled, "Tink may have been a little mean. Maybe she teased you a lot, but she loved you and even if she couldn't go. She would have wanted you to go explore and follow your dreams."

Dingba glanced up at her, "But I'm leaving you."

Singka chuckled, "You aren't leaving me. You're entering a new chapter in your life. A scary... and uncertain chapter, but a new chapter, nonetheless. I think it'll be good for you."

Dingba smiled then looked up at Tong.

Tong looked around, "Don't look at me. She said basically what I wanted to say. I even asked Jordan to take you along with him."

Singka snapped her gaze to Tong. "Tong!?"

Tong looked around, "What? I thought it'd be good for her. I had her best interest at heart."

Dingba laughed quietly then it grew harder until she was crying from laughter.

Tong and Singka watched her with smiles on her face.

After a moment Dingba regained her composure.

Tong tilted his head, "Well?"

Dingba took a bite of her sapper, "I'll think about it."

THE CHOICE

THE DAY CAME for Jordan to leave. He stood at the edge of the village. His legs fidgeted in front of the crowd; the sides of his lips twitched if he smiled too wide. He didn't know what to do with his hands or where to look, so he kept fixing his hair and clothes. With every fairy that joined the crowd, he would stand up straight, only to deflate when it was someone other than Dingba. His shoulders slowly drooped, and he let out a deep sigh. He could only stall for so long before it became awkward. Once he noticed that Singka and Tong were also missing from the crowd; He waited a little longer. Just in case.

A voice chastised him from the crowd. "Didn't I tell you not to wear those?"

Jordan looked up to see Dingba walking towards him with two medium bags. She scowled as she approached.

Jordan struggled with a toothy grin as she drew closer, "I told you I only have these things."

"Here." Dingba handed him a bag. "Go change and come back. You can't leave here looking like a bum."

Jordan took the bag and dipped into a nearby hut to change. A few moments later he reemerged dressed in leaf clothing. The crowd "Ohs" once they get a look at him.

Dingba nodded, "That looks much better."

Jordan posed for her, "So, I assume the other bag is for you?"

Dingba smirked, "Someone has to make sure you stay out of trouble."

Jordan chuckled, "I supp—"

Dingba interrupted, "Plus, your common is still bad, can't have you accidentally selling yourself."

There crowd chuckled. After a moment Tong and Singka finally join the farewell party.

Tong walked up with three small boxes. "Before you two leave..." He walked up to Dingba and Jordan. "One for each of you." He handed the boxes to them. "And..." He turned to Singka, "One for you." He handed one to Singka, much to her surprise.

The trio gave each other looks before opening their respective boxes. Jordan's and Dingba's boxes contained a small blood leaf pendant that is shaped like moth wings. The sun illuminated the finer details of the pendent. The wings had thin layers of leaves added on to give it a delightful texture and more personality.

In Singka's box was another bloodleaf creation and instead of a pendent it was a statue of her, Dingba, and Tink all holding hands, much like the cherished painting. Singka gasped deeply and covered her mouth.

Dingba smiled and hugged her as Singka tried to keep her composure. "Thank you Tong."

Tong smiled and gave her a gentle nod. He turned his attention to Dingba and Jordan.

"I packed a bunch of food and water for you both. And some money and a map. The nearest town is called Chesterpeak. The map is old, but they should be friendly. Dingba's mother used to travel there quite often. Maybe you can find a lead there. She has sharp wings like a yellow jacket, her name was Fooua."

Dingba hugged him. "Thanks Tong."

Singka walked up and hugged them both. "Be careful you two and take care of each other."

They hugged her back.

Dingba squeezed tighter. "We will."

Dingba let go and glanced up at Jordan. "Ready?"

Jordan nodded. "Ready."

The two turned and begun their march out of the town and onto their adventure. But before they got too far Tong called out.

"Ah. Young Jordan wait."

Jordan turned around as Tong hobbled towards him.

Once Tong caught up he took a deep breath, "I'm old..." He chuckled and looked up at Jordan. "I just remembered something. In all the excitement I forgot to tell you. The name of the second extinct race was Abomination."

Jordan's eyes widened, "Wait like that Noritaibu guy?"

Tong nodded, "I didn't realize it at first. I don't really look at the bounty books. Though I guess I should from now on..." He glanced at Dingba, "Anyway, the reason I didn't realize it was them, is because Abomination wasn't their original name."

Jordan tilted his head, "Oh? What was?"

Tong shrugged, "That I don't know. But one of the things that started the war between Humans and Abominations were the Humans calling them that and having it catch on. Though, they eventually embraced it to empower themselves which supposedly the Humans didn't like."

Jordan sighed as memories of Earth flooded back.

"*God damn us.*"

Tong stroked his beard, "So yes, it seems the Abominations are back, though they may have never left. Either way, I'd be careful. You may not remember them, but they might remember you."

Jordan nodded, "Thanks. I'll be careful."

Tong smiled, "Good, now go have fun and be safe."

Jordan rejoined Dingba and they left. Dingba quickly led them to the edge of the trees. The sun was still rising in the cool morning air. The open plains stretched out in front of them as far as the eye could see. The sun peaked over the horizon towards them as the morning light bathed the plains in a golden glow. Gentle waves of mists rolled throughout the area welcoming them.

Jordan inhaled deeply. The air chilled his nose.

Dingba floated in front of him, "Are you ready?"

The light bent around Dingba's frame outlining her body as she hovered in front of Jordan. Her face was tight with excitement.

Jordan nodded his head.

Dingba gave him a toothy grin, "Good. Let's go see," She stretched out her wings, "Reverba."

End of part 1

Sign-up for Jordan's newsletter to be the first to know about new releases in the Tales of Reverba series. jspicerwriting.com

If you liked A New Ember, I would be very grateful for an honest review. The reviews help other readers decide on their next book that much easier.

ABOUT THE AUTHOR

Jordan Spicer is a young African-American, who longed to write stories with faraway worlds filled with gigantic monsters, new races, exotic foods, colorful characters and lots of magic. If you wish to support him on this journey you can find out more about him and his books by going to

jspicerwriting.com

or by following him on Amazon.com.